Love and Lies

at Martha's Hair Done Right

MICKEY DUBROW

Chapter One

THE SHOPKEEPER'S BELL rang as Polly Swift entered Martha's Hair Done Right. She breathed in the smell of hair spray, perming lotion, shampoo, and heated air. Some people hated the smell, especially the perming lotion. Polly loved it. She looked over the shop, one large open room with a reception area, front desk, four styling stations, two manicure stations, and three dryers. The wet stations for shampooing had to be in the back. The building was old. The faded wallpaper was a garden of pink flowers. It was the kind of wallpaper that should only be found in a wallpaper museum.

On the waiting room table were copies of People magazine and the Christian equivalent, Charisma Magazine. Seated behind the front desk was a woman who looked to be in her late sixties. She wore cat-eyeglasses and a pinched face. She looked Polly over with open curiosity.

"Hello," Polly said. "I'm here to see Martha Swafford."

"How do you know I'm not Martha Swafford?" the woman asked.

"I didn't until now."

"Oh really?"

"If you were Martha, you would have said, 'I'm Martha Swafford. How can I help you?'"

The woman let out a loud braying laugh.

"You're right. I'm not Martha. My name's Crystal. Crystal Beaver. No vagina jokes, please. I hang out here because I'm retired and have nothing better to do with my time. I'll warn you right now. I'm a nosy busybody and a terrible gossip. Or a great gossip depending on your opinion of gossip."

"Is Martha in or should I come back later?"

Crystal brayed again.

"Sorry. I do get carried away. Martha's using the little girl's room. Should be back any minute."

Polly thanked her and sat in the reception area. A minute later, a woman in her late forties wearing a black nylon salon smock came out of the back of the shop. She was an attractive woman. Her auburn hair had streaks of gray. Polly jumped to her feet and smoothed her dress with her palms.

"Hello," Polly said. "You must be Martha Swafford."

"I am," the woman replied. "And you must be Polly Swift." The women shook hands.

"You didn't tell me you were interviewing anybody today," Crystal said.

"You're right, I didn't," Martha said. "Because it's none of your business."

Crystal grinned, obviously more amused than offended. Martha turned to Polly.

"We can talk in my office," Martha said. "Crystal will let me know if anybody comes in."

"I don't work for you," Crystal said.

"You got anywhere else you got to be for the next half hour?"

"Can't say that I do. I'll let you know if anybody comes in."

Martha led Polly around a corner to a hallway that took them past the two wet stations. Across from the wet stations were two bathrooms, one for men and the other for women. In this estrogen rich territory, Polly wondered if anyone ever used the men's room. At the end of the hallway, Martha ushered Polly into a cramped office. Martha sat at the desk and Polly took the visitor's chair.

Martha opened a manila folder on her desk and plucked out Polly's resume. She looked it over as if she hadn't already studied it carefully.

"Your work history is very impressive," Martha said, tapping the resume. "I may live in this little town, but I've heard of these places. They're high-end salons. You haven't bounced from place to place like some stylists do. You spent a good amount of time at each salon. Shows they liked your work."

"What can I say?" Polly said. "I love what I do."

Martha laid Polly's resume on her desk and stared at Polly. Polly squirmed in her seat but didn't lose her smile.

"I don't know what to tell you, Ms. Swift," Martha said. "I can't pay you anywhere near what these big city salons pay or guarantee the amount of business they get. I have four chairs out there, but I can only keep two of them busy. I had one employee, but her husband got a job in Denver. You're from Atlanta. How did you even find out I had an opening?"

"You posted an ad in the Dillard Register. They have an online version of the paper."

"But why on Earth would you want to work in Red Fox, Georgia?"

Polly clasped her hands in her lap.

"I grew up in a place just like Red Fox. I moved to Atlanta because I wanted to live in a big city. I thought it would be exciting and that I'd meet interesting people. The longer I lived in Atlanta, the less exciting and interesting it became and the more I missed living in a small town. So, I searched small town newspapers on the Internet and found your ad."

Martha studied Polly's face. She didn't know what to make of this girl. It would be great to have someone with Polly's experience, but maybe she'd lived in the big city for too long and picked up too many bad habits.

"I understand the salons in cities like Atlanta attract a lot of people with questionable morals," Martha said.

"Questionable morals?" Polly asked.

Martha leaned forward.

"A lot of gay men are hairdressers. Did you ever have to deal with homosexuals at the places you worked?"

"Every place I worked there was always at least one or two gay men."

"How did you deal with them?"

Polly grinned. "Well, they didn't have much to do with me for obvious reasons."

"I don't understand."

"I'm not a man."

Martha leaned back and crossed her arms.

"Well, you won't have to deal with those kinds of people in Red Fox. This is a good Christian town. We're not perfect but we're blessed."

"That's good to know."

Martha had nothing more to ask Polly. She trusted first impressions and her first impression of Polly was that she was hiding something. Probably she was running from a bad relationship. Most times when love turned sour, it was the woman who left town. Though in Martha's case, it was her husband who ran off, leaving her to raise their son on her own.

They heard the shopkeeper's bell ring, but Martha ignored it. A moment later, Crystal knocked before opening the door.

"The queen is here," Crystal announced.

"Of course, she is," Martha said. She stood. "We're pretty

much done. Thank you for coming in, Polly. I'll let you know what my decision is by the end of the week."

Polly got to her feet. "Thank you for considering me. If you don't mind me asking, who is the queen?"

Crystal entered the office and closed the door behind her.

"Tammy Baggs," Crystal said. "She's the pastor's wife at the church me and Martha go to. She never makes an appointment. Just shows up whenever it pleases her and expects Martha to drop whatever she's doing and wait on her hand and foot."

Martha grimaced. She didn't like Crystal telling tales to strangers, though she should have been used to it by now. On the other hand, since it was Tammy they were talking about she couldn't resist joining in.

"She's impossible to please," Martha said. "Nothing I do to her hair is right. She doesn't like anything I suggest."

"She used to make Susie cry," Crystal added. Noticing the confusion on Polly's face, she continued. "Susie Murphy. It's her job you're applying for. I think Susie convinced her husband to find a job in Denver just so she could get away from Tammy. I tell you that woman is a sadist. She likes to inflict pain."

"Don't exaggerate, Crystal," Martha said. "Tammy puts on airs because she's the pastor's wife. She feels entitled to act the way she does."

"You would think a pastor's wife would be humble since her husband serves the Lord," Polly said. Martha and Crystal stared at Polly. "I'm sorry. I shouldn't have said that. However, may I make a suggestion?"

"What's on your mind?" Martha said, crossing her arms.

"Let me do Ms. Baggs hair today. It will give me a chance to show you what I can do and if I make her happy then that might influence your decision about me."

"And if you make her angry, then what?" Crystal asked.

"You said she's never happy no matter what you do, so what do we have to lose?"

Martha rolled her eyes.

"Sure, why not? You can use Susie's station."

Martha led the way as the three women entered the main salon. Tammy sat in the salon chair at Martha's station. She furiously flipped through the pages of a People magazine.

"It's about time," Tammy barked as she tossed the magazine to the floor. "I haven't got all day. I have church business to attend to."

"Sorry, Tammy," Martha said. "I've been busy interviewing candidates to replace Susie. This is Polly Swift. She's one of the top stylists from Atlanta."

"Atlanta?" Tammy said, giving Polly the once over. "Are you familiar with Fuse or VonDavid?"

"Oh, you've been to them?" Polly said. "If you went to Fuse, I hope you asked for Krista. She's the best. I love Von and David to death, but like all brothers they're always arguing, so I only worked for them a couple of years before I moved to Botticelli."

"Botticelli? I tried to get an appointment there, but they were always booked up."

Polly put her forefinger on her cheek as if she'd just had an amazing idea.

"Maybe I can make it up to you. Let me do your hair today. If that's okay with you and Martha."

Tammy scowled at Martha. Martha shrugged her shoulders.

"It's okay with me."

"Is this going to cost extra?"

"Same rate as always."

Tammy grinned at Polly. "Let's do it!"

Martha showed Polly to Susie's old station. Polly made sure she had everything she needed. The building might be old, but the equipment was newish. Polly had her own gear in her car, which were much better quality, but she didn't want to waste time fetching it. She had Tammy sit in the salon chair and spun it around to face the mirror. Polly stood behind her.

Tammy had severe features: a sharp nose, a sharp chin, and narrow eyes. There were hints of softness in her, but they were carefully buried. Her dark brown hair was done in a long wavy formal style. Tammy was trying to look like a classic pastor's wife with the long flowing locks of a virtuous woman of God. But that wasn't who she was. No wonder she was never satisfied with her hair.

Polly used to have a client who was a dominatrix. She was one of the nicest people Polly ever dealt with. The dominatrix explained that since she had to be cruel all day, she didn't have the strength to be mean outside of work. She and Tammy had similar features.

"I have just the thing for you," Polly said.

Polly took Tammy to the wet station and washed her hair.

"You have strong hands," Tammy said.

"Pilates," Polly said.

Polly brought Tammy back to chair and started cutting Tammy's hair. As she worked, Tammy chatted and Polly listened, occasionally adding an appropriate yes, no, and really, I had no idea. Martha pretended not to watch Polly's every move. Crystal didn't pretend at all. When Polly was done, she turned Tammy around to see the results.

Tammy stared in disbelief as she fingered the tips of her hair. Polly had given her a classic Bettie Page cut with short bangs and long waves. All Tammy needed to look completely like a dangerous vixen was bright red lipstick and a black leather bustier.

"I like it," Tammy said. "But I feel like something is missing."

"Your hair is the wrong color," Polly said. "It needs to be pitch black, darker than the darkest night.

"You're right. Let's dye it."

"Not yet. You should live with this cut a few days to make sure. Would you like to make an appointment for a dye job next week? You can cancel if you decide you want to keep your natural color."

"Sounds good to me."

Tammy paid Martha for the haircut and handed Polly a five-dollar tip before making an appointment for the following Monday. She bounced out of the salon humming a hymn. As soon as she was gone, Polly located a broom and swept up Tammy's cut hair on the floor.

"I wouldn't have believed it if I hadn't seen it with my own eyes," Crystal said. "You tamed the Wicked Witch of the West."

"You gave her a great haircut and got her to make an appointment," Martha said. "Are you capable of any other miracles?"

"Oh, I didn't do anything special," Polly said. "I just got lucky. But I hope you'll consider this when you make your final decision."

"Like I'm going to find somebody better?" Martha said. "Polly, you're hired."

Polly's face lit up and grabbed Martha's hands, but then she blushed and dropped her hands to her side.

"You won't regret this. I promise."

"When can you start?"

"Tomorrow if that's okay."

"Really? Don't you need to give your employer a two-week notice? Don't you need to pack your things?"

"I quit two weeks ago, and all my stuff is in my car. I'll be honest. I have a list of other small-town salons looking for a stylist. If you didn't hire me, I was going to apply at the next one and the next one until someone did."

Martha was now convinced. Polly was running away from a bad relationship and wasn't ready to admit it. Giving her a job was the Christian thing to do.

"In that case," Martha said. "You can start tomorrow. We'll do all the paperwork then. Do you have a place to stay?"

"I saw a motel when I drove in. I figured I would stay there until I found an apartment."

"That's the only motel in town," Crystal said. "They have rooms with a kitchenette that you can rent by the month."

"Sounds perfect," Polly said. "Thank you so much, Mrs. Swafford."

"Call me Martha."

"Okay, Martha. See you tomorrow."

Polly bounced out of the salon and spun in a circle on the sidewalk. Martha watched her as she got into her purple car and drove away.

"So, what do you think, Crystal? Did I make a mistake in hiring that girl?" Martha said.

"Only time will tell," Crystal said. "Only time will tell."

Chapter Two

TRACIE LOOKED OUT the picture window in her living room, and then hurried down the hall to the kitchen to glare at the kitchen table. Then, she raced back to the living room. Duane Anderson was almost done cutting and trimming her yard. Back in the kitchen, Tracie's five-year-old son, Connor, was seated at the kitchen table tearing his bologna sandwich into smaller and smaller pieces. Her three-year-old daughter, Harper, had already been put to bed for her nap, but Connor claimed he wasn't sleepy.

"Finish your juice," Tracie said.

Connor drained his glass and then continued the destruction of his sandwich. The whiskey Tracie had slipped into his apple juice was taking longer to take effect. She had done it too many times and he'd built up a tolerance. When it came to handling his liquor, Connor took after his father.

Tracie went back to the living room. The yard was finished. Duane was packing up his equipment. He would be at the back door any second for his check and once he had his check, he would leave. Unless the children were asleep.

Tracie raced back to the kitchen. Connor had gotten bored

with his sandwich and was pulling napkins out of the napkin holder and ripping them into pieces.

"You feeling sleepy, honey?" Tracie asked. "You want to lie down and rest your eyes."

"No, Mom. I'm not sleepy at all. Can I have some more juice?"

Tracie fetched the apple juice from the frig and refilled Connor's glass halfway. She added whiskey until the glass was full. Skyler's fifth of Evan Williams was almost empty. She'd have to run out to the liquor store and get a replacement bottle before he came home tonight.

Tracie set the apple juice in front of Connor. He gulped a quarter of the glass. Unlike his little sister, he no longer grimaced at the taste.

The knock on the door made her jump. Wiping her palms on her pants, she went and opened the door. Duane stood there with a wide smile on his face. He smelled of sweat and freshly cut grass.

"All done," he boomed. "You want to come out and take a look?"

"No, I trust you," Tracie said. "You always do excellent work. I suppose you'll be wanting your check."

"If you don't mind."

"Of course not. Come on in and have a seat. I'll get the checkbook. Would you like a glass of cold lemonade?"

"Water would be fine." Duane entered the kitchen and closed his eyes. "Oh man, that air conditioning feels good."

Tracie got a glass out of the cabinet and loaded it with ice cubes. Then she filled it to the brim with cold water. She handed it to Duane. She watched his Adam's apple bob as he drained the glass. He wiped his mouth with the back of his hand. Tracie stared at him. His bald head was shiny and his T-shirt, drenched in sweat, stuck to his body showing off his huge pecs and six pack abs. Though the man was in his late forties, he was in phenomenal shape thanks to a lifetime of physical labor.

"About that check," Duane said.

"Right, the check," Tracie said, snapping back to reality.

She scurried down the hall to the den. She could have written the check earlier but had waited until now. She always waited until the last moment to write Duane's check.

She filled it out with a feeling of resignation. She was angry with Connor even though she knew she shouldn't blame him. If anyone was to blame, it was her and her wicked desires. They had taken control of her better judgement and made her abuse her precious children. Once Duane was gone, she would make it up to Connor and Harper. She'd treat them to cherry Icees.

Back in the kitchen, Duane leaned against the kitchen counter. Tracie handed him his check. He folded it carefully and slipped it into his jeans pocket. Then he picked up a glass and took a sip. Tracie noticed that it wasn't the water that she'd given him earlier. The glass was smaller, and the liquid wasn't clear. It was amber. Duane was drinking Connor's apple juice.

"I wanted to see what you'd given him this time," Duane said, pointing at Connor.

The boy had keeled over and was snoring softly into the remnants of his bologna sandwich.

"It's not half bad," Duane said as he took another sip. "I might have to start mixing my liquor with apple juice."

Tracie wiped smashed food off Connor's face and lifted him into her arms.

"I'll put him down and then meet you in the bedroom," she said. "You want to shower first?"

"I thought you liked me all sweaty."

"You know I do."

Tracie carried Connor to his bedroom and put him under his covers. She left his door cracked open in case he called out for her. She peeked inside Harper's room. She had pushed off her covers. Tracie pulled the cover back over her daughter.

When she got to her bedroom, Duane's sweaty clothes were piled on the floor, and he was lying naked on the bed. The same bed she slept in every night with her husband, Skyler. The same bed where she and Skyler had created Harper.

Tracie closed the bedroom door and began to disrobe.

"Wait," Duane said. "Take them clothes off slowly. And when you get to the pants, turn around so I can watch that glorious ass of yours."

Tracie loved it when he told her what to do. As she unbuttoned her shirt, she hesitated between each button. She slipped off the shirt and tossed it onto the figure eight Buttblaster exercise machine sitting on a chair in the corner.

She still couldn't believe Skyler had the nerve to get her that torture device for her birthday. He complained that she had gotten a fat ass since they married nine years ago.

When she walked down the aisle with Skyler, she had a cute little butt, almost like a boy's butt. Birthing two children had changed her. The babies were large when they were born. Harper was nine pounds and Connor was a whooping eleven pounds. Her hips had spread out to make room for them to exit her body.

Tracie pulled down one strap of her bra and then the other. Then she leisurely pulled the bra down until her breasts popped out. During pregnancy, her former bee sting tits had ballooned from an A cup to a C cup to accommodate the milk the babies needed for nourishment. She used her forearms to squeeze them together.

"Nice," Duane said.

Most men would have loved to have their wife transform from a skinny tomboy into a voluptuous woman with big tits and a curvy ass, but not Skyler. Having children didn't dampen Tracie's sexual needs so if Skyler wasn't interested in her, she would quench her desire in the arms of the yard man.

And what a yard man. Tracie gazed at Duane's naked body and had to wipe her mouth to keep from drooling. She never thought she'd feel such lust for a Black man. Red Fox was a small Georgia town. Starting at a young age she was taught to love Jesus, hate liberals, and fear anyone who wasn't white. The first time she was with Duane, she compared her pale skin to his dark skin. She felt a mixture of revulsion and excitement so great that when he finally entered her, she almost puked and came at the same time.

That first time was an act of revenge on both Skyler and her parents. It was also an act of desperation. But now, she counted the days until the next time she was in bed with Duane Anderson.

Tracie turned her back on Duane and unbuttoned her jeans. She looked over her shoulder at him and winked. Swinging her hips from side to side, she worked her jeans down to her ankles and then stepped out of them. She hooked her thumbs into the elastic of her panties and inched them down, exposing her wide ass.

"I wish your grass grew faster," Duane said. "Then I'd have an excuse to come over more often."

Tracie climbed into bed with the yard man. By the time Duane fertilized her a second time, Tracie had stopped caring if she woke the children. Her screams of ecstasy echoed through the house.

Once their passion was spent, Tracie relished the weight of Duane's body on top of her. After a minute, he rolled off her. They were both drenched in sweat. Duane sat up and drained the glass of water he'd left on the bed stand. He got out of bed and put on his sweaty clothes. Tracie would have to do a load of laundry before Skyler got home.

She put on her bathrobe and escorted Duane to the door.

"See you next time," Duane said as he walked toward his pickup truck.

"Drive safe," Tracie called back.

She closed the door and went to check on the kids. They were both asleep. She went back to the bedroom. It smelled of sex and freshly cut grass. As she stripped the sheets off the bed, she wondered what to make for dinner.

Chapter Three

Travis and Gus were none too happy about their escorts. The delivery men from JH Restaurant Supply were supposed to install a replacement freezer and haul the dead one away. Something they did all the time. They didn't need two restaurant employees following their every move. It was bad enough that they had to wait in their truck outside a metal gate for half an hour before they were finally allowed onto the premises, now they had to endure this crap.

The level of security and surveillance at Kitsune restaurant rivaled that at banks and federal government buildings. There were cameras watching visitors from the moment they entered the front gate, but that was nothing compared to how closely management watched their own employees. Cameras kept watch on the employees preparing the food in the kitchen, serving the customers, tending the fields where the food was grown, and even watched them relaxing in their cabins.

An outsider might think this was a ridiculous amount of caution to ensure that something like Kitsune's recipe for sautéed asparagus and field peas didn't fall into the hands of competing restaurants, but Kitsune had always been shrouded in mystery. That was a part of the restaurant's appeal.

Nobody in the nearby towns had ever eaten here. The restaurant was for rich people. They came from miles away. They drove up Red Fox Mountain and through the woods in their fancy cars to this secluded location for the privilege to dine here.

"What kind of food do you serve here?" Travis asked as he and Gus wrestled the new freezer into the space where the old one had been.

"You wouldn't be interested," escort number one said.

"Just making conversation."

"It's vegan cuisine," chirped escort number two.

Escort number one gave escort number two the stink eye. The escorts wore pressed khakis and black polo shirts with the name Kitsune in white and the restaurant's log, an illustration of a fox's head, stitched on the breast.

"Vegetarian?" Gus said. "I don't like vegetables. I like meat."

"If you could afford to eat here," escort number one said, "you would quickly change your mind."

"Kitsune is more than a vegan restaurant," escort number two said, his voice rising with excitement. "It's more than the greatest restaurant in the world. The purity of Mr. Kite's cuisine allows us to achieve enlightenment and transcendence. Mr. Kite's spiritual guidance and sublime sustenance has given our lives meaning and filled us with a happiness you can't begin to fathom."

Escort number one slapped escort number two's face. The smack echoed off the kitchen walls.

"You're talking too much," growled escort number one. "When Terrence hears of this, I wouldn't be surprised if you ended up as dishwasher."

Escort number two rubbed his cheek. "But I just graduated to prep cook."

"You can kiss that good-bye."

Travis and Gus ignored them and continued to install the freezer. Travis plugged it in. A soft hum filled the room. The glass doors began to fog from the influx of cool air.

"That ought to do it," Travis said.

The two escorts pretended nothing had happened between them as they examined the new freezer.

"Yes, this is satisfactory," said escort number one. "You may haul away the old freezer."

"Before we do, do you mind if I use your bathroom?" Gus said.

"The bathrooms are for paying guests only," said escort number two. "Hold it in until you're outside the gate and then you can do your business in the woods."

Gus glared at Travis. Travis shrugged. They put the defunct freezer on a dolly, rolled it into the back of their truck, and tied it down. Their escorts stood guard until the deliverymen climbed into the cab of the truck.

Travis got behind the wheel and drove to the front gate.

"I'm with you, Gus," he said. "A meal's not a meal without some kind of meat on the plate."

They didn't have to wait for the gate to open to leave. It swung toward them as they approached it. The security guard in the control room followed the truck on the surveillance cameras as it drove out of the restaurant's property.

However, the guard failed to see the person using the truck as a shield by running behind it. The guard also failed to see the person dive into the bushes next to the stone wall once the truck had passed through the gate.

"Stop the truck," Gus said.

"Why?" Travis said. "Did you see something?"

"No, I need to take a piss and I'm going to piss on their goddamn gate."

Travis chuckled. "They're going to see you."

"Good! I want those stuck-up bastards to see me."

With the truck idling, Travis turned on the radio to a classic rock station. "Jim Dandy" by Black Oak Arkansas filled the cab. The gate had a sign attached to it with the same Kitsune and fox head logo that was on the employees' polo shirts. Gus sauntered over to the gate, unzipped his fly, pulled out his dick, and released a stream of urine aimed directly at the fox's face.

The security guard the control room called for someone to go clean the gate. As he watched Gus, Gus watched his stream of urine splash against the fox's face, and Travis watched the road ahead. No one saw the person hiding in the bushes race to the back of the truck, open the roll up door, climb inside with the busted freezer, and pull down the door. Travis had the radio up so high he didn't even hear the door clang as it closed.

Once his bladder was empty, Gus zipped up and climbed into the cab. Travis looked in the rear-view mirror. Someone wearing a Kitsune polo shirt had come outside the gate with a bucket and a rag.

"Now look what you made them do," Travis said.

"It's their own fault," Gus said. "They should have let me use the fucking bathroom."

Travis put the truck in drive, and they rumbled away.

"You notice all them rows of vegetables they had growing behind the restaurant," Travis said.

"Yeah," Gus said. "What about them?"

"I bet you dollar to donuts that everything they serve they grow and produce themselves."

"What's your point?"

"These people are fucking weird."

"Hell, I could've told you that."

Thirty minutes later, Travis and Gus drove into Red Fox, Georgia. They stopped at Kemp's Garage for gas. While Travis filled the tank, Gus went inside to buy a pack of Marlboros. Neither of them noticed the person who'd caught a ride with them slip out the back of their truck and dash into the women's bathroom.

With a full tank and a fresh pack of coffin nails, Travis and Gus headed down the mountain toward JH Restaurant Supply in Dalton, Georgia.

Chapter Four

MOST MODERN MOTELS looked alike, and the Fox Creek Falls Inn was no exception. A long rectangular building housed two floors of rooms. The lobby sat next to the rooms. The lobby's walls and furniture were various shades of beige while the carpeting was a relaxing sea of light blue.

When Polly entered the lobby, there was no one in sight. She tapped a shiny call bell on the reception desk, causing a clear ding. Fifteen seconds passed before a South Asian man appeared from an inner office.

Polly looked him over and liked what she saw. Tall dark, and handsome. There was no better way to describe him. He looked to be in his twenties. His jet-black hair hung over his piercing brown eyes. His skin was the color of dark chocolate. He had the beginning of a five o'clock shadow on his chiseled chin. His blue Oxford shirt and pressed beige khakis were tight enough to reveal that he had the muscular body of a dedicated gym rat.

"How may I be of service?" he asked.

Polly liked how his words tumbled past his soft full lips. He was sexy as hell and smelled like smoked lemons. Polly caught herself arching her back so that her breasts thrust forward.

"I understand you rent rooms with kitchenettes by the month," Polly said.

"Indeed, we do," he said.

"Well, that's what I want."

He studied her body so blatantly that Polly was tempted to cover herself. His head snapped up as if he'd been in a trance.

"I will need to check to see if we have any available."

He disappeared into the inner office. Polly waited for a full minute, but he didn't come back. She tapped the bell again.

A short plump South Asian woman with a friendly face emerged.

"Hello," she said cheerfully. "Would you like to check in?"

Polly pointed at the doorway to the inner office.

"I just told that other guy that I wanted to rent a room for a month."

"Would you like one with a kitchenette?"

"Yes," Polly said. "That's what I told the other guy."

The woman turned and shouted into the inner office. "Mansoor! Mansoor! Get out here now."

The young man came out. He kept his head down except to steal worried glances at Polly.

"I'm so sorry," the woman said. "My nephew is normally a very polite man. I don't know what came over him. Mansoor, apologize."

"My deepest apologies," he said.

"We have a room with a kitchenette available. It has a nice view of the mountain."

"Do you have internet?" Polly said.

"We are one of the only establishments in Red Fox that has reliable internet despite the mountains."

Polly signed the necessary paperwork and paid with a credit card. The plump woman handed Polly a room key.

"Just drive down to the far end of the building," she said. "It's room thirteen. If you need anything, just ask. I'm Lata and this is my nephew, Mansoor."

"Thank you, Lata," Polly said.

"Do you need any help with your luggage?" Mansoor asked.

If Mansoor had asked earlier, Polly would not only have said yes, she would have engaged in a little harmless flirting, but his odd behavior had turned her off. Besides, she suspected he was only offering as a way to avoid getting reamed by his aunt once Polly left the reception area.

"No, that's okay," Polly said. "I can handle it myself."

The disappointment on Mansoor's face was painfully clear.

Polly went out to her battered Pontiac Vibe that she called the Purple Beast and drove to the other end of the motel. She found a parking space right in front of room thirteen.

She opened the door and was greeted with the chemical smell of motel room cleaning supplies. The mattress felt solid and from the window she really did have a great view of Red Fox Mountain. Polly carried in her few boxes and suitcases. She had chucked everything she felt was non-essential before she left Atlanta. The few remaining possessions represented everything she had in the world.

She slipped off her sandals and got out of the flower print peasant dress she'd worn for her interview. She put on a pair of worn jeans, a black long-sleeved T-shirt, and sneakers. She tied her long blonde hair into a ponytail. She briefly checked her appearance in the mirror before she grabbed her purse and left her motel room. She got into the Purple Beast and drove to the parking lot exit. Downtown was to the left. Polly turned right.

Chapter Five

THERE ARE PEOPLE who like to smoke after sex. Henry Nix liked to smoke during sex. He sat in his rickety office chair and puffed on a no filter Camel cigarette while a young woman kneeled between his legs. He tapped his ashes into a Styrofoam cup with an inch of coffee in the bottom. The ashes hissed as they hit the brown liquid.

"You got the most appropriate name of anyone I know," he said. "Anita Cox. I-need-a-cock. That's you."

Anita stopped going down on Henry, got to her feet, and put her hands on her hips.

"Do you want to talk, or do you want to fuck?" she said. "I ain't got time for both."

Henry laughed which turned into a rasping cough. He spat into the Styrofoam cup and then leaned back in his chair. His pants and dirty underwear were bunched around his ankles.

"Don't rush me," he said. "It'll ruin the mood. By the way, how's your momma doing?"

"How the hell do you think she's doing. She's drunk on her fat ass and fucking Black men. Same as always."

"Don't bad mouth your momma. You should thank her for teaching you how to suck dick like a pro. Now show me that sweet pussy of yours."

Anita hiked up her skirt. She wasn't wearing panties. She didn't believe in shaving her pubes and was proud of her hairy bush.

Henry dropped his cigarette butt into the cup. It sizzled before dying out. Henry grabbed Anita's arm and pulled her into his lap. He smelled of cigarettes, motor oil, and rank body odor. Anita doubted he'd bathed in days. Ever since high school when she hung out with boys who spent hours working on their cars, Anita had been turned on by the smell of gasoline and grime. And nasty sex. Nothing turned her on more than having a disgusting man run his grubby hands over her young, tender body.

Henry jammed his nicotine-stained fingers inside Anita. She responded by spreading her legs. If it weren't for the fact that Henry was always hungover on a Sunday morning, he would have gone to church and thanked Jesus for taking this petite blonde-haired babe with the perkiest tits and tightest ass he'd ever seen and turning her into a nymphomaniac for ugly assholes like him. Plus, she could cuss worse than a sailor with his dick stuck in a two-dollar whore's ass.

As Henry played with Anita, she gazed at his messy office. Piles of old receipts and coffee cups overflowing with cigarette butts littered his desk. Crappy bookshelves along the wall were filled with obsolete auto parts and fishing trophies left behind by the previous owner. A layer of dust covered everything. A cockroach skittered across the floor.

"Remember last time I was here?" Anita asked.

"How could I forget?" Henry said. The truth was he'd been too drunk last time to remember any details.

Anita quickly undressed, tossing her clothes on the desk.

"I was on the floor on my hands and knees. You took me

from behind like I was nothing more than a junkyard dog. You held onto my hips while you plowed into me. You dug your fingers in so hard, you left bruises. I was black and blue for a solid week."

"Yeah, what about it?"

"Do it again. Now."

Anita got on her hands and knees. Henry positioned himself behind her. Once he was inside her, the outside world and all its baggage dissolved away as pleasure spread throughout her body. What Henry said was true. She was addicted to sex and would suffer any humiliation to obtain it.

Their rutting was interrupted by a loud crash that sounded like metal hitting concrete.

"What the hell!" Henry shouted as he tugged on his pants. "Somebody's trying to rob me."

He took his handgun from a desk drawer and headed for the door.

"Are you just going to leave me here?" Anita asked.

Henry looked back at Anita standing naked in the middle of his office.

"You got a gun?" he asked.

"This is the Bible belt. Everybody has a gun."

"Then I suggest you get it. Stay here until I get back."

Henry left the office. Anita glanced at her watch. She didn't have time to wait for him to come back. She had only stopped by for a quickie before her shift started at the Rejoice Diner. Gathering her clothes, she examined the oil stains on her shirt. Though she hated the way her boss frowned at her when she showed up at work looking like she'd been wallowing in a grease pit, there was no way she was going to change into her clean waitress uniform in this dump.

As she put on her dirty clothes, Anita thought about how much Henry loved this place. Kemp's Garage was one of the last remaining combination gas pump and garages left in Georgia if not the whole U.S. of A. Henry had inherited Kemp's Garage from the original owner, Albert Kemp.

Henry had worked for Albert until the old man died while rebuilding a busted transmission. Even though Albert didn't have any family, Henry was still shocked and touched that Albert had left Henry the garage in his will, so touched that Henry hadn't changed a thing since the day he became the owner thirteen years ago.

Anita opened the office door and listened. She heard a clang followed by Henry cussing, so she guessed that he'd bumped into something.

She really had to pee. Anita might get off on dirty sex, but when it came to using the bathroom, she preferred a clean toilet and Henry cleaned the bathrooms as often as he cleaned the rest of the place, which was never. Her bladder told her she couldn't wait until she got to the diner. She would just have to squat over the women's room toilet.

The bathrooms were outside on the side of the building. Keeping in mind that there might be a thief lurking about, Anita dug her gun out of her purse and held in ready as she entered the bathroom.

There was a gasp, a flash of movement, and the sound of shoes echoing off the tile floor. With adrenaline pumping through her veins, Anita held her gun ready. She kicked open the only stall. A young Black woman stood on the toilet with her hands raised in the don't-shoot-me position.

Anita wasn't sure why she didn't shoot intruder. It was a split-second decision, but time seemed to have slowed down. She saw the fear and desperation in the woman's face. Anita lowered her gun.

"What the fuck?" she said.

"I'm sorry," said the woman. "Just don't shoot me."

"Come on out of there." Anita motioned with her gun hand.

The woman scurried out of the stall. She kept her hands raised. Anita put her gun in her purse, pulled up her skirt, and sat on the toilet forgetting that she didn't want her butt cheeks to touch the nasty seat.

With great relief, Anita emptied her bladder. As she did, she studied the woman standing outside the stall. She put her hands down and stared at the floor so that she wasn't watching Anita do her business. Anita guessed that she was in her early twenties. Anita was twenty-four.

Anita didn't care for Black people, but she was sympathetic to any woman in trouble and this girl had to be in serious trouble if she was hiding in Henry's god-awful bathroom.

"You got a name?" Anita said.

"Dani," the woman stammered. "Dani Lewis."

"Glad to meet you, Dani. My name's Anita."

Anita finished peeing. She fished a tissue out of her purse and used it to wipe herself. She pulled down her skirt and got a bottle of hand sanitizer out of her purse. She squirted the clear goop onto her hands and rubbed it in.

"You work for Kitsune?" Anita asked.

"What makes you think that?" Dani said.

"You got their logo on your shirt."

"How do you know so much about Kitsune?"

"It's been around long enough for even us simple town folk to know some things about the place."

Dani rubbed her fingers on the logo patch.

"Do you know who Kitsune is? He's the Fox God. Kitsune isn't just a restaurant. It's an evil place run by an evil man."

Anita looked at her watch. If she didn't leave now, she was going to be late. She wasn't worried about getting fired, she just wasn't in the mood to listen to her boss gripe about her tardiness.

"This Kitsune guy sounds like a real prick and I'm sorry he

did you wrong, but I got to skedaddle," Anita said. "You be careful. Henry's out there with a gun. He thinks you're trying to rob him."

"Please don't leave me here," Dani said, blocking the door. "I swear I didn't try to steal anything. In fact, I haven't left the bathroom since I hid in here this morning."

"You've been in here all day? How the hell did you survive the stink of this shithole?"

"I was afraid to leave. I figured when it got dark, I'd make a run for it. But I have nowhere to go."

"You weren't in the garage just now?"

"No."

Four gunshots rang out. Dani threw her arms around Anita. She was shaking with fear.

Anita was once this frightened. When she was a little girl, she would hide under her covers in bed while her parents yelled at each other. She was afraid their anger would bust into her room and consume her. For years, Anita had carried a prickly ball of fear in her stomach until she found strength and security in the arms of boys. Then later, she found strength in herself. This was the first time someone had sought strength in her arms. It annoyed and thrilled her at the same time.

Anita peeled Dani off her.

"Calm the fuck down. You can stay at my place until you figure out where you want to go," Anita said. "But first, I'm going to see who Henry shot."

"And then you'll come right back?" Dani said.

Anita put her hand on Dani's shoulder.

"I'll be right back. Okay?"

Dani nodded but seemed dubious. Anita peeked out the door. Henry came marching by the bathrooms carrying the biggest, ugliest rat she'd ever seen. The rat and Henry could have been brothers. Henry was holding the vermin by the tip of its disgusting tail. Blood dripped out of the dead rat's mouth, and it had a large meaty hole in its midsection.

"Weren't no thief after all," Henry said. "It was this big ass motherfucker."

"Damn, Henry," Anita said. "You sure there aren't more of them fuckers living back there."

"Gawd, I hope not. While I was trying to kill this guy, I shot a hole through the tire of a car I was working on. Now I got to give the owner a free tire." Henry turned the deceased rodent from side to side and then grinned at Anita. "Hey, what do you say we pick up where we left off?"

The man never was much for sweet talk.

"Naw," Anita said. "I got to go to work. Maybe some other time."

Henry pouted but didn't argue and headed for the dumpster to dispose of the rat. Anita waited until he was out of sight before she led Dani out of the women's bathroom.

When they were two blocks from the garage, Anita paused. The Rejoice Diner was just down the street. Her house was a mile away in the opposite direction.

"Hell, I better call him," Anita said as she took out her cellphone. She called the diner. Her boss, Owen Tew, answered.

"Rejoice Diner. Praise the Lord and pass the taters."

"Owen, it's Anita. I'm going to be late."

"Goddamn it, Anita! Put your panties on and get your ass in here pronto."

"The longer you bitch at me on the phone the later I'm going to be. I'll see you when I see you."

Anita hung up.

"Come on," she said. "I live that way."

"Where's your car?" Dani said.

"Don't have one."

Anita considered a car an unnecessary expense. Everything

she needed was in Red Fox and if she wanted to go somewhere, there were plenty of men willing to take her. She didn't even need to blow some of them for the ride.

Dani shook her head. "Somebody will see us. Is there another way to get there where we won't be out in the open?"

"Yeah, but it takes forever."

"You don't understand. Kitsune will send somebody to find me. I can't let anyone see me."

Anita groaned. Why did helping people have to be so damn hard?

"Lucky for you I grew up here and know all the back roads. Now let's go. I'm already late for work."

Anita took a dirt path that led behind a row of houses. Dani stayed close behind her.

Chapter Six

POLLY PARKED THE Purple Beast in front of a white bungalow. The old house was showing its age. The paint was peeling, and the front porch sagged. A sale sign in the front yard was almost completely obscured by weeds.

The boards creaked loudly as Polly stepped onto the porch and she prayed it wouldn't collapse as she peered into a dirty window. Other than a wooden chair with a missing leg and a dust covered vase, the interior was empty. Except for a house on the corner, none of the homes on the street were occupied.

While weeds had claimed the front yard, the backyard was a dirt square with a few pitiful islands of grass. A patch of woods fifty yards wide separated the homes on this street from the homes on the next street. Polly walked along the edge of the woods until she detected a ghost of a trail.

She followed the trail, pausing next to a tall pine tree to listen to an early rising owl. After so many hours driving from Atlanta to Red Fox, it felt good to stretch her legs. The trail ended at the edge of a half-acre lot. The yard was well-kept with plenty of shade trees including a majestic oak next to a three-story colonial home.

In contrast to the street where Polly had left the Purple Beast, there were no empty houses on this street. The colonial and its neighbors were inhabited by people who obviously took great pride in their homes and their spacious yards. There wasn't a single rusting car on blocks.

Though there was an exterior staircase that led to the third floor of the house, Polly opted to climb the adjacent oak tree. She ascended quickly, rarely pausing to test a limb to make sure it wouldn't snap under her weight. The limbs allowed her to step directly onto the roof. She walked over to a third-floor window. The drapes were pulled shut so she couldn't look inside. As she suspected, the window had been left unlocked. She opened the window and listened.

When Polly felt certain that no one was inside, she parted the drapes and climbed in. The air smelled stale. She turned on the light switch. She was in a living room with a couch, easy chair, and coffee table. Walking from room to room, she turned on lights and explored the entire floor. There was a bedroom, living room, bathroom, kitchenette, study, and two closets. In the hall closet was a cardboard box sealed shut, otherwise she would have been tempted to look inside.

There were lots of windows that would let in plenty of light when the drapes were pulled open. Though it was furnished, there was nothing personal on the walls or the shelves to indicate who had lived here. The lack of dust indicated that someone kept it clean. It felt like a hotel room waiting for a guest to arrive.

Polly sat on the living room couch and imagined how she would decorate the place.

The sound of a car approaching sent Polly running to the

window. A red minivan came up the driveway and parked next to the house. Her new employer, Martha Aldridge, got out.

Polly quickly turned off all the lights, climbed out of the window and onto the roof. She pulled the window shut and walked softly across the roof. When she reached the oak tree, she hesitated.

She listened to the front door open, and slam shut. Martha was inside the house. Polly could feel her heart beating a mile a minute as she climbed down the oak tree. When she reached the ground, she hid behind the trunk.

From her vantage point, Polly could see into the kitchen. Martha entered and opened the kitchen window. She filled a kettle with water from the tap. Once she had the kettle on the stove, she got a ceramic cup and dropped a teabag into it. Then, her phone rang.

With the window open, Polly could hear Martha's side of the conversation.

"Hello? Yes, Crystal, I made it home without any problems... Of course, there was no traffic. This is Red Fox, Georgia. The closest thing we have to traffic is the annual Christmas Parade... What am I doing tonight? Nothing. That's what I'm doing... What's that?... Okay. See you tomorrow."

Martha hung up. The kettle whistled and she poured steaming water into her cup. With the cup in hand, she left the kitchen. Once she was out of sight, Polly hurried across the yard and into the woods.

When she reached the barren yard on the other side of the woods, Polly noticed she was sweating heavily and that her jeans were covered with beggar's lice. The green seeds stuck like Velcro. With her attention on removing the annoying suckers off her pants, Polly didn't see the police car parked behind the Purple Beast until she was in the front yard.

Her first instinct was to run and hide, but the policeman

standing by his patrol car had already seen her. Her heart sank. She had gotten greedy and had ruined her plans before she even got started. She gave the officer a weak smile and waved. He waved back.

"Where were you?" he said. "I looked all around the house, but I couldn't find you."

"I was in the woods," Polly said.

Her legs were shaky as she walked toward him. She stopped by the Purple Beast. He sauntered over and leaned against her car.

"The woods, huh?" he said as he hooked his thumbs in his belt. "Well, that makes sense."

She was sure that he was toying with her, but she wasn't going to make it easy for him. She would let him ask the questions. Then again, if he asked her why she was spying on her new boss, she had no idea what she would say.

"May I see your license and proof of insurance?" he said.

"My purse is in the car," Polly said.

She got her keys out of her jeans pocket and started to unlock her car door.

"Hold on, Miss," the officer said. "Do you have a gun in your car?"

Polly took a step away from her car.

"No, officer. I don't own a gun."

He rubbed his chin. His mirror shades hid his eyes so Polly couldn't begin to guess what he was thinking.

"Okay," he said finally. "Get your purse."

Polly got her purse from the front seat, took her license and insurance card out of her wallet, and handed them to the officer.

"Wait here," he said.

He got into his patrol car. Polly took a deep breath. She had nothing to worry about. She had given him a legitimate driver's license. The car was legally hers.

Five minutes took their dear sweet time passing before the officer returned. He handed her license and insurance card back to her. Polly stuffed them into her purse, which she had been clutching to her stomach.

"Red Fox is a small town. Strangers stand out," the officer said. "I haven't seen you around here before. You passing through?"

"I just moved here. Today, in fact."

He took off his round brim hat and mirror shade sunglasses. He put the sunglasses in his pocket and held the hat in his hands. Polly had always been a sucker for men with dark hair and blue eyes, and his eyes were the deepest blue she'd seen in a long time. Her knees weakened for reasons other than fear and she had to put her hand on her car to steady herself.

"Back when I was a kid, I used to play in those woods," he said, pointing where Polly had just been. "Me and my best friend spent hours back there messing around. His house is not too far from here."

"Really?" Polly said. Her mouth was dry, so she had trouble getting the words out. "So, you live in this neighborhood?"

"Naw. I live about four miles thataway. Listen to me ramble on. Where are my manners? My name's Skyler Aldridge. I'm a deputy with the Red Fox Police Department. And you are?"

"Polly. Polly Swift."

They shook hands. His strong grip sent a jolt through her as she tried not to stare at his handsome face with his blue eyes, thick eyebrows, and the kind of lips that girls like to kiss. His only imperfection was a broken nose which only made him sexier.

"You're probably wondering why I'm out here," Skyler said. He didn't wait for her to respond. "Mrs. Hensley is the only neighbor left on this street. She called the police. She claimed she saw you breaking into the old Miller house. We knew that couldn't be right. It's been a dog's age since Mr. Miller died and he didn't leave a damn thing worth stealing. But we had to send somebody to check it out and here I am."

"And here you are," Polly said.

"You know you can do better."

"I don't think that's possible."

"Then this house? Sure, you can."

"Oh right. The house."

"There are plenty of places available that aren't near as run down as this one. Besides, do you really want to live across the street from nosey Mrs. Hensley?"

Polly looked at Mrs. Hensley's house. An old woman was at the window glaring at them.

"I'm not ready to buy," Polly said. "I was just being a looky-loo."

Skyler put his hat on his head.

"Well, I better get back to the station. I'm sure I'll be seeing you around."

"That would be nice. It was a pleasure to meet you, Deputy Aldridge."

"The pleasure was all mine, Ms. Swift."

He got into his car and drove away. Polly looked back at Mrs. Hensley's house. The old busybody was still giving Polly the evil eye. Polly decided to leave before she called the police again.

But first, Polly was going to get the beggar's lice off her jeans. As she picked them off, she scolded herself for almost getting caught. She got lucky this time. She might not be so lucky next time. She had to be extra careful from now on.

Chapter Seven

Terrence Grigsby was in a good mood. The restaurant was full. The dinner crowd had arrived on time, and no one complained about having to wait at the front gate while their reservation and identity were validated. Happy chatter filled the dining room. More than once, Terrence had seen a customer sneak their smartphone out and take a photo of their food. Kitsune had a no photography rule, but it was the only one of their rules that was never enforced. Smuggled food photos added to Kitsune's mystique.

Terrence entered the kitchen, and his mood went from good to practically giddy. Mr. Kite wasn't yelling at the cooks.

Mr. Kite was Kitsune's head chef and culinary visionary. His long hair flowed out from under his chef's hat and his bushy beard covered half of his white apron. He ambled from station to station enlightening his crew on the proper way to achieve gastronomic nirvana.

Mr. Kite showed a cook the proper way to decorate the carrot crepes with petals and sunflower seeds. He tasted the charred cauliflower and potato soup and advised the cook to add more kale. He took one look at the miso-marinated Portobello carpaccio and tossed it into the garbage, and then told the cook to start over.

A prep cook fell to his knees when Mr. Kite approached his station and bowed down so that his lips touched Mr. Kite's feet. Everyone froze. There was a time and place to bow to the master but never during the dinner rush hour. Terrence froze too, his good mood wavering.

To everyone's relief, Mr. Kite smiled and bid the young man to stand and go back to chopping vegetables. Terrence relaxed and took a moment to breathe in the wonderful aromas drifting from the stoves and ovens. He had purposely skipped lunch and the smell made his stomach rumble. Like a junkie who puts off shooting up until his body is in desperate need of a fix, Terrence had been putting off eating one of Mr. Kite's sublime dishes until he couldn't wait any longer. The time was coming soon.

Terrence went upstairs to his office and found Lorenzo waiting for him. The worried look on the head waiter's face immediately killed Terrence's good mood.

"What's wrong?" Terrence said.

"We just found out," Lorenzo said. "We would have discovered it sooner, but we thought maybe there'd been a change in the schedule that we forgot about or maybe she got sick. It happens. People sometimes get sick at the last minute."

"What in the name of the holy Fox God are you talking about, Lorenzo?"

"Dani Lewis. She's missing. She was scheduled to be a waiter tonight, but she didn't show up. We found a replacement."

Terrence wasn't worried about finding someone to take Dani's place. Every disciple on dishwasher or janitor duty would kill for a chance to move up to waiter. The real question was why wasn't Dani Lewis out there right now taking orders and carrying trays to hungry customers?

"When did you first figure out, she was missing?"

"After the dinner shift began. It wasn't until things got busy that we noticed we were missing a waiter. Once we got someone to cover her shift, we checked Dani's cabin."

Terrence sat at his desk and nibbled on his thumb. People were always trying to get inside their world. And who could blame them? Kitsune had created a heaven on earth. Once they gained entrance, nobody in their right mind would want to leave. That was what worried Terrence the most. Only someone truly disturbed would leave this heaven and such a person wouldn't hesitate to spread terrible lies about Kitsune.

"Should I tell Mr. Kite?" Lorenzo asked.

Terrance glared at Lorenzo.

"You'll do no such thing. He mustn't be disturbed. Get back to work. I'll handle this."

Lorenzo left the office. Terrence drummed his fingers on his desk. He needed to find Dani, but it had to be done quietly. Mr. Kite entered the office without knocking. He sat in the visitor's chair and propped his feet on the edge of Terrence's desk.

"I understand that a waiter has gone missing," Mr. Kite said as he stroked his beard.

"How did you find out?" Terrence asked.

"We're a close-knit family. News travels faster than a falcon swooping down to snatch a mockingbird from the sky. Which waiter is missing?"

"Dani Lewis."

Mr. Kite twirled the tips of his mustache.

"Remind me who she is."

Terrence had to think a minute before he could picture her.

"African American. Round face. Cute."

"Hmmm. Does she have what the boys crudely refer to as a bubble butt?"

"That's her."

"I remember now. She was among the group scheduled to compete for my special enlightenment at our next ceremony."

Terrence rubbed his forehead. This was bad. A true believer would give his right arm for a chance to receive Mr. Kite's special enlightenment. If Dani was avoiding the ceremony that meant there had been a heretic in their midst.

"There's no way she could've gotten out of the compound," Terrence said. "The security guards would have seen her. She must be hiding. Don't worry. We'll find her."

"I'm not worried," Mr. Kite said. "But need I remind you that our compound covers ten acres? That's a lot of hiding places."

"What do you suggest we do?"

"Unless she's running around naked, she should be wearing some article of clothing provided by Kitsune. Don't forget, all those clothes have the Kitsune logo."

"Of course! Every Kitsune logo has a tracking device sewn into it. All the security guards need to do is zero in Dani's GPS coordinates."

Mr. Kite gave Terrence his most benevolent smile, which was sometimes mistaken for a smirk.

"Feel better?" Mr. Kite said.

Terrence did feel better. He had calmed down enough to feel hunger again.

"Thank you, Mr. Kite. As always, you're brilliant."

"That's why I'm the Fox God."

Chapter Eight

POLLY ENTERED HER motel room. She was sweaty and dirty. She needed a shower, but she wanted to get on her computer first. It wasn't until she had booted up that she realized that she had forgotten to get the Fox Creek Falls Inn's internet password. She called the front desk.

"Front desk. How may I assist you?"

Polly recognized Mansoor's deep, smooth voice.

"Hi, I just checked in today. I'm in room thirteen."

"Yes, Ms. Swift. How can I be of service?"

Polly was glad he couldn't see her blushing over the phone.

"Uh, I forgot to get the internet password."

"Yes, of course. Do you have something to write this down?"

Polly dug through her purse for a pen and a scrap of paper to write on.

"Got it. Go ahead."

"It's jaldi karo and then an exclamation point."

"I'm sorry. What?"

Mansoor chuckled. "Let me spell it for you."

He spelled it slowly and Polly wrote it down. She stared at what she had written.

"Is this Hindu?" she asked.

"It is indeed. It means hurry up. It's Aunty Lata's little joke. When it comes to an internet connection, we all desire that it be quick, so we tell it to hurry up and connect already."

Polly laughed. "Tell Lata that I like her joke."

"Just a moment, Ms. Swift. Since this is your first day as a resident of Red Fox, may I have the pleasure of buying you dinner? There is a lovely diner close by."

"Are you asking me out on a date?"

"A date? No. I would not call it a date. We've only just met. Think of me as the unofficial welcoming committee. And I would like to make up for my rude behavior this morning."

"Well in that case, how can I say no? Can you wait an hour? I have some things I need to do."

"No problem. When you're ready, I'll be in the front office."

Polly hung up the phone. She got on the internet and checked her Facebook page. She always looked at the page of her friend, Bobby, first. He loved posting photos. He took wonderful pictures considering he was an amateur. It helped that he lived in a beautiful place. She chose three of his landscape photos and downloaded them onto her desktop. She avoided photos of Bobby and his girlfriend.

She got off Facebook and checked her email. There were no messages. Polly wasn't surprised. Before leaving Atlanta, she had narrowed down her circle of friends to just those individuals that she was extremely close to.

She logged off the email server and logged onto her second email server. She had one new message. Polly wasn't surprised by this either. Only one person was aware of this email address and the single message was from her. She wanted Polly to know that she liked the last batch of photos, but why weren't there any selfies? She also asked about the weather.

Polly responded to the email. She attached the photos she'd downloaded from Bobby's Facebook page and then wrote: Mom, here are my latest photos. It's nice out. Lots of sun and people are still wearing shorts, but fall is coming soon. I miss you. Have a blessed day.

She finished the message and hit send. She shut down her computer and then took off her dirty clothes. She made a mental note to see if the motel had a laundry room. Polly was disappointed at how sore she felt. Hiking through a small patch of woods and climbing an oak tree was hardly excessive physical activity. Starting tomorrow she would start jogging again.

Polly got into the shower and let the hot water soothe her muscles. After the shower, she wrapped a towel around herself before digging through her suitcase for something to wear on her non-date with Mansoor. She didn't want to get too dressed up and give him the wrong impression.

In different circumstances, she would have worn something slinky and revealing. She would have put on her best fuck-me shoes. After purging so many of her possessions, Polly was down to just one pair of fuck-me shoes.

But Polly was on a mission in Red Fox, and she couldn't let anyone, even someone as sexy as Mansoor, distract her from her goal. So instead, she put on a beige blouse, clean jeans, and sandals.

The sun was setting as Polly walked from her room to the lobby. The crispness in the air meant Fall would be here soon. She breathed in deeply. After years of Atlanta's polluted air, she'd forgotten how sweet clean air smelled.

Mansoor was busy checking in a middle-aged couple, so Polly waited in the lobby. While the couple had their attention on the paperwork, Mansoor caught Polly's eye and winked. Polly blushed and blushed some more.

The couple got their key and left.

"I'll be right with you," Mansoor said.

He went into the inner office and took his sport coat off a coat rack. Aunty Lata sat at the desk and went over the maid's time sheets. She smiled at her nephew.

"You going to dinner now?" she asked.

"Yes," Mansoor said. "Would you like me to order you something? I can bring it back with me."

"No. Your uncle promised me that he was going to get off his lazy butt and make dinner tonight." Lata came around the desk and peeked into the lobby. "She looks very nice. I'm glad to see you're finally going on a date. I was beginning to think you were becoming a hermit."

"It's not a date. I'm just welcoming Polly to Red Fox."

"Two young people going out together. That's the very definition of a date."

"Okay, it's a date. Just don't tell her. If she found out, she might change her mind."

Chapter Nine

Deputy Skyler Aldridge was attacked the moment he entered the living room. His son, Connor, tackled one leg, and his daughter, Harper, grabbed the other.

"Daddy's home! Daddy's home!" they chanted.

Skyler could smell meatloaf cooking. His favorite. He swung his legs, carrying the heavy loads clutching his thighs. The children enjoyed the ride. Tickling loosened their grip and left them giggling on the floor.

"So, what did you two do today?"

"I don't remember," Harper said, shrugging her tiny shoulders.

"The yard man came with his big machine," Connor said. He made motions with his hands as if he were pushing a mower. "He went brrrr, brrrr, brrrr and then there was no grass."

Skyler left the kids in the living room and joined Tracie in the kitchen where she was mashing potatoes. She glanced over her shoulder at him and smiled.

"Hey, how're you doing?" she asked cheerfully.

"You're in a good mood," Skyler said. "For a change."

"And there you go trying to ruin it."

Skyler held up his hands. "Sorry. You're right. I'm glad you're in a good mood. Hey, I'm in good mood too."

"Good."

Skyler leaned against the kitchen counter and crossed his arms.

"How much are we paying Duane to cut the lawn?"

Tracie froze for a moment and then resumed mashing the potatoes.

"I'll have to check. Whatever we're paying him it's not enough. He does such a good job."

"Sure, he does, but how good does our yard have to be? We're not competing for best yard in the neighborhood."

"What are you suggesting?"

Skyler shrugged. "I just figured we could use the money we're giving Duane on something else. Like paying bills and saving up for a vacation. Besides, I'm fully capable of mowing my own damn yard."

Tracie struggled to remain calm. If she freaked out, he might become suspicious.

"Okay," she said. "But this better not be one of those situations where I end up having to do it for you. The only reason I hired Duane in the first place was because you said you were so busy at work that you didn't have time to cut the lawn."

"Yeah. That's true. Let me think about it."

"Dinner will be ready in about fifteen minutes."

Skyler opened the frig and took out a can of beer. Fifteen minutes. That gave him time to catch up on some stuff in his man cave. He went down a flight of stairs to the basement. Football trophies lined a bookcase and NASCAR posters were taped to a wood panel wall. A computer and an empty ashtray sat on a card table in the middle of the room. Two metal filing cabinets stood behind the desk chair.

Only Skyler was allowed to come down here. It was the

only room in the house where he could get any privacy. A man needed time alone where no one bothered him. It never crossed Skyler's mind that Tracie might need a room of her own for the same reason.

Skyler unbuckled his leather belt and placed it on the top shelf of the bookcase. He locked his gun in a metal cabinet. He sat down at the card table and turned on the computer. While he waited for it to boot up, he lit up a cigarette. This was the only place inside the house he was allowed to smoke in.

When the computer was up and running, he checked his Facebook page before briefly surfing his favorite porn sites. Then, he switched over to his home surveillance system. He called up the cameras he'd installed in the living room, kitchen, kids' rooms, front yard, back yard, and garage. The eight feeds came on the screen as two rows of four squares. The kids were watching TV and Tracie had the stove door open as she inspected the meatloaf.

Skyler tapped on the keyboard. The live camera feeds were replaced with the DVR connected to the hidden camera in his bedroom. When he installed the security system, he didn't tell Tracie about this camera.

He fast forwarded through the video from today's recording. It was like watching a Benny Hill episode as he and Tracie sped through their morning routine. Once they were dressed and gone, the only activity for hours was from sunbeams moving across the floor as they shone through the window.

Mid-afternoon, Duane Anderson entered the bedroom. Skyler stopped fast forwarding and hit play. Duane removed his clothes and lay naked on the bed. Tracie came into the bedroom five minutes later and did a strip tease for Duane before climbing into bed with him. Skyler leaned closer to the monitor as his wife and his yard man fornicated on his bed.

Skyler was thankful the video had no audio track.

He had suspected for some time that Tracie was cheating on him, and now he had proof. He turned off the video. Any other man would have stormed upstairs and confronted his wife. Maybe even have given her face a well-deserved slap. But Skyler was not any other man.

Skyler was heartbroken, but not because Tracie had cheated on him. He was heartbroken because he didn't care. Skyler didn't love Tracie. He never had.

Why did he get married?

Tracie was guilty as sin, but so was Skyler. He was the one who proposed. He let her get pregnant.

The basement door opened, and Connor shouted down to him.

"Mom says dinner's ready!"

Skyler shut down the computer.

"It's about time!" he shouted back. "I'm starving."

Chapter Ten

"So, what do you think of Red Fox so far?" Mansoor asked.

"It's charming," Polly said. "I think I'm falling in love with this town."

Mansoor drove to the center of downtown Red Fox. The buildings were old but well preserved. The streets were clean. The sun had gone down, and families walked on the sidewalks.

Mansoor parked in front of the Rejoice Diner. The heavy aroma of fried chicken and bacon fat greeted Polly as they entered. The place was half full of customers, which considering it was a weeknight suggested that the food was good.

The dining room was one long room. Booths with red vinyl seats were on one side and a long counter with counter stools was on the other. The ceiling fans turned slowly over the checkerboard tile floor. A football pre-season game played on the television mounted on the wall. The rest of the wall was covered with photos of fishermen holding up their prize catches. Ironically, the diner didn't serve fish of any kind.

A sign said to take any seat that wasn't already taken so Mansoor suggested an empty booth. Polly slid in.

"Have you ever eaten at a place like this?" Mansoor said.

"A meat and three?" Polly said as she looked over the menu. "Sure. They have places like this in Atlanta, but I grew up in a small town just like Red Fox. This place reminds me of home."

A waitress came to their table. She was a petite blonde with blue eyes and a button nose. She wore a pink waitress uniform with a black apron and ankle socks with pom poms.

"Hey, Mansoor," she said as she took out her order pad. "Sorry you had to wait. I'm running behind tonight."

"No problem," Mansoor said. "Anita, this is Polly Swift. She just moved to town today."

"Is that right?" Anita said. "What the hell made you decide to move here?"

Polly liked Anita's candor. She could tell this was a no bullshit girl.

"I wanted to get out of Atlanta and move to a smaller town," Polly said. "I found out that Martha's Hair Done Right needed a new hair stylist."

"You do hair?"

"I do indeed."

Anita pushed a strand of hair out of her eyes.

"I've been cutting my own lately and as you can see, it's a mess. Can you cut my hair?"

"Sure. I start tomorrow. Just call the shop and make an appointment."

"Well, all right. Do you know what you want, or do you need a minute?"

Polly chose the grilled chicken breast with collard greens and a salad with oil and vinegar. Mansoor ordered a vegetable plate with mashed potatoes, black-eyed peas, collard greens, Waldorf salad, and macaroni and cheese. They both ordered unsweetened iced tea. Anita rushed away and returned shortly with their iced tea.

"So, were you born in America, or did you move here?" Polly asked as she squeezed lemon into her tea.

"I grew up in Mumbai. I lived there until three years ago when I was exiled to America."

"Exiled? That's pretty harsh."

Mansoor shrugged.

"There's no better way to describe it. My parents forced me to move here to work for my aunt and uncle. Don't get me wrong. I love my aunt and uncle and I enjoy working at the motel, but it was not my choice to come here."

Polly sipped her tea and wished that she'd ordered the sweet tea instead. She tore open a sugar packet and poured the contents into her glass.

"You're going to make me work for this, aren't you?" she said. "Very well. Why did your parents exile you to America?"

Before he could answer, Anita arrived with their food. It was steaming hot and smelled delicious. The portions were more than generous and included a basket of cornbread.

Polly took a bite of her chicken and smiled. "Just like Mom used to make. Okay Mansoor, tell me your story."

"Like most tragedies, this one involves a girl. Her name is Riya. I met her at a party, and it was love at first sight. But I knew from the beginning that she would not be acceptable to my parents, so I didn't tell them about her. I managed to keep our relationship a secret for over a year before they found out. They were horrified. To keep me away from Riya, they sent me here. They figured that there was no chance that I would ever meet someone like Riya in a tiny American town like Red Fox."

Polly smeared a tab of butter on a slab of cornbread and took a bite. Her mother never made cornbread this good.

"I don't really understand the caste system in India," Polly said. "I didn't realize people still discriminated according to your class."

"This had nothing to do with the caste system," Mansoor said. "My parents didn't want me to be with Riya because she is a *hijra*."

"What's that?"

Mansoor pushed his food around on his plate before answering.

"A ladyboy. A transgender woman. A chick with a dick."

Polly put her fork down.

"I see," she said.

Mansoor smiled at Polly.

"Can you imagine how shocked my parents would be if they knew I was having dinner with a transgender woman right now?"

Chapter Eleven

POLLY SWIFT HAD been looking forward to her meal, but that was before the handsome man seated across from her ruined her appetite.

"Mansoor Amin, you don't know what you're talking about," she said. "I'm not what you think I am."

"Whoever performed your surgery did an excellent job," Mansoor said, "but there are little details that only someone who has spent a lot of time in intimate company with a transgender woman can see. You've had facial reconstruction, your Adam's Apple shaved, breast augmentation, and are presently taking hormones. You're still tucking so you haven't had sexual reassignment surgery yet. Did I miss anything?"

Polly covered her face with her hands. This was a disaster. She'd been in Red Fox for less than a day and already her hopes and dreams had crashed and burned.

Anita came by the table.

"Ma'am?" she asked. "Are you okay?"

"She's fine, Anita," Mansoor said.

"I didn't ask you. I asked her."

Other diners started to take an interest in what was going on. Mansoor glanced around nervously. He knew what it looked like. The dark-skinned man was upsetting the white woman.

"Please, Polly," he said. "People are watching."

Polly took a deep breath. She put down her hands and looked up at Anita.

"I'm fine. Thank you for asking."

Once Anita had left, Polly narrowed her eyes at Mansoor.

"I don't know what you thought was going to happen, but you can forget it," she said. "I'm not scared of you."

Polly grabbed her purse and scooted out of the booth, leaving her mostly untouched dinner on the table. Mansoor watched dumbfounded as she walked out of the diner. The Rejoice Diner was about a mile from the motel, and it was a pleasant night for a walk. Polly just wished she had worn sneakers instead of sandals.

Chapter Twelve

Tracie washed the dishes in the kitchen while Skyler watched a baseball game in the living room. Connor sat next to his father on the couch and begged Skyler for a sip of his beer.

"What do you think?" Skyler called out to Tracie. "Should I let Connor have a taste or is he too young?"

"One little sip won't hurt," Tracie replied.

Tracie scrubbed vigorously to remove bits of meatloaf stuck to the sides of a baking dish. The sound of the baseball game floated in from the living room. She didn't notice Skyler enter the kitchen until he opened the refrigerator door. He took out a beer can, popped it open, and leaned against the kitchen counter.

"You'll never believe what just happened," Skyler said. He took a sip.

"You left the empty can of the beer you just finished in the living room and expect me to throw it away for you?" Tracie said. "I believe it. I totally believe it."

Skyler ignored her nagging. She hated to have to nag him, but not as much as she hated that he paid no attention to her nagging.

"I handed my beer to Connor and told him to just take a little sip," Skyler said. "Instead, he guzzled it. I had half a can left and he emptied it before I could stop him. If I had drunk that much beer when I was his age, I would have passed out."

Tracie's stomach rumbled and she felt light-headed.

"Oh my God, Skyler. You shouldn't have let him do that."

"I thought he'd take one sip, make a face, and complain about how terrible it tastes. Nobody likes beer the first time they try it. Instead, Connor says he likes how it tastes. Says it tastes like apple juice. Ain't that something?"

Tracie could feel bile rising in her throat. She wasn't sure she could make it to the bathroom in time. She let go of the baking dish and it dropped through the soapy water to the bottom of the sink. Holding her hand over her mouth, she pushed past Skyler making him spill beer on his shirt. He started to complain, but she was already down the hall and in the bathroom.

Tracie locked the bathroom door. The toilet seat was already up because Skyler was incapable of remembering to lower it. She got to her knees and vomited into the bowl.

When she was done, she flushed and sat on the floor with her cheek against the cool porcelain edge of the toilet. Emptying her stomach made her feel better. She washed her face and brushed her teeth. She looked at herself in the mirror. Her cheeks were flushed. She rarely threw up, even back in high school when she used to drink like a fish.

It could have been something she ate, but nobody else got sick. There was another reason why women threw up. Tracie opened the medicine cabinet and checked her birth control pills. She hadn't missed a dose. But the only birth control that was one hundred percent effective was abstinence. Every so often, the others don't work. Could this have been one of those times?

When Tracie came out of the bathroom, she found that Skyler had returned to the living room to watch the baseball game. She was hurt that he hadn't checked on her to see if she was okay. But it was just one more hurt to go with all the others. She finished washing the dishes and cleaned the kitchen.

Exhausted, she went into the living room and sat in the easy chair. The game was still on, but Skyler and Connor had both fallen asleep on the couch with Connor curled up under Skyler's arm. Most mothers would have taken a photo to capture this adorable moment, but Tracie was too tired to move.

She was also too terrified to move. What if she was pregnant? She and Skyler hadn't had sex in almost a year. He was bad at math, but not that bad. Even if she could convince him that he had gotten her pregnant, once she gave birth to a dark-skinned baby, he would know the truth. Everybody in Red Fox would know the truth. It was bad enough that she had screwed someone other than her husband, but the other man was Black. In this town, there were few sins worse than that.

Tracie waited until the game was over, and then she threw away the empty beer cans and tucked Connor into his bed. She didn't wake Skyler and went to bed alone.

Chapter Thirteen

POLLY TRIED AND failed to keep the tears from coming. She curled up on her motel bed with her face buried in the pillow and sobbed. It wasn't fair. She had planned everything so carefully. She had done everything right. Then this strange man showed up and ruined her life. The chances that a guy like Mansoor would be in Red Fox, Georgia were beyond astronomical. Obviously, God was punishing her for thinking her plan would work.

It didn't help that Mansoor Amin was so damn attractive. If circumstances had been different, she would have easily fallen for him. Good thing she found out he was an evil bastard before she did anything stupid.

Polly wiped her tears with a tissue and poured herself another glass of white wine. She'd bought the wine from a Piggly Wiggly that she passed on her way back to the motel. Normally, she wouldn't have touched alcohol the night before starting a new job, but she desperately needed a drink after the experience she'd had at the diner.

The more she drank, the less reason she saw in going to work in the morning. She should pack her things and drive back to Atlanta tonight. Don't even bother telling Martha. Just go.

Polly emptied her glass in one gulp. The wine stung the back of her throat. She began to pack her belongings but was interrupted by a knock on the door. She looked through the peephole. Mansoor stood outside her door. He was holding a white plastic bag.

"Go away," Polly said.

"Please, Polly," Mansoor said. "Let me in. We need to talk."

"No, we don't. Go away."

"I brought you your dinner." He held up the plastic bag. "You left before you had a chance to eat. I'm sure you are very hungry."

Her stomach growled which meant he was right. She was so upset that she forgot that she hadn't eaten. That would explain why the wine made her head spin so quickly.

Polly cracked open the door and held out her hand. Mansoor gave her the bag. Polly pulled it into her room and slammed the door in his face. In the bag was a Styrofoam clamshell containing the food she'd ordered. Mansoor must have had the diner give him a fresh dinner because the food was hot. She put the clamshell on the table, tore open the clear plastic bag with plastic utensils, and dug in. She chewed rapidly and washed it down with wine.

She paused halfway through her meal and looked through the peephole. Mansoor hadn't moved. Polly knew she was going to regret it, but she opened the door and waved Mansoor inside. Polly went back to her dinner and Mansoor sat on the corner of the bed.

"I don't understand what you're angry about," Mansoor said. "I thought you would be pleased to know that there was someone in this desolate town who you could relate to."

Polly resisted the urge to throw her collard greens in his face.

It would be a waste of delicious collard greens and would do little to mar his perfect cheekbones.

"I admit it," Polly said. "I'm transgender. I have a penis. Are you happy now?"

"Happy isn't the word I would use to describe my feelings at this moment," Mansoor said. "I reached out to you in a friendly way, and you completely misinterpreted my intentions."

Polly slammed her wine glass on the table.

"Friendly? You took me to a public place and ambushed me! What do you want from me?"

Mansoor's eyes widened.

"I wasn't trying to ambush you. Quite the opposite. I figured out your secret and so I told you mine."

Polly attacked her food, jabbing the chicken and salad with her fork, transferring her anger at Mansoor onto her innocent meal.

"What exactly is your terrible secret? You like ladyboys? Big deal. Unless you're caught making out with one, nobody can prove it."

"Personally, I don't care who knows, but my parents made me promise that I would tell no one. Not even my aunt and uncle. My parents were too ashamed to tell them."

Polly emptied the last of the wine from the bottle into her glass.

"Now that we know each other's secret, what happens now?"

Mansoor stared at his polished shoes.

"I was hoping that I had finally found someone that I could talk to who wouldn't judge me."

Polly put down her fork. There was a stabbing pain in her stomach.

"I get it, Mansoor, I really do but here's the thing. All I have left to do before I become a complete woman is my bottom surgery. Once I have that, there's no going back. Before I make that final decision, I want to experience life as a woman. I couldn't do that in Atlanta. Too many people knew me. I had to move someplace where I was a complete stranger and more importantly, a place where nobody knew I was trans. To the people of Red Fox, I'm a woman. They treat me like a woman. They talk to me like I'm a woman. I can finally see what it's like to really be a woman."

Mansoor clenched his fists.

"I won't tell anyone. I promise. They wouldn't believe me anyway."

"Even if you swear, you'd never tell, there's a chance you'll get angry and tell everyone out of spite."

Mansoor sprang to his feet.

"I would never do that!"

"That's not the only problem, Mansoor. You ruined my chance to live here as a woman. I didn't even get through one day before you took it all away from me. Don't you see? As long as one person knows, then I can't live as a woman. Not really."

Polly could see the pain in Mansoor's eyes. He was crushed. Now he knew how she felt.

"So, does that mean you're leaving?" he said.

"Probably. I'm going to think it over tonight and decide in the morning. Right now, I'm exhausted and I've had too much to drink."

Mansoor left Polly's room with his head down so low Polly was surprised he didn't run into the door. She closed the clamshell on her unfinished dinner and threw it in the garbage can.

Chapter Fourteen

TERRENCE GRIGSBY SAT at his desk pouring over the work schedule. Mr. Kite had promoted more employees into cook positions than there were spots available. Terrence had the frustrating task of finding a shift for everyone. One floor below him, the kitchen was empty. He heard footsteps coming up the stairs, so he put his paperwork aside. There was a soft knock on his office door.

"Come in," he said.

Ginny Spencer and Corey Chan entered. Even though they had just finished a ten-hour shift, their Kitsune polo shirts were neatly tucked in, and they looked clean and alert. They stood at attention like soldiers.

"You asked to see us, Mr. Grigsby?" Ginny said.

"Yes," Terrence said. "Sit down." He gestured at the visitors' chairs.

They sat with their backs straight and their hands clasped in their laps. Terrence leaned back in his executive chair and made a steeple with his hands.

"Mr. Kite personally chose you two for a very important mission," Terrence said.

Terrence was lying. He had chosen them and had planned their mission as well.

Ginny and Corey could barely contain their excitement. They had to grip the armrests of their chairs to keep from leaping out of them.

"Whatever Mr. Kite wishes for me to do, I will not fail," Ginny said. "You can depend on me."

"Me too," said Corey.

"Mr. Kite and I have complete confidence in both of you," Terrence said. "That's why we chose you. I mean, it's not like we would have chosen you because we expected you to fail."

Terrence grinned at his little joke. Corey and Ginny stared at him with stony faces.

"A member of our family has gone astray," Terrence continued. "She somehow managed to slip past our security guards and get outside the wall. We need you to find her and bring her back home. We traced her GPS tracker to the city of Red Fox, but then we lost the signal. We suspect she's hiding somewhere, but eventually she'll have to come out. When she does, you'll be there to pick up her signal."

Corey held up his hand. "Excuse me, Mr. Grigsby. Who are we looking for?"

Terrence frowned.

"I thought you of all people would know. When was the last time you spoke to your girlfriend?"

"Dani? She ran away?"

"You really didn't know?"

Corey squirmed in his chair.

"We aren't exactly a couple anymore."

Terrance glared at Corey.

"Are you suggesting she won't listen to you? Perhaps Mr. Kite was hasty when he chose you for this mission."

"I promise you, Mr. Grigsby. Dani will listen to me."

Ginny held up her hand.

"This isn't a classroom," Terrence said. "You don't need to raise your hand when you want to ask a question."

"What if Dani doesn't listen to Corey?" Ginny asked. "What if we're forced to apprehend her against her will?"

"Let's hope it doesn't come down to that. We're not angry at Dani. We want to help her. I think once you remind Dani that we're only interested in what's best for her, she'll want to come home peacefully."

Terrence opened his desk drawer and took out Corey and Ginny's personal wallets, the key to Terrence's BMW, a cellphone, and a tablet computer with Dani's GPS tracker information already loaded in.

"You have credit cards and cash in your wallets," Terrence said. "The car has enough gas to get you to Red Fox. You may need to hang around town for a few days so go back to your rooms and pack your civilian clothes. Check into the local motel. To avoid suspicion, share a room. Pretend you're a couple on vacation."

Ginny grabbed the car key and the phone. Corey was left with the tablet.

"Don't worry about a thing, Mr. Grigsby," Ginny said. "You can depend on me."

"Yes, I believe you mentioned that earlier," Terrence said. "Ginny, could you wait a moment? Go ahead, Corey. I need to discuss something with Ginny that's completely unrelated to your mission."

"Yes, sir," Corey said.

Once he had left the room, Terrence had Ginny close the door and sit back down. He opened a different desk drawer and took out a handgun, a box of bullets, and a leather holster. He placed them at the center of his desktop.

"Do you know how to use a gun?" Terrence asked.

"I do, sir," Ginny said.

"Don't let Corey know I gave you this. Use it only as a last resort."

Ginny stared at the handgun's gleaming metal barrel.

"Should I not trust Corey, sir?"

"Corey's not the one I'm worried about. I'm afraid Dani might try to do something that would harm Kitsune, and I can't allow that to happen. I need Corey to focus on luring Dani back home. Your job is to step in if Dani refuses to listen to reason."

"After we return with Dani," Ginny said as she loaded the gun. "Is there any chance I might have a private cooking lesson with Mr. Kite?"

"You're ambitious," Terrence said. "We like that at Kitsune. I'll pass your request directly to Mr. Kite."

"That would be most excellent, Mr. Grigsby."

Chapter Fifteen

ANITA ENTERED HER front door and stood in the foyer. Other than the ticking of the Dale Earnhardt wall clock in the living room, the house was silent.

"You still here or did you skedaddle?" Anita called out.

There was no answer. She walked from room to room, but there was no sign of the Black girl she found in the women's bathroom of Kemp's Garage.

"I thought you might be hungry, so I brought you something from the diner."

Anita held up a white plastic bag with a Styrofoam clamshell inside. The hallway closet door creaked open, and Dani poked her head out.

"I figured that would flush you out," Anita said.

"I had to make sure you were alone," Dani said.

Dani followed Anita to the kitchen. Anita got out of a plate and utensils. She offered Dani a glass of Mountain Dew, but Dani asked for water instead. Anita opened the clamshell and transferred fried chicken, macaroni and cheese, black-eyed peas, and cornbread onto the plate. They sat at the dining room table. Dani poked at the food and frowned.

"What's the matter?" Anita said. "Aren't you hungry?"

"I'm starving," Dani said as she pushed the plate away. "But I can't eat this."

"Why the hell not?"

"Please don't be offended. It's just I've been eating the world's finest vegan cuisine for the last four years. My stomach can't handle meat or anything that wasn't prepared in Kitsune's kitchen. This food would probably make me projectile vomit."

Anita went to the kitchen and got herself a PBR tall boy of the refrigerator. She popped it open and took a long swallow. The beer bubbled out and she sucked the foam off her fingers. She came back to the dining room, plopped down in her chair, and slammed the beer on the table.

"Then I guess you'll fucking starve," Anita said. "I didn't have to take you into my house along with whatever bad situation you brought with you and I sure as hell didn't have to buy you dinner and carry it home for you. So, don't eat it. See if I fucking care!"

Tears welled up in Dani's eyes.

"You bought this?" she asked.

"They don't give food away at the Rejoice Diner. Unless you're really down and out."

Dani pulled the plate back and speared two black-eyed peas with her fork. She grimaced as she put the fork in her mouth. She chewed slowly and swallowed.

"That's not bad. How were the peas seasoned? It tastes familiar, but I can't place it."

Since Dani had mentioned the word vegan there was no way in hell Anita was going to tell her that the seasoning was pork fat.

"I have no idea," she said. "My boss, Owen Tew, guards

his recipes like he guards his porn collection. Nobody's allowed to see it but him. You want a beer or is Pabst Blue Ribbon not fancy enough for you?"

"I haven't had a beer in years. Any brand will do."

Anita got another tall boy out of the frig and brought it to Dani. She hadn't been in close proximity to a Black person since high school and had forgotten what they smelled like. She knew that they didn't smell like regular people. The ones in high school stank something terrible, but not Dani. She was dirty and sweaty, but she smelled okay. Almost normal.

"Is there somebody you want to call?" Anita said. "You can use my phone."

"My family lives in Portland, but I don't dare call them," Dani said. "Kitsune's security guards are worse than the NSA. They've probably bugged my parents' phone."

"I'm pretty good friends with the sheriff here in town. I could have him come over and talk to you."

"I have no way to prove what's been going on up there. He'll think I'm crazy."

"Then what's your plan?"

Dani looked down at her plate.

"I don't know. I was hoping I could stay here for a few days until I figure out what to do."

Anita sipped her beer. She belched, covering her mouth as she did and wondering where these manners were coming from.

"You're welcome to stay. As long as you tell me what the fuck is going on."

Dani ate a few more beans and washed them down with beer.

"It all started four years ago. I was living in Seattle with my boyfriend, Corey. He was a software developer, and I was a graphic designer. Seattle is crazy expensive, but with our combined income we made enough money that we could eat out a lot. We ate out so much, we became foodies."

"Foodie?" Anita said. "Is that that sexual fetish where you smear food on your body?"

"Uh, no. A foodie is someone who's really into finding new dining experiences. They're always on the lookout for the best restaurants and the best food and drink. It's a first world hobby for sure. We had a podcast called Tooti Frooti O'Foodie. We talked about tracking down hidden gem restaurants and described what it was like to eat there. No place was too far away. If we heard about a great tapas place in Portland or amazing barbeque ribs in a tiny restaurant located in a back alley in Savannah, we'd go there.

"We first heard about Kitsune when we were in Sweden. We were eating dinner with some fellow foodies at this remote farmhouse restaurant. The thing about eating with other foodies is that you spend half the evening rating the food and the other half trading information about which restaurants to go to next. I don't remember who it was, but someone brought up Kitsune. Everyone at the table agreed that it was not only the best vegan restaurant, but it was also one of the top five restaurants in the world.

"Corey and I were shocked because we'd never heard of it. I should add that we were the only Americans at that table. It was like every foodie on the planet knew about this place but us and it was in our own country. We had to go there."

Normally, Anita didn't care for people who took forever to get to the point, but she was willing to listen to the long version of Dani's story if she eventually got around to dishing the dirt on Kitsune.

Nobody in Red Fox had ever eaten at the fancy pants restaurant. Nor would they ever eat there. For one thing, they only served vegetables. A meal wasn't a meal without some kind of meat on the plate. But the main reason the town avoided Kitsune was because they didn't much care for the fact that these big city folk bought up a piece of their mountain, built an upscale restaurant, gave it a fucked-up name, and made it so expensive that only rich out-of-towners could afford to eat their undercooked vegetables while looking down their noses at the blessed but not perfect citizens of Red Fox.

"First chance he got, Corey called the restaurant for a reservation," Dani said. "Their first opening was in two months. Corey made a reservation for four and invited our closest foodie friends to come with us. We made a special occasion out it. We flew into Atlanta and took a limo to the restaurant."

"A limo?" Anita said. "It's at least a two-hour drive from Atlanta."

"I know, right? But it was worth it. Kitsune far exceeded our expectations. It was a beautiful space, our waiter was amazing, and the food, oh my God, I had the best meal of my life. We topped off the meal with a glass of cognac and that's when things started to get weird. Corey noticed the busboy looked exactly like a famous food critic for the New York Times. Corey talked to the busboy. Turned out he was the famous food critic. He had quit his job so that he could work for Kitsune."

"You're right," Anita said. "That's weird."

Dani finished the black-eyed peas and moved on to the macaroni and cheese and cornbread. She had pushed the fried chicken to the far end of her plate, so Anita had taken a wing. Anita pulled off strips of meat from the bones and popped them into her mouth.

"It gets weirder," Dani said. "When we got back to Seattle, Corey asked around and found out a lot of people associated with the foodie world had dropped everything in their lives to work for Kitsune and learn how to cook like Kitsune's mysterious chef, Mr. Kite."

"Mr. Kite?"

"That's what we call him. Nobody knows what his real name

is or where he came from. But I'm getting ahead of myself. We should have known something wasn't right, but Corey insisted we go back for another meal. We ended up going once a month. We would have gone more but reservations were so hard to get. Corey was obsessed. He loved Kitsune's food, but he wanted to know what it was about this restaurant that made people devote their lives to it.

"Every time we went, Corey talked to more people who worked there. Finally, someone told him that learning to cook like Mr. Kite was about more than making great food. Mr. Kite had shown them a path to spiritual enlightenment through his cooking."

Dani got to the spiritual enlightenment part just as Anita was taking a swig from her PBR tall boy. Anita guffawed and beer came out of her nose.

"You're making that up," she said. "That can't be for real."

"I wish I was," Dani said. "I wish Corey and I hadn't fallen under Mr. Kite's spell to the point where we sold all our things and left the wonderful lives we had in Seattle so that we could work at Kitsune. We weren't paid a salary. We lived in a big commune. We did whatever Mr. Kite asked us to do. Kitsune is more than a restaurant. It's a cult and Mr. Kite is the cult leader. It took me four years to realize it and I escaped with nothing but the clothes on my back."

Anita yawned and looked at up at the Dale Earnhardt clock.

"Damn, it's late," she said. "I want to hear more but if I don't go to bed soon, I'm going to pass out here at the table. You must be pretty whipped too."

Dani looked down at her empty plate.

"I ate more than I thought I would. Yeah, I'm beat. Thank you so much for taking me in, Anita. You saved my life today."

"Well, somebody would say it was the Christian thing

to do, but I ain't much of a Christian. Here, I'll show you to your room."

They put the dishes in the sink and then Anita led Dani to a bedroom in the back of the house. There were camouflage sheets on a single bed, a rebel flag on the wall, plastic horses, and race car models on the top shelf of a bookcase. The rest of the shelves were filled with paperbacks. Dani glanced at the spines. There were science fiction, fantasy, and mystery novels along with literary novels.

"There's a bathroom through that door there," Anita said pointing. "There's toothpaste in there but no toothbrush. You'll have to use your finger until I can get you one. You're taller than me so I can't lend you any of my clothes. But you're in luck. You and my mom are about the same size, and she left a whole closet of her stuff behind. She's got terrible taste, but the clothes are clean."

"Yes. Clean clothes would be awesome," Dani said. "Is this your room?"

"It was before my parents moved out. I'll go get you those clothes."

Dani wanted to thank Anita again, but she had already left. Dani went into the bathroom. There was a stale smell which told her that it hadn't been used in a while. But there were clean towels in the linen closet and an unopened bar of soap in the medicine cabinet. She stripped off her clothes and sniffed her shirt. It stank of the nasty gas station bathroom she'd hidden in earlier that day.

The hot water in the shower was a gift from heaven. Dani could feel her tense muscles unwinding. She was too exhausted to think of the future. The only thing she felt sure of was Anita. She was convinced that she could trust this strange redneck girl and that she was safe as long as she stayed inside this house, though that Confederate flag over the bed had to come down.

When Dani got out of the shower, the mirror had steamed over. She rubbed toothpaste on her teeth and then rinsed her mouth out. On the bed, she found that Anita had left her an unopened 3 pack of thong underwear, a sleep shirt that read "I'm great in bed. I can sleep for days," a pair of skinny jeans, and a black t-shirt with the word "Diva" spelled out in rhinestones.

Dani stuffed her dirty clothes in a trashcan and put on a pair of panties and the sleep shirt. The panties were a bit loose, but the sleep shirt was a perfect fit. She climbed under the covers. The sheets were a bit musty, but the bed felt wonderful. She would fall asleep in no time.

But she didn't. Even though she was bone tired, she was too scared to sleep. She kept imagining security guards from Kitsune breaking down the door and dragging her back up the mountain. Dani got out of bed and went through the dark house, peeking into rooms until she found the master bedroom. Anita was curled up on the right side of a king-sized bed.

"Anita?" Dani whispered.

"You don't have to whisper," Anita said. "The only person you're going to wake up is me and you've already done that."

"I'm sorry. It's just I can't sleep."

"I've got some Xanax."

"I was wondering. That is, if you wouldn't mind."

Anita sat up and stared at Dani. She appeared as a silhouette in her doorway. Anita knew what Dani was trying to ask her. The very idea of allowing a Black person in her bed was absurd. She should be firm and let this uppity negro know that there were limits to Anita's generosity.

"Sure," Anita said. "Hop in. There's plenty of room."

Anita couldn't believe she'd just invited this stranger to share her bed, but she'd heard the words pop of her mouth clear as day so either deep down her must have thought it was okay or she was so worn out she was talking nonsense.

Dani rushed over and slipped under the covers. Again, Anita noticed that Dani didn't smell the way she expected Black people to smell. In fact, now that she had showered, she smelled nice.

"Just so you know," Anita said. "I'm not into carpet munching. I like men. Period."

"That makes two of us," Dani said.

Anita curled up so that she was facing away from Dani. She worried that she wouldn't be able to relax knowing there a Black woman behind her, but she fell asleep moments after she closed her eyes.

Chapter Sixteen

THE SHOPKEEPER'S BELL rang as Polly Swift entered Martha's Hair Done Right. The ding-a-ling bounced around inside her skull before leaking out of her ears. She kept her sunglasses on, afraid to reveal her bloodshot eyes. She was paying the price for drinking a bottle of cheap wine the night before. It had been quite some time since she'd had a hangover and of course it was happening on her first day on a new job.

Martha came out from the back of the shop. Instead of the black nylon salon smock she'd worn the day before, she had on a pink cotton smock with her name embroidered above her left breast.

"Good morning," Martha chirped. "You're early. We don't open for two hours."

"I wanted to make a good impression on my first day of work," Polly said. "And I wanted plenty of time to set up my chair."

"Right. Speaking of your chair." Martha stood in the middle of the salon chairs. "You have three to choose from, Susie's old chair or one of these two empty chairs."

For Polly, it was an easy decision. Susie's chair was closest to Martha's. Polly removed her sunglasses, packed up Susie's gear, and put her bag on the styling station. She took out her brushes, clips, spritzer, rollers, and curling iron and placed them where she could reach them easily. She set up her disinfecting jar and dropped her combs and clippers into the blue liquid. The ritual of setting up her station calmed her and eased the jackhammering in her head. The last thing she did was place her Georgia cosmetology license where her customers could see it.

Martha put her hands on her hips as she examined Polly's station.

"Looks like you're all set up," Martha said. "Let's get some coffee."

"Wonderful idea," Polly said.

Normally, Polly was unable to function until she had her first cup of coffee, but today she had skipped her usual caffeine fix. The Fox Creek Falls Inn served guests coffee and assorted muffins in the lobby, but after last night's confrontation with Mansoor Amin, she wanted to avoid him and there was a better than even chance that he would be working the front desk.

To make matters worse, Polly had really needed the coffee's calming effect this morning. Mansoor discovered her secret. She barely knew him and had no reason to trust him when he said that he wouldn't tell anyone. She didn't decide to stay in Red Fox until she got into her car this morning. As she pulled out the motel's parking lot, she said to hell with Mansoor. She wasn't going to let that prick ruin her plan.

Martha's coffee maker was in the small break next to her office. There was a collection of mismatched mugs in the cabinet. Martha chose a cup with a Cross and Romans 10:13 on it and Polly got a cup with a photo of a kitten. Martha stirred hazelnut-flavored non-dairy creamer into her coffee. Polly drank hers black. They sat in their salon chairs and sipped their coffee.

"I love your shoes," Martha said. "What are they?"

Polly's shoes were teal Mary Janes with wide aqua straps. She turned her foot back and forth so Martha could get a better look.

"Thank you," Polly said. "They're Fluevogs. Very fancy, expensive designer shoes, but here's a little secret. There's a website where you can buy them used."

Martha nodded. "I might have to check that out. If they have shoes to fit your big feet, then I shouldn't have any trouble finding my size."

Luckily, Martha was looking at the Fluevogs and didn't see the brief panic on Polly's face.

"Yeah, I do have big feet," Polly said. "It's really embarrassing."

Crystal arrived and settled into the front desk in the reception area. An overweight ten-year-old girl was their first appointment of the day. Martha cut her hair as the girl's equally overweight mother talked non-stop. After they left, the rest of the morning became a blur for Polly as a parade of women came in to get their hair styled or their nails done or both. They ranged in age from eight to eighty. Most were delighted to meet Martha's new employee while others complained openly that they missed Susie. But one thing they all agreed on was that Polly's shoes were outstanding.

Knowing her craft helped Polly fall into a comfortable routine. She was at home in a beauty salon. The gossip flowed, the spritzers misted the air, and the snipped off hair floated to the floor. As familiar as it all was, Polly noticed differences between the conversations in Martha's shop and the salons in Atlanta.

In Atlanta, most of the customers were young, upwardly mobile metrosexual men and hipster women. They talked about going to nightclubs and concerts, their careers, boyfriends, girlfriends, and most of all, themselves.

In Martha's Beauty Salon, the customers were all women

and girls. Polly wondered where the men got their hair cut and decided to ask Martha later. The women of Red Fox talked about jobs, health problems, children, church, husbands, and who was doing something they ought not to be doing.

As she listened, it dawned on Polly that the social economic differences between Atlanta and Red Fox was more than just urban white collar versus rural blue-collar. Red Fox was suffering economically. She had seen the empty storefronts and the boarded-up houses. The biggest topic of conversation was a gift shop that had gone under. Everyone knew the former owners. They had seen them at church and their kids had gone to school with their kids. But now they had moved away. Red Fox was dying. Polly knew it was selfish to feel the way she did, but she was thankful that she had come here before it was too late.

As for passing as a woman, Polly received two comments that indicated that they viewed her as a fellow female. The first came when she was searching the bathroom's medicine cabinet hoping to find a bottle of aspirin to help alleviate some of the pain from her hangover. She didn't think to shut the bathroom door. Martha poked her head in.

"They're in the bottom drawer next to the sink," Martha said.

Polly opened the drawer and found it was filled with tampons.

"Thank you," she said. She took one out of the drawer.

"I saw how pale you looked this morning and figured it must be that time of the month. There's also some Midol in the medicine cabinet."

Polly closed the bathroom door and put the tampon back in the drawer. She found regular aspirin next to the Midol. As she swallowed two tablets, she wondered if maybe she should get a hangover once a month.

The second and most wonderful comment came later. Martha was trimming an elderly woman's long white hair while Polly was busy buffing a teenage girl's nails and discussing what color nail polish she wanted. The girl was trying to decide between bubblegum pink, shimmer pink, or sunrise pink.

The elderly woman's name was Eloise Otey. She narrowed her eyes at Polly.

"Polly," Eloise said. "That's your name, right?"

Polly looked up and smiled.

"Yes, it is."

"I noticed that you don't have a ring on your finger. Is that because you take it off when you're working or is it because you aren't married?"

"I'm not married."

"You're not! How old are you?"

"Now, Eloise," Martha said. "You know it's rude to ask a woman her age."

"I don't care. How old are you, Polly?"

"Twenty-eight."

"Oh, dear sweet Jesus. You'd better find yourself a man and get married. You need to start having babies before you get too old."

Everyone laughed. Polly blushed. If she had been born a woman she might have been annoyed, but instead she was thrilled because the comment made her feel like she was truly living as a real woman.

Chapter Seventeen

SKYLER WALKED OUT of the Fox Food Mart with a large cola Icee in one hand and a bag of pork rinds in the other. He opened the door of his police cruiser, tossed the pork rinds onto the passenger seat, and sat behind the wheel. He pried the dome-shaped clear plastic cover off the Icee. The dome always made him think of a nicely rounded tit. Looking around to make sure no one was watching; Skyler retrieved a pint bottle of Evan Williams in a brown paper bag from under his seat. He chugged a glob of the frozen soft drink down his throat and screwed up his face while he waited for the brain freeze to pass. He refilled the cup to the brim with bourbon. He put the plastic dome back on the cup and inserted a straw. He sucked down some of his frozen bourbon and cola and breathed a sigh of relief. He might make it through another day after all.

Skyler drove into the town square in search of a spot where he could get drunk and eat his pork rinds in peace. The sidewalks were busy with people on their lunch break no doubt headed toward one of Red Fox's three eating establishments. Those who took the time to pack a lunch were seated on park benches enjoying the early days of Fall weather when it was sunny but not too hot or too cold.

Skyler hit the brakes when he spotted a gorgeous blonde wearing big sunglasses, a gray top, faded jeans, and funny green shoes. The car behind Skyler honked and he quickly pulled into a parking space. He sipped his drink as he watched the blonde enter the Rejoice Diner.

It was Polly Swift, the woman that Mrs. Hensley claimed was trying to break into the old Miller house but turned out she was just house hunting. She had made a big impression on Skyler. He even remembered her name and he was terrible about remembering names.

Skyler sat in the cruiser and went through all the reasons why he shouldn't go into the diner and talk to Polly. He was a married man and had no business flirting with a single lady. As an officer of the law, he was supposed to set a moral example. He was a complete mess and no good for anybody.

The Evan Williams in his Icee melted away each reason. His wife certainly didn't believe in honoring their marriage vows so why should he? He wouldn't be the first Red Fox policeman with questionable standards. He was just going to talk to the young lady. Talking wasn't cheating. In fact, it was his duty as a civil servant to do whatever he could to make a newcomer feel welcome.

Skyler stuck his ring finger in his mouth to loosen his wedding ring. He slipped off the gold band and stuffed it into his pocket. He left his Icee and bag of pork rinds in the car and hurried over to the diner.

Inside, the human activity and multiple conversations combined with the alcohol coursing through his system caused Skyler to become temporarily disoriented. He felt a wave of dizziness that quickly passed when he spotted Polly sitting by herself in a booth. He casually walked over to her table and then awkwardly pretended that he just happened to see her as he was passing by.

"Hey, it's you," he said. "Polly? Right?"

Polly peered up from her menu and her face lit up.

"Wow, you remembered my name," she said. "I'm flattered, Deputy Aldridge."

"I'm flattered too. That you remembered my name. But you can call me Skyler," He wobbled a bit as he grinned stupidly at her. "Hey, I just happened to come in for lunch and I just happened to see you sitting here. You know, I hate to eat alone."

Polly gestured at the other side of the booth.

"Would you like to join me?"

"I hate to intrude."

"Not at all. I also hate to eat alone. I would love your company."

Skyler slid into the other side of the booth. The waitress came over to take their order. She was in her early sixties. She had short red hair and was curvy without being plump. Her face was pleasantly plain. She narrowed her eyes at Polly.

"Are you Polly?" she asked.

"Why yes, I am," Polly said. "How did you know?"

"My name's Gloria Medley. I live next door to Crystal Beaver. If you don't already know, the woman loves to gossip. A day doesn't go by that she doesn't come over to my house and tell me every little thing that happened in town whether I want to hear it or not."

As Polly and Crystal continued chatting, Skyler felt a wave of panic. If Crystal Beaver found out that he had lunch with Polly, she'd blab it to everybody in town. And once folks knew, they would blow the whole thing out of proportion. Instead of him and Polly sharing a friendly meal, people would swear that the two of them were making out in the booth with his hand under her shirt.

But then, Skyler relaxed. Gloria was the opposite of Crystal. She didn't talk about anybody. In fact, he was surprised that Gloria was talking so much to Polly since normally she acted like her face would break if she had to speak more words than were absolutely necessary.

When the two women finally quit yakking, Gloria took their order. Polly asked for a tuna fish sandwich on wheat bread with a side of coleslaw and an unsweet tea. Skyler ordered a bacon cheeseburger with fries and a Coke. Gloria waved away his alcohol breath and suggested he get black coffee instead of the Coke. Skyler sheepishly agreed.

Gloria returned shortly with their drinks and then hurried off to wait on other tables. Skyler sipped his hot coffee. Gloria was right. He needed coffee.

"How you liking Red Fox so far?" Skyler asked.

"I love it," Polly said. "The people here are so warm and genuine."

"We do our best."

They fell into an easy conversation. Polly talked about wanting to move to a small town and how fortunate she was that Martha had an opening at the beauty salon. Skyler talked about the other deputies on the police force and how it's easy to keep the peace in a town where you know everybody. Twice he caught himself about to say something about his kids and changed the subject.

They barely noticed when Gloria brought them their meals. Skyler couldn't remember the last time he'd felt so comfortable talking to someone. He wasn't much of a talker period, but this was different. It was if he'd known Polly his entire life.

He tried to pay for her lunch, but she wouldn't let him. She glanced at her watch and gasped.

"I better hurry on back," Polly said. "I'm going to be late."

Skyler only had seconds left to say what he'd been working up the nerve to say since he first sat down at her booth.

"Would you like to go to a movie?" he blurted out.

Polly froze and stared at him.

"It's okay," he said. "You barely know me. I just thought it might be a nice thing to do."

"Yes," Polly said. "I'll go see a movie with you. Maybe we could have dinner before we go."

Happy feelings rushed through Skyler's body.

"Yes, we could. I mean we will. I mean I'll call you later."

He got out of the booth to leave.

"Skyler," Polly said.

He quickly sat back down.

"Yes, Polly."

"Let me give you my phone number. You know, so you can call me."

"Oh right. Good idea."

Polly took a pen out of her purse and wrote her number on a napkin. Skyler folded it and put it into his breast pocket. They left the diner together and then Polly headed in the direction of the beauty salon. Skyler stood on the sidewalk and watched her cute butt as she walked away. He knew he shouldn't stare, but he couldn't help himself.

Chapter Eighteen

Corey Chan's stomach growled. Sitting in a restaurant with nothing but a cup of hot coffee while surrounded by people eating generous portions of overcooked vegetables and various species of fried meat didn't help calm his appetite. He tried closing his eyes but that made the smell more acute and his hunger more torturous.

"We should order something other than coffee," Corey said. "We look suspicious."

"Nobody's paying attention to us," Ginny Spencer said. She sipped her coffee and made a face. She took out a packet of Starbuck's instant coffee and poured the powder into her cup.

"There's a cop right over there." Corey nodded toward a booth at the end of the row. "He's going to think we're up to something."

Ginny turned around in her seat and stared openly in the direction Corey had indicated. A handsome deputy and an attractive blonde were deep in conversation. Ginny turned back around and faced Corey.

"The only thing that cop notices right now is that woman's

tits," Ginny said. "And what if he does see us? We haven't done anything."

"We would blend in more if we ordered food," Corey groused.

"What could we possibly eat here that wouldn't make us sick? When was the last time you ate meat?"

"It's been four years since I've eaten meat. God, I miss meat. We could order a vegetable plate."

"I'm sure everything here is cooked in pork fat. You'd end up puking all over the table."

"What about that Mexican place around the corner? Those little out of the way places always have the best authentic tacos."

"What is wrong with you, Corey? It's not like you haven't eaten."

The motel room they were staying in had a kitchenette. Every day, Ginny prepared sliced vegetables and kidney beans and served them with olive oil. It was enough to keep Corey from dropping dead, but hardly enough to satisfy his hunger.

"It's been a week," Corey said, changing the subject. "We still haven't picked up Dani's signal on the GPS tracker. Let's face it. She's probably miles away from here."

"We don't know that for sure," Ginny said.

Corey had the tablet computer with Dani's GPS tracker information on the table in front of him. He poked the tablet with his index finger.

"There's no signal. I think we should call Mr. Grigsby and tell him Dani's not in Red Fox. We should go back to Kitsune."

"Not until we complete our mission. We don't go back without Dani."

Corey sipped his coffee. It tasted nutty and tangy but wasn't bright enough to be considered outstanding. Still, considering that he expected it to taste like something wringed out of a dirty rag, it wasn't half bad. Though he had learned to appreciate the coffee, Corey thought coming to the Rejoice Diner every day during the lunch rush was a waste of time. Since it appeared to be the town's most popular restaurant, Ginny decided there was a chance that Dani would wander in thinking she was safe. Or they might hear someone mention her name and then they would somehow convince that person to tell them where Dani was hiding.

Corey tried to question her logic, but Ginny shut him down. Any time he challenged her decisions, she accused him of not trusting Mr. Kite as if he was somehow telepathically sending her orders.

Corey desperately wanted to return to Kitsune. The longer he was away, the more conflicted and adrift he felt. Life was simple when all he had to worry about was how to please Mr. Kite. He had jettisoned everything else in his life including his connection to Dani.

He had jettisoned his sex drive as well. He could give pleasure if that was what was required of him, but he didn't feel it himself. He was convinced his sexual desire was dead and buried until sharing a motel room with Ginny Spencer brought it clawing back to the surface.

Corey supposed the main reason he'd become attracted to her was because she spent most of her time in the motel room nude. When they were done for the day, Ginny stripped off her clothes, took a shower, and then stayed naked. She slept in the bed next to him naked. She had small breasts and stubby legs, but she was in great shape. Her ass was especially in great shape. She exercised daily and badgered Corey into exercising with her. Of course, she exercised in the nude.

At first, he didn't react to her nudity. She was just a body occupying the same space with him. But the friction she caused with her insipid arguments, the way she smirked when she caught him staring at her breasts, and the soft mound of light red pubic hair around her labia took their toll on him.

He was constantly trying to hide his erections from her. If she had noticed his raging hard-ons, and he suspected she did, she didn't acknowledge them or tease him about them. At night, Corey waited until Ginny was asleep before going into the bathroom to masturbate. As he jerked off, he imagined taking her from behind while smacking her tight ass. That offered some relief but being in bed just inches from the body he wanted to ravage was maddening.

Sitting in the diner, suffering from hunger pains and blue balls, Corey desperately wanted to go back to Mr. Kite's cabin and serve the master chef. He could forget about Dani and Ginny. He would eat good food and experience spiritual enlightenment. He would gladly get on his knees and show his devotion to Mr. Kite.

"Hey, are you listening to me?" Ginny asked.

Corey snapped out of his thoughts. Ginny was of Irish descent with pale skin, curly red hair, and freckles. Her cheeks glowed with a faint pink color when she was angry. At first, he saw that pink as a warning sign, the same way red meant danger. But now, it was just one more thing about her that turned him on.

"Sorry," Corey said. "I zoned out. What were you talking about?"

"What are those dots?"

Ginny pointed at two blue dots pulsing on the tablet's screen.

"That's us. Just like Dani, we're carrying GPS trackers. I think they're in our wallets. Isn't it strange that Kitsune keeps track of its employees' every move? Why do they do that?"

"Mr. Kite is our shepherd and we're his flock."

"So, what does that make us? Sheep?"

"You're definitely a sheep. I'm one of his herding dogs."

"This conversation is depressing."

"Hey, you told me what those two dots were. What about the third dot?"

"Third dot?"

Corey studied the tablet. A third dot had appeared on the screen that hadn't been there before. He did a quick location search.

"It's Dani!" Corey said. "She's two miles from here."

"Told you she was still in Red Fox."

Corey took a ten-dollar bill out of his wallet and put it on the table.

"Come on," he said. "The sooner we get Dani the sooner we can go home."

"You've finally said something I agree with."

Chapter Nineteen

For a first date, Polly couldn't have wished for things to have gone any better. Even the things Skyler did that could be considered mistakes were done with such good intentions that they weren't mistakes at all. Skyler arrived at her motel room on time in a clean shirt and khakis, and an overdose of Axe Body Spray. He drove them down the mountain to have dinner at a Cracker Barrel in Ringgold. From the way he strutted around Polly could see that Skyler hadn't taken her there because the chain restaurant was inexpensive. He really liked Cracker Barrel and wanted her to enjoy it as much as he did.

After dinner, they went to a multiplex in Fort Oglethorpe. Two new action movies had opened that night, but Skyler suggested they see a romantic comedy. Polly would have preferred one of the action movies but was so touched that he was willing to sit through a chick flick because he thought it would make her happy that she pretended to be thrilled with his selection.

Skyler bought a tub of popcorn and a giant soda. Polly wasn't hungry, they had just had dinner, but took a couple of handfuls just to be nice. He ate the rest of the tub himself. All that popcorn must have made him sleepy because he nodded off about two thirds of the way through the movie. Polly thought the story was predictable and hated the lead actress. Watching the light from the projector dance on Skyler's delicate features as he slept was much more interesting. She was tempted to kiss him to see if it brought him back to life like Sleeping Beauty. She didn't because this was a first date. Making out in a movie theater was something you saved for a third or fourth date.

Polly decided to have a bit of impish fun with Skyler on the way back to her motel room. She asked what he thought about certain scenes in the movie that she knew he slept through. But instead of talking about things that actually happened, she made up stuff that wasn't in the movie.

"What did you think about that scene where Mark leaves Bridget on her deathbed and runs off with Jack?" Polly said.

"Uh yeah, that was pretty messed up," Skyler said.

"I should have guessed that Mark and Jack were gay after that scene where they were making out while Bridget was in the next room changing the baby's diaper. I thought they were just doing it to pass the time."

Skyler scratched the back of his head.

"I don't remember that scene."

"You don't? It was a very funny scene. It made you laugh."

"Well, maybe I do."

"We never saw what happened to the baby after Bridget accidentally left it in a cab. I guess we'll have to wait for the sequel to find out."

"I guess we will."

When they got to the Fox Creek Falls Inn, Skyler got out and opened Polly's car door for her. They stood outside her motel room. If Skyler was waiting for Polly to invite him inside for coffee, he was out of luck. It wasn't going to happen. At least, not tonight.

Instead, it was that classic moment when a boy takes a girl home from a date and the girl waits for the boy to kiss her goodnight. There were so many times when Polly dreamed of being that girl and here she was. She wanted to slow down time and savor every second.

"I had a great time tonight," Polly said.

"Me too," Skyler said. "Let's do it again real soon."

"I'd like that."

He leaned in with his eyes closed. Their lips met and Polly was filled with warmth. Skyler took her in his arms, his strong hands on her waist. She pressed her body against his as she wrapped her arms around his neck. Polly almost changed her mind about inviting him in for that coffee. But it was too soon to share her secrets with him.

Or was it? Maybe now was the right time. She could feel his desire pressing against her belly. Her reservations about having sex with him too soon were melting quickly.

They sensed that they weren't alone and pulled apart. Mansoor stood a few feet away from them. He looked so sad Polly almost felt sorry for him.

"Hey, Mansoor," Skyler said. "What's going on?"

"Room eleven requested an extra blanket and pillow," Mansoor said.

Sure enough, Mansoor held a folded blanket and pillow under his arm. He knocked on room eleven's door. An Asian man opened the door. They heard a woman inside the room shout, "Who's out there, Corey?" Corey looked over his shoulder and said, "It's the guy from the front desk."

Mansoor handed Corey the blanket and pillow. Corey thanked him and shut the door. Mansoor nodded at Skyler and Polly and hurried away.

Skyler tried to pick up where they had left off, but Polly had cooled down and regained her senses.

"I should go in," she said. "I have to get up early."

"Yeah, me too," Skyler said. The disappointment in his voice was achingly clear.

Polly unlocked her door and went into her room. She stood at the window and peeked through the curtain. She watched Skyler get into his car and drive away.

Two minutes at the most, that was how long Mansoor had stood near Polly and Skyler, but it had been long enough to ruin her special moment with Skyler. Sure, Mansoor probably stopped her from making a big mistake, but if only he had waited until after the kiss. That almost perfect goodnight kiss. Mansoor always managed to ruin something for Polly every time he was around her.

Chapter Twenty

Henry Nix parked his pick-up truck in front Anita Cox's house. The truck was old and beat up, and the name Kemp's Garage stenciled on the doors was fading away. It often broke down, which amused Anita to no end. More than once she had told Henry that it was bad for business to have an unreliable company vehicle, especially his business. Why would anyone trust him to repair their car when he couldn't keep his own on the road?

"If I'd known we was going to end up at your house, then we could've done it on your bed instead of the floor of my office," Henry said.

"I only let you drive me home," Anita said. "You're not coming inside."

"Now that I think on it, I've never seen the inside your house. How come you've never invited me in? Are you ashamed of me?"

"That's got nothing to do with it. I don't allow men inside because once you let 'em in, it's almost impossible to get 'em out."

Henry chuckled. "Girl, you are something else."

"Alright. I got to go. Thanks for the ride."

"What? No kiss goodnight?"

"Don't make me laugh."

Anita got out of the truck and Henry drove away leaving a trail of smoke. Before they left the garage, he'd given her a cold beer. She was reluctant to take it at first. She didn't like to accept anything that could be considered payment for sex. But then, he took out a cold one for himself, so she saw no harm in having one too.

She was down to suds in the bottom of the can. Her garbage bin sat on the curb under the lone streetlight on her block. She lifted the lid and was about to toss the can inside when she noticed something made of black fabric inside. Anita pulled it out. It was Dani's Kitsune polo shirt. Dani had been too scared to even look out the window much less venture outside. She must truly hate this thing to come all the way to the curb to throw it away.

Shame to waste a perfectly good shirt. Anita didn't want it. She decided to donate it to Faith Inc. Thrift Store. She dropped the beer can into the bin and carried the shirt inside the house to the closet where she kept her compact clothes washer/dryer combo and tossed the shirt into the washer.

In the kitchen, Anita found a note attached to the frig with a magnet. It read, "Made veggie chili. Help yourself." Anita found a Tupperware container filled with a red, lumpy stew. She took out a spoon, tasted the chili, and nodded her approval. She scooped a generous portion into a bowl and heated it up in the microwave. Instead of sitting in the dining room, Anita ate while leaning against the kitchen counter. She took a tall boy out of the frig to go with her meal.

As she ate, she marveled at how odd this past week had been. Rather than sit around the house all day, Dani had made herself useful. She cleaned the house. In fact, Anita couldn't remember when she'd ever seen the house this clean. Neither she nor her mother were very good housekeepers.

Dani had given Anita a grocery list. Anita was none too happy about spending her hard-earned money so that Dani could make the kind of hippy dippy vegetarian food that only her delicate stomach could tolerate. But then, Dani had cooked enough for her and Anita, and Anita discovered that vegetarian food could be mighty tasty.

Dani saved the grocery receipt and added it to the tally she was keeping of how much money she owed Anita for letting her stay in her house. Despite Anita's insistence that Dani didn't need to pay her back, Dani promised that once she got back to Portland, the first thing she was going to do was write Anita a check and mail it to her. It was the very least she could do.

When Anita finished eating, she washed the bowl and put it in the dish drainer. Before Dani arrived, Anita would have waited until the sink was full of dirty dishes and then force herself to wash them. Dani's constant cleanliness had rubbed off on her and now she cleaned her dishes at the end of every meal.

Anita still had half of her tall boy to drink. It was her second beer of the night but so what. She was a grown ass woman in her own home. She could be like her daddy and drink until she passed out on the floor.

She went into the dark living room. Dani kept the curtains always drawn in case someone from Kitsune drove by. Anita pulled aside the curtain and watched a raccoon amble down the middle of the street. She closed the curtain, sat on the couch, and sipped her beer.

Anita took pride in being honest with herself. She didn't give a fuck that the town considered her a slut. A head shrinker could probably explain her addiction to disgusting men, but she was happy with her life as it was right now. Or rather she thought she was happy. That was before she found Dani hiding in the women's bathroom of Kemp's Garage.

For years now, Anita had lived alone and thought she

had liked it that way. Now she knew that she had accepted it because she had no other choice. She had no siblings. Her parents divorced years ago. They both moved out of the house, basically abandoning her. She seemed incapable of sustaining close friendships and the type of men she screwed were hardly what you would call boyfriend material.

Anita enjoyed Dani's company. She looked forward to coming home to hang out with her. Yet Anita knew damn well that Dani would eventually get up the nerve to call her parents and go home to Portland.

Then there was the problem with Dani's skin color. Anita was proudly racist. As she liked to say, "It ain't that I'm prejudice, I am." But here she was living under the same roof with a Black woman. Anita couldn't decide if she was a racist who changed her tune once she got to know a person of color or if maybe, just maybe, she never actually hated Black people. Was that humanly possible?

Maybe Anita only hated Black men because one had seduced her mother away from her father. Or maybe she just hated her mother and anything her mother liked; Anita hated.

Anita finished her beer in one determined gulp. She tossed the can in the kitchen trash bin and then went to her bedroom. The bed was empty. She pushed aside her disappointment and took a hot shower to wash off the grease and dirt from Henry's grimy hands. After brushing her teeth, she put on a worn T-shirt with a pair of men's boxer shorts. She left the master bedroom and walked softly to the other side of the house.

Anita peeked into her old bedroom. Dani was sitting up in the bed.

"Did I wake you up?" Anita said.

"No," Dani said. "I heard you come in."

"Did I scare you?"

"Not at all. I'm much better than I was a week ago. I can even look out the window without freaking out."

"You did more than that. I found your shirt in the trash. I put it in the wash. I'm going to clean it and then give it to the thrift store."

"As long as it's out of my life."

Anita sat on the side of the bed.

"Why are you in here?"

"I figured you were tired of me cowering in your bed like a frightened child."

Anita twisted a strand of her hair.

"You didn't have to leave. I didn't mind."

Dani smiled.

"When I was in college, my little sister used to visit me on weekends. My roommate was never around on weekends. My sister could have slept in my roommate's bed, but we preferred sharing a bed even though it was small. As small as this one."

Dani pulled back the covers. Anita curled up next to her and Dani draped the covers over her. They spooned. Anita panicked when Dani wrapped her arm around Anita's waist. Maybe she'd given Dani the wrong idea. She waited for Dani's hand to inch toward her breast or her pussy. If she did, Anita would just leave without saying anything. But Dani's hand didn't move. A minute later, Anita could feel Dani's steady breathing on her neck. Dani was asleep. Her body felt warm against Anita's. Anita decided that they should sleep in here from now on.

Chapter Twenty-One

TERRENCE'S GOLF CART bumped over rocks as he navigated hair pin turns on a dirt road that wound through the forest. The road was heavily used by Kitsune employees. Terrence wanted to have it paved, it could be treacherously muddy after a rainstorm, but Mr. Kite liked the rural charm of a dirt road that led into the mountains and away from the restaurant. Trees blocked out the late afternoon sun making it seem like dusk, but then Terrence arrived at a clearing and was bathed in orange sunshine.

The grassy field was large enough to accommodate a football game and rested on the northernmost end of Kitsune's ten acres. On one end of the field was a row of small cabins, home of Kitsune's employees. Parked in front of the cabins were more golf carts. Most of the restaurant's fifty employees were busy preparing for the evening's special ceremony. Long tables were set with white tablecloths and silverware. Multi-colored streamers hung above a wooden stage. Mr. Kite's throne was adorned with wildflowers. Employees scooted out of the way of Terrence's golf cart and waved as he rolled past them. He parked in front of Mr. Kite's log cabin.

The original cabin had been built decades earlier but had been expanded over the years. During the sixties, indoor plumbing was added along with a bathroom. During the eighties, a second bedroom was added, and the kitchen was expanded. The latest renovation took place after Kitsune began to make a profit. The old cabin had exploded into a luxury lodge with a wraparound porch, gourmet kitchen, massive fireplace, five bedrooms, four bathrooms, a wine cellar, and a hot tub.

Terrence entered the lodge's screened porch and was greeted by Mr. Kite's leash of tame red foxes. They sniffed his shoes with their pointy noses and wagged their bushy tails. The front door was locked, and Terrence cursed himself for forgetting to bring his copy of the key. He knocked on the door.

"Mr. Kite cannot be disturbed at this time," said a woman's voice inside.

"It's me, Cheryl," Terrence said.

A woman in her early forties with short auburn hair wearing only a Kitsune polo shirt and panties opened the door. She beamed at Terrence.

"Hey, hon," she said.

"Where is he?" Terrence asked.

"Where else? In the kitchen."

Terrence walked past Cheryl and went to the kitchen where Mr. Kite was preparing his special tasting menu that he would bestow on the two employees that he felt were ready to receive the ultimate culinary enlightenment at the climax of this evening's ceremony. The preparation was a sacred and private ritual. Mr. Kite was naked except for an apron that read "Free Hot Dog, Bring Your Own Bun" with an arrow pointing toward his crotch.

"Terry, my man," Mr. Kite said. "Would you care for a taste?"

"No, thank you," Terrence said. "I need to keep a clear head tonight."

Only three people knew what exactly was in Mr. Kite's special tasting dishes and all of them were in the house at this moment. The appetizer was raw cannabis and kale salad. The main dish was psilocybin mushroom risotto. For dessert, there was chocolate moonshine cake. Mr. Kite grew the weed, brewed the moonshine, and picked the magic mushrooms himself.

Some of the ingredients were added in smaller amounts to dishes that he feed the employees at every stage of their indoctrination into the Kitsune culinary clan. Mr. Kite once explained to Terrence that the mind-altering substances expanded his employees' consciousness so that they could accept the Nirvana that he was offering them.

"I just got off the phone with Ginny Spencer," Terrence said. "She and Corey located Dani's GPS signal."

Mr. Kite paused from stirring the mushroom risotto to taste it. He nodded his approval and continued stirring.

"That's awesome!" he said. "You know what we should do? We should add Dani as a third recipient of tonight's special tasting menu. I know she's not competing, but it will show her that we forgive her and accept her back into the family."

"Ginny and Corey haven't found Dani yet," Terrence said. "Her signal appeared on their tracker for about ten minutes and then disappeared again. They followed the signal into a residential area before losing it. They couldn't get a definite location."

Mr. Kite opened the oven and poked a toothpick into the cake. It came out clean, so he put on a pair of oven mitts and removed the chocolate moonshine cake from the oven. The room filled with the wonderful smell of freshly baked cake. He put the pan on a wire rack and turned his attention back to the mushroom risotto.

"Don't look so gloomy," Mr. Kite said. "Until today you weren't even sure Dani was still in Red Fox."

"That's true," Terrence said. "I told Ginny and Corey to

stay right where they are. The next time Dani pokes her head out of her hiding place, they'll be there to pick her up and bring her home."

Terrence leaned against the kitchen counter and looked out the window. The sun was dropping behind the forest. He could hear a Stevie Nicks song coming from the loudspeakers mounted on poles in the field. During the ceremony, they'll play a mix tape of songs by Mr. Kite's favorite Southern rock bands.

"We've built something really special here," Terrence said. "I don't want to see it come tumbling down."

"And it won't, Terry," Mr. Kite said. "Stop being so negative. You're starting to harsh my mellow, man. The ceremony will be starting soon. You should go out there and enjoy the community we built together."

"Yeah, I guess you're right."

"Tell you what, Terry. Since I'm going to be tied up all evening with the two latest inductees into the sacred circle, I'm going to have Cheryl stay with you tonight."

Terrence grimaced. His partnership with Mr. Kite had brought him more wealth and prestige that he ever imagined, but there were two things about Mr. Kite that he hated with a red-hot passion that he couldn't control or bury. The first was having to get Mr. Kite's permission to spend the night with his own wife. The second was being called Terry. He hated that name.

"Thank you, Mr. Kite," Terrence said, swallowing his pride once again. "That's very generous of you."

"Hey, I'm a generous guy."

Terrence's flesh crawled with anger. He bit his tongue and lumbered out of the kitchen. Once outside the lodge, he could breathe easily again. Everything was ready for the ceremony. The employees milled about in groups, laughing and chatting about the latest cooking technique bestowed upon them by the great Mr. Kite.

Terrence had seen the ceremony many times over the years and wasn't in the mood to watch it again. While everyone lived out here on the northern end of the Kitsune property, Terrence's house was behind the restaurant at the southern end. The evening had gotten dark enough for the employees to light the bamboo torches. Meanwhile, Terrence got into his golf cart and headed for home.

Cheryl helped Mr. Kite arrange his completed special tasting menu on a rectangular table in the living room. She had put on a blouse and jeans. He hung up his apron and had put on a fox fur loincloth, fox fur leggings, and a fox fur hat. His hairy chest, arms, and legs were bare. Cheryl peeked out the window.

"The natives are getting restless," she said.

"I don't blame them. It's time to get this party started." Mr. Kite put his hand on the doorknob and hesitated. "I told Terry you'd be staying with him tonight."

"Why? Did I do something wrong?"

"Not at all. It's just I'll have my hands full with the new inductees and I sensed that Terry was feeling a bit out of sorts. I think a night with you will cheer him up."

Cheryl nodded. "Yes, that would be nice."

Mr. Kite stepped onto the screened in porch. His foxes got to their feet and gathered around him. He squatted to pet them, and they mugged him with affection.

"Alright Ronnie, Patsy, Duane, Stevie Ray, Selena, and Butterbean. Let's go get us something to eat."

As he emerged from the porch with his foxes at his heels, Stevie Ray Vaughan & Double Trouble's "Pride and Joy" played on the loudspeakers. His employees cheered and kept cheering until he took his place on his throne with his foxes seated at his feet. He held up his hand for silence.

"What a glorious night," Mr. Kite said. "I'm surrounded by glorious people and we're about to partake of glorious food that will fill our bodies and our souls."

The employees cheered.

Mr. Kite held up his hand again. Silence.

"So, what are we waiting for? Let's get this party started."

Kitsune dishes was served along with bottles of wine. People became so enraptured by the experience of eating the most spiritual food on the planet in their elite community that they jumped from the table to sing and dance. They fed, kissed, and fondled each other in an orgy of happiness.

After they had eaten, Cheryl got on the stage.

"I know I don't need to remind anyone here what the word Kitsune means," she said.

"Fox!" the employees shouted.

"That's right. Kitsune is Japanese for fox, but I'm not talking about the kind of cute bushy tail foxes like Ronnie and Pasty sitting there at Mr. Kite's feet. I'm talking about the fox from Japanese folktales. That Kitsune is a shapeshifter fox that can take human form. That Kitsune has superior intelligence, can live hundreds of years, and has magical powers. That Kitsune is like a god. A Fox God!"

"Fox God! Fox God! Fox God!" the employees chanted.

"And what do we call our Fox God? The Fox God who fills our empty bellies and empty souls with the goodness from the land?"

"Mr. Kite! Mr. Kite! Mr. Kite!"

"Yes, our own Mr. Kite. He is our spiritual leader, our master chef, and our Fox God!"

The employees cheered. They formed a circle around Mr. Kite's throne and pranced around him. The foxes held their ears back as they watched them go by.

Mr. Kite stroked his bushy beard and smiled benevolently.

When it looked like the employees might collapse from so much prancing, he held up his hand. They stopped mid-prance and went back to their seats.

"As much as I would like to bestow all my secrets to each and every one of you, I must hold back and parcel them out to only those who are truly ready," Mr. Kite said. "My secrets are too powerful to share with anyone who isn't worthy."

The employees murmured their agreement.

"Let the judging begin," Cheryl said.

Four plates were presented to Mr. Kite. They were prepared by the four top contenders to receive the ultimate culinary enlightenment. He took a single bite from each dish before placing the plate on the floor so that his foxes could scarf down the rest.

Judging the entries was just for show. Mr. Kite had already chosen the two lucky inductees: Rachel because of her enormous breasts and long legs, and Anthony because of his cute ass and blue eyes. He whispered his choices into Cheryl's ear. She waited to announce the winners until after he vacated his throne and walked back to the lodge. The foxes trotted after him.

"The winners are Rachel and Anthony," Cheryl said.

The crowd cheered and the losers pouted. Rachel squealed and hopped up and down causing her breasts to jiggle. Anthony grinned like an idiot. Cheryl gave them instructions to go to the lodge, knock on the door, wait for Mr. Kite to invite them in, and then do whatever he instructed them to do.

Rachel and Anthony were too nervous to talk as they walked across the grassy field to the cabin. The foxes were curled up on the porch. They were nodding off to sleep and barely acknowledged the couple's presence. Anthony knocked on the door and immediately Mr. Kite invited them inside. They found him standing behind a table with the special tasting menu laid out in front of him. The only illumination came from black lights casting dark purplish shadows and providing an eerie glow. Pink Floyd's trippy album "Ummagumma" provided background music.

"Come closer," Mr. Kite said waving his hands. "Don't be shy."

Rachel and Anthony edged closer to the table. They breathed in the scent of the mushroom risotto and the chocolate cake.

"Where are the plates and utensils?" Rachel asked.

"Kitsune is more than the best restaurant in the world," Mr. Kite said as he walked around the table. "It's a religion. It's a way of life." He took two cushions from the corner and dropped them on the floor in front of the two inductees. "Kneel and accept this sacred offering."

Rachel and Anthony kneeled on the cushions. Mr. Kite stood over them and spoon fed them the tasting menu like a mother bird feeding her chicks. In between bites, he gave them sips of water. He fed them slowly so that they could savor the flavors and textures of each dish. By the time he got to feeding them the chocolate moonshine cake, the marijuana in the salad and the psilocybin mushroom in the risotto were taking effect.

Rachel and Anthony giggled like children as their drugged minds struggled to find new superlatives to describe the food. Their bodies tingled as they became too stoned to stay kneeling. They slouched over and eventually lay on their backs. They pointed at imaginary comets shooting across the ceiling.

Mr. Kite helped them to their feet and led them to the master bedroom. A king size bed with rabbit fur blankets dominated the room. Rachel and Anthony sat on the bed and ran their fingers through the soft fur.

"Why just your fingers?" Mr. Kite said. "You've eaten the food provided by this land. Now experience the creatures you share the land with." Rachel and Anthony tilted their heads in confusion. "Get naked so you can feel the fur all over your body."

The inductees fumbled with their clothing, but they were

too stoned and couldn't get them off. Mr. Kite undressed them. They writhed on the fur blanket as they reveled in the sensations rippling through their bodies. Mr. Kite took off his hat and leggings and stood on the bed.

"I have one more special dish to share with you," he said. "Come. Kneel before me and receive my most precious gift of enlightenment."

Rachel and Anthony knelt before Mr. Kite. He took off his loincloth and pulled their heads toward him. As he ran his fingers through their soft hair, they took turns taking him into their hungry mouths. They followed Mr. Kite's directions without hesitation. For hours, he gave them new combinations to perform. Whenever they were close to orgasm, he had them hold off until they were begging him for release. He finally relented. Their fluids soiled the fur blanket. Mr. Kite ejaculated on their faces and had the couple clean each other with their tongues.

The two inductees slept curled up on either side of Mr. Kite. In the morning, he made them breakfast wearing only a pair of pajama pants. While they ate, he made them swear that they would never reveal a single detail about the sacred ceremony to a living soul and especially not to a fellow Kitsune employee or else it would ruin the experience for the next inductees.

Mr. Kite had Rachel and Anthony do the dishes, while he went out on the porch to pour dog food into bowls for his foxes. A cool breeze blew through the screens and brought the scent of pine. Once they were done cleaning the kitchen, Rachel and Anthony joined Mr. Kite on the porch. He could tell from the way the couple stared off into space that they were still a bit blurry from the drugs he'd fed them the night before.

"So, what do we do now?" Rachel asked.

Mr. Kite stretched his arms and yawned.

"Head on back to your dorm. Tonight, Terry will tell you which position you've been promoted to in the kitchen."

They started to leave, but Mr. Kite grabbed Anthony's arm.

"I'd like you to stay here for a few days," he said. "You'll assist Cheryl with maintaining my cabin."

Rachel's face burned with envy as she hurried across the field to her dorm.

Mr. Kite pulled Anthony close to him. He placed Anthony's hand on his crotch as he grabbed Anthony's cute ass. Mr. Kite's beard tickled as he kissed Anthony's neck. Anthony slipped his hand inside Mr. Kite's pajama pants.

"Is this how I'll be assisting Cheryl?" Anthony asked.

"Smart boy," Mr. Kite said. "You go to the head of the class."

Chapter Twenty-Two

TRACIE HADN'T BEEN to this part of town since high school. She and her friends used to buy pot from a guy who lived in the neighborhood. Back then, she thought the houses looked cheap and run down. She could see now that they weren't any different from the houses in the neighborhood she grew up in. The people here were working class but not dirt poor.

The house she lived in now was much nicer than her childhood home. Skyler's deputy salary wouldn't have gone far in a big city, but it provided a level of comfort in Red Fox that was better than most folks in town. Right now, Connor and Harper were alone in that nice house. Tracie had left them in front of the TV, absorbed in their cartoons. If she hurried, she would return before they noticed her missing.

Tracie found the house she was looking for. She was surprised to see that the yard was overgrown and full of weeds. She supposed that if your job was to maintain other people's yards, you would be too worn out to do your own.

She parked in the driveway behind Duane's pick-up truck. She checked to see if anybody was in the adjacent yards or walking past the house. Other than the singing cicadas, the neighborhood was quiet. Tracie rushed from her car to the front door and knocked.

Duane opened the door immediately. He held it open, and she dashed inside. Tracie was surprised again. She knew Duane was divorced and lived with his teenage son. With two men living together without a female, she expected the house to be a smelly pigsty. Instead, the house was immaculate. The furniture was old, and the carpeting was worn, but they were well kept. A bookcase filled with football trophies dominated one wall.

"I wasn't sure you'd be home when I called," Tracie said. "I've been putting off coming to see you, but I can't wait any longer."

"I've been wanting to see you too," Duane said.

He came up behind her, reached around, and grabbed her breasts while grinding his groin against her butt.

"No, Duane," Tracie said. "That's not why I'm here."

"You don't have to pretend. Everybody needs an occasional booty call."

Duane pulled up her blouse and yanked it over her head before she could stop him. Tracie retreated to the kitchen. He followed her. She held up her hands as if that would ward him off.

"We need to talk, Duane," Tracie said. "This is important."

He removed his T-shirt, showing off his broad shoulders and beautifully sculpted chest. He swiped her hands aside and wrapped his massive arms around her. He pressed his lips on hers before she could speak. His tongue forced its way into her mouth as he grabbed her ass.

Though she was upset and furious that he wouldn't listen to her, her body responded to his advances. She closed her eyes and arched her back. His rough hands slid up her back and in one deft move, he unsnapped her bra and yanked it off.

"We really do need to talk," Tracie said weakly as she tried in vain to maintain a shred of control.

"Talk?" Duane said. "Like dirty talk? I can do that. You a naughty girl and I'm going to punish you by doing all kinds of dirty things to you."

Duane teased Tracie with his hands and his tongue until she was beyond the point of protesting. She let him have his way with her on the cool tile kitchen floor.

There was no more dirty talk, only their bodies responding to each other's need, matching each other's thrust, and mingling their sweat. Duane held Tracie tightly when he climaxed, which caused her own orgasm to ripple through her.

They lay silently on the floor for a minute before Duane rolled off Tracie. He filled two glasses of water and gave her one of them. They didn't look at each other as they dressed.

"This isn't the reason I came over here," Tracie said.

"Could have fooled me," Duane said.

"I'm serious."

Duane looked at the wall clock.

"Say what you got to say and then you got to go. My boy's coming home from school soon."

Mentioning Duane's son reminded Tracie that she had to hurry home to her own kids. Taking a deep breath, she faced Duane.

"I'm pregnant," she said.

Duane drained his glass of water and put the glass in the sink.

"Oh, I get it. Once you got three children, you won't be able to afford me no more. You didn't need to come all the way over here to tell me that. I have a phone."

"You don't understand. I had to tell you in person." Tracie's eyes filled with tears. "You're the father, Duane. I'm pregnant with your baby."

Chapter Twenty-Three

Corey Chan woke up with a stiff neck and a wicked headache. Ginny made him sleep on the floor as punishment for losing Dani's GPS signal. He argued that it wasn't his fault, but she wouldn't listen.

He threw the thin blanket aside, got to his feet, and stretched his aching back. He checked his watch. It was 5:00 a.m. Ginny was curled up in the middle of the warm comfy bed. Corey went into the kitchenette for a glass of water. As he drank the water, he glared at the large bottle of olive oil on the counter. The idea of another meal of sliced vegetables and kidney beans in olive oil was more than he could stomach.

Corey took his clothes and his wallet into the bathroom and locked the door. He was going to get some solid food damn it, but he didn't want Ginny, or anyone associated with Kitsune to know where he was going. He had to find his GPS device. He had learned that Dani's device was embedded in her Kitsune polo shirt, but he wasn't sure where the security guards had hidden his.

After searching his clothes, his shoes, and his watch, he felt something hard inside the lining of his wallet. He tore open the stitches and found a wafer-thin plastic disk. In case he had any doubts, the words GPS Finder were etched into the plastic.

He considered flushing the disk down the toilet, but he was worried that if his signal suddenly disappeared, the security guards would know he found it. He put it in the pocket of his pants for the time being.

Once he was dressed, he eased out of the bathroom. Ginny was snoring. Corey left the motel room as quietly as possible. It was hazy and cool. The sun hadn't broken the horizon yet. He walked toward downtown. Fog rolled over the road. When he was a half mile from the motel, he hid the GPS disk under a rock next to the road.

He arrived in downtown Red Fox an hour later. As he walked along the sidewalk, Corey was reminded that Red Fox was a very small town. He counted four traffic lights.

Everything was closed, including the Piggly Wiggly, so he continued on Main Street to the edge of town. He saw a lone store on a dirt lot about a quarter mile away and headed for it.

The hand painted sign over the doorway read Zorro Deli and Groceries. The neon Open sign in the window was glowing red. Corey went inside and was greeted by the smell of burnt pork, stale coffee, and motor oil. It was a ramshackle store with three aisles overloaded with a mix of Mexican and American items. There were bags of tortilla chips next to bags of sour cream onion potato chips. There were packages of dried chilies and cans of refried beans next to cans of creamed corn and jars of mayonnaise. Spicy lollipops sat next to Milky Ways.

Corey wandered through the store, his stomach growling loudly. He got a large bag of plantain chips off the shelf, and a bottle of Jarritos Mango soda from a walk-in cooler that smelled like something had gone sour a long time ago. He carried his items to the front counter. Next to the counter were glass display cases filled with prepared food. Corey's foodie instincts went into overdrive. Here was the real treasure.

There were heaps of chicharrones, crispy and oily. There were stacks of burritos individually wrapped in foil, and rows of gorditas. The smell coming from the display case was heady and strong, and combined with Corey's lack of protein it made him light-headed.

A Mexican man appeared at the counter. He wasn't fat, but he was very large. His smile was large as well. He wore a clean white apron over a tight T-shirt. Taped to the wall behind him were Polaroids of hunters and the deer they killed. Written in Magic Marker at the bottom of the photos was the hunter's name and the score for the buck.

"Buenos dias, amigo!" the man said. "If you're hungry, you came to the right place. We have the best burritos in town. Actually, we have the only burritos in town."

"I am hungry, and would love a burrito," Corey said. "What kind do you have?"

"I have pork, chicken, beef, and plain black bean."

Corey rubbed his chin. Since he hadn't eaten meat for so long, he should probably get the black bean burrito, otherwise he might become violently ill. But the smell of seared animal flesh was making him crave meat in the worst way.

"I can also make you a huevos rancheros burrito."

Corey's eyes lit up.

"That sounds perfect."

"Why don't you have a seat in the deli, and I'll bring it to you. You can take your chips and soda with you."

"Should I pay first?"

"You can wait until you're finished eating. There's no hurry."

The deli was a small room with a cracked linoleum floor and a wobbly overhead fan. There were four tables with plastic tablecloths and metal folding chairs. On the tables were napkin dispensers and flatware in wax paper sleeves. On the walls were framed children's drawings. Corey sat at the table in the back. He tore open his bag of plantain chips and twisted off the cap of his soda. As he savored the chips combination of sweet and sour, Corey felt he was beginning to think clearly for the first time in days. Hell, for the first time in years.

Now that he'd spent some time away from Kitsune, the spell it had on him was beginning to wear off. He tried to recall the details of the night he'd been chosen to receive Mr. Kite's special tasting menu and experience culinary enlightenment. Ginny was his fellow inductee. At the time, Corey was sorry Dani wasn't the second inductee, but later was thankful that she hadn't been there. Corey had smoked plenty of pot and had done ecstasy a few times, but he'd never been as high as he was that night. He wasn't sure how he and Ginny ended up in Mr. Kite's bed. Corey wasn't gay but when Mr. Kite told him to go down on him, Corey did it without hesitation. In the morning, Mr. Kite had sent Ginny away and for the next month, Corey stayed in the lodge, cleaning it during the day and having sex with Mr. Kite at night. Sometimes, Cheryl Grigsby joined them or slept in a separate bedroom.

The month ended and Mr. Kite sent Corey back to the dorm. When it was time for the next ceremony, Corey understood that Mr. Kite would choose a new inductee to clean his lodge during the day and get sodomized by him at night.

Corey went back to work in the restaurant but now he was confused. The food that he once worshipped gave him stomachaches. He should have left then, but Kitsune had become his life. He couldn't leave. He buried his doubts and completely devoted himself to Kitsune and Mr. Kite. Eventually, the pain in his stomach went away.

Corey's thoughts were interrupted by the arrival of his food. The burrito was steaming hot. There was a pool of refried beans and a scoop of rice next to the burrito.

"And no meal is complete without this," his server said as he put a bowl of salsa next to the plate.

"This is awesome," Corey said.

"Gracias. You're not from around here, are you?"

"No. Just visiting."

"Welcome to Red Fox. My name is Pepe Martinez. I own this place be it ever so humble."

They shook hands.

"I'm Corey Chan and I can't wait to dig into this."

"Of course. Don't let me keep you."

"You can join me if you like. I wouldn't mind the company."

Pepe glanced at the front door.

"Sure," he said. "Nobody usually comes in for another hour."

He sat in the chair next to Corey.

"If nobody comes in, why do you open so early?" Corey said.

"Once in a while someone like yourself comes by. When it's early morning and you're really hungry, it's important that someone be there to feed you."

Corey picked up the burrito and took a bite. The eggs were firm, and the sauces were divine. If he was still doing his podcast, Tooti Frooti O'Foodie, he would have devoted an entire episode to this place that would have sent his fellow foodies trekking up Red Fox Mountain to eat breakfast in Pepe's tiny dining room.

"What made you decide to visit Red Fox?" Pepe said. "Do you like to go hiking? Fishing? The fishing is good here. I like to fish when I can find the time."

"Actually, I'm looking for a friend."

"Really? What does your friend look like? A lot of people come through my store. Maybe I've seen them."

Corey spooned salsa onto his refried beans.

"This is going to sound really weird. I don't want to find her anymore. The place I work for asked me to do it, but I don't think I want to work for them anymore."

Pepe sat back and crossed his arms.

"And just who do you work for?"

"Kitsune."

Pepe rolled his eyes.

"Those pendajos!"

"Exactly. Those pendajos."

The front door opened, and a petite woman came in She had blonde hair tied in a ponytail. She wore a T-shirt and torn jeans.

"Excuse me," Pepe said. "I'll be right back." He got up and waved at the woman. "Anita! What are you doing here so early in the morning?"

"I told my friend Dani that you make the best breakfast burritos in the whole fucking world," Anita said. "But she didn't believe me. I dragged my sorry ass out of bed this morning and came down here so I could prove it to her."

Corey dropped his burrito when he heard the woman named Anita say Dani's name. He felt his old stomachache come back. He watched Anita as she paced in front of the counter.

"One huevos rancheros burrito coming up," Pepe said.

"Make that two," Anita said. "I'm not going to sit there and watch her eat without having one myself. I'm going to get me a couple of them Mexican Coca Colas too."

"Sure. You know where they are."

Anita moved out of Corey's line of sight, but she returned shortly carrying two bottles which she placed on the counter. Corey looked down at his burrito and stole glances at Anita and Pepe. They made small talk as Pepe prepared her order. Corey picked enough of their conversation to figure out that Pepe wanted to do something sexual with Anita, but she didn't have time for it.

Corey just knew that Dani was hiding in Anita's house. He could follow Anita. Once he knew where she lived, he could get Ginny and together they could convince Dani to come back to Kitsune. He would be a hero to Terrence and Mr. Kite.

Or he could stay right where he was and enjoy this amazing food.

After Anita left with her burritos, Pepe came back to join Corey.

"So, how long have you worked for Kitsune?" Pepe asked.

"Long enough to know that it's time for me to move on," Corey said.

"Sounds like you're planning on putting in your two-week notice."

"To hell with that. I'm quitting today. In fact, I've already quit."

A man wearing a John Deere baseball cap came in followed by a middle-aged woman wearing cat eyeglasses. Pepe went to wait on them. By the time Corey finished eating, the other tables were occupied. He paid Pepe for his meal, shook his hand, and left.

On the walk back to the motel, Corey noticed that Pepe's food had not made him sick. If anything, he felt better than he had for months. The decision to leave Kitsune was easier than he imagined. A weight had been lifted off his shoulders. Soon, Kitsune would be nothing but a bad memory.

He thought about finding Dani and asking her to join him. It was his fault that they ended up at Kitsune. Maybe escaping together would make up for getting them trapped by Mr. Kite. A wave of guilt came over Corey. He'd caused Dani enough grief. From the way that woman Anita talked, Dani was doing all right on her own.

Ginny started screaming at Corey the second he entered their motel room.

"Where the hell have you been? Why didn't you tell me you were going out? What have you been eating? I can smell your shitty breath from here!"

Corey ignored her and began stuffing his clothes into his

suitcase. Ginny stood beside him and continued to berate him. As usual she was naked. Corey had to admit that he liked how when she was angry her freckles stood out on the skin between her breasts.

"What are you doing?" she yelled. "Are you leaving? You can't leave. We haven't found Dani. You can't abandon our mission. I won't let you!"

"I've had enough of this crap," Corey said. "I'm leaving and you can't stop me."

"You can't leave. I won't let you. I'll tell Mr. Grigsby and he'll tell Mr. Kite of your betrayal."

Corey glared at Ginny.

"And what will they do? Fire me? Fuck them. I quit!"

Ginny's mouth dropped open.

"Did you just curse the name of Mr. Kite?"

"Yeah, I guess I did. What are you going to do about it?"

Ginny pummeled Corey with her fists. Caught off guard, he retreated to the kitchenette. He cowered against the sink while she swung her fists at him and kicked him.

During her assault, something broke inside of Corey. Kitsune had already beaten him mentally and emotionally. Now he was being beaten physically. He'd had enough abuse and wasn't going to take it anymore.

He pushed Ginny as hard as he could. She toppled to the floor. He grabbed her long curly hair. She howled in pain as he dragged her across the room to the bed. He wrapped his arms around her waist. She swung her arms and legs, but he was blinded by anger and impervious to her blows.

Corey threw Ginny on the bed. He took off his belt and used it to bind her wrists together. It was a trick he'd learned when he and Dani had experimented with light bondage. Using the other end of the belt, he pulled her arms over her head and tied the belt to the headboard. Ginny struggled in vain to get loose.

"Help!" she screamed. "Help! I'm being raped!"

Corey rushed back to the kitchenette and got a dish towel. He rolled it up and tied it over Ginny's mouth. Her eyes raged at him as the gag muffled her screams. He put the Do Not Disturb sign on their door.

He stood at the foot of the bed. Ginny was bound and gagged. And naked. On the bed. And Corey realized he had an erection.

Well, he'd gone this far.

Corey took off his clothes. Ginny's eyes widened when she looked at his crotch. He grabbed the bottle of olive oil off the kitchen counter. He pushed Ginny's legs apart and poured the oil on her. The golden liquid soaked her pubic hair and dripped down between her legs and around her labia. Corey rubbed it inside her. Ginny shut her eyes and moaned.

"You like that, don't you?" Corey asked.

She shook her head no.

"Lie all you want. Your body gives you away."

Corey slid his fingers in and out of her, slowly at first and then quickening the pace. Ginny whimpered helplessly as she opened for him. Corey leaned over and bit one of her nipples. That was the last straw. She climaxed. Her legs shook and only Corey could hear her muffled moans. Crushed by how her body had betrayed her, tears rolled down her face.

"That was just the beginning" Corey said.

He climbed onto the bed. Ginny silently pleaded with him to stop, but he had already passed the point of no return. He grabbed her ankles and spread her legs.

Corey paused to enjoy that magic moment when a man enters a woman. It reminded him of why men spend so much time and energy pursuing sex. It was the best feeling in the world. Better than the finest meal from the greatest restaurant.

And then the moment passed. All the pent-up sexual tension created by Ginny constantly parading around naked was released as Corey ravaged her.

At some point, Corey let go of Ginny's ankles. He embraced her as she wrapped her legs around his waist. They both needed this more than they realized.

After much sweating and groaning, Corey climaxed. Exhausted, he collapsed on top of her. They stayed like that with his body pressing down on hers for a minute before Corey rolled off Ginny and sat on the edge of the bed. It was as if he'd had a fever and the fever had broken, leaving him ashamed of the way he'd abused her.

"I'm sorry, Ginny. I don't know what came over me. I wouldn't blame you if you hated me."

Corey untied the belt and freed her wrists. He stood in the corner and waited. He deserved whatever punishment he was about to receive. Ginny pulled the gag off her mouth and rubbed her wrists.

"Why didn't you tell me you were into bondage?" she asked.

"I don't know. I guess I didn't know I was into it until now," he said.

"I love bondage!"

Ginny slid off the bed and hugged Corey.

"Next time," she said. "I want you to spank me."

"Next time? Ginny, weren't you listening? I'm leaving."

"You can't leave now. We're just getting started."

Chapter Twenty-Four

"WHAT MAKES YOU SO sure I'm the father?" Duane said. "What about your husband?"

"Skyler and I haven't had sex in a year," Tracie said. "You're the only person I've slept with."

Duane leaned against the kitchen counter and crossed his arms. The kitchen still smelled of sex.

"I thought you were on the pill."

"I am on the pill, but it's not a hundred percent foolproof. Once in a while women on the pill get pregnant."

"And you're sure you're pregnant?"

"I peed on a stick and got a plus sign. Besides, after two kids I can tell. I'm definitely pregnant."

"I guess my sperm was super strong. It couldn't be stopped."

"What are we going to do?"

Duane narrowed his eyes at Tracie.

"There is no we. This is your problem, not mine."

"But you're the father."

Duane left the kitchen, went into the living room, and sat on a couch. Behind him was the bookcase filled with football trophies. Tracie followed him and sat on an easy chair.

"You think you the only white girl in Red Fox that I've been with?" Duane said. "The white women in this town been lining up for my big Black dick since I was barely out of my teens. But you the first one stupid enough to come to me when they got knocked up."

He made it sound like the women he impregnated were solely responsible, as if he had nothing to do with it.

"If people found out, it would be bad for both of us," Tracie said.

"Worse for you than me," Duane said. "This ain't the sixties. They don't lynch Black men for screwing white women anymore."

"I can't have this baby. I have to get an abortion."

"Then do it and stop bothering me."

Tracie rubbed her temple. She was getting a terrible headache. She hated that his seed was inside her now.

"I don't have the money. Skyler gives me an allowance and after buying groceries and paying the bills, there's hardly any left for me to do even little things like get my hair done. I have nothing in savings."

"Can't you borrow the money from somebody?"

Tracie looked at Duane. Her lower lip trembled. He shook his head.

"Oh no. Do I look like a bank to you?"

Tracie pointed at the football trophies.

"Everybody knows half the colleges in the SEC want to recruit Shaun," she said. "Don't they give him money to sign with their school?"

Duane jumped to his feet. His fists clenched as he glared at Tracie.

"Don't you bring my son into this! He's got nothing to do with this."

Tracie shrank back in the chair.

"I didn't mean it like that. I just thought you might have plenty of money right now."

Duane's features softened and he plopped down on the couch.

"Sorry. I'm just very protective of my boy. It hasn't been easy as a single parent to raise a child on my own. My landscape business has been steady, but I only make enough to scrape by."

Tracie crossed the room and sat next to Duane. She took his large hand in hers.

"Isn't there some way you can help me? Please?"

"You could work for the money. Probably wouldn't take you more than a couple of nights."

Tracie jumped to her feet and glared at Duane.

"Despite what you might think of me, I'm not a whore!"

Duane leaned back.

"You think I chose to cut lawns for a living? This town chose my job for me. They made sure the only work I could get was the kind where I bust my ass all day and before I get my money, I have to say yes sir and yes ma'am to all the happy white folks looking down on me. Don't tell me how you're too good to be a whore."

Tracie stared at the football trophies as if they would have the answer.

"There is no way in hell I'm going to sell my body for money. I'll just have to find the money someplace else. You're obviously not going to help me."

She was almost out the door when Duane caught her arm.

"Think about it," he said. "You got the kind of body that turns a man on. Why not use it? You can make good money for just a few hours on your back doing what comes naturally."

Tracie hung her head.

"I'd never be able to live with myself afterwards."

Duane put his hand on Tracie's stomach.

"Whatever you're going to do, you'd better decide soon. You'll start showing before you know it. If you decide to follow my advice, let me know. I can hook you up with the right people."

Tracie pushed Duane's hand away.

"I won't change my mind. Goodbye, Duane. By the way, we won't be needing your services anymore. Skyler wants to mow the yard himself."

Chapter Twenty-Five

POLLY CARRIED THE garbage to the dumpster. When she returned to the beauty shop, Martha was waiting for her at the back door.

"I just made a fresh pot of coffee," Martha said. "Would you like a cup?"

"I'd love some," Polly said.

They went into break room and Martha filled two cups with steaming black coffee.

"Can I talk to you in my office?" Martha said.

Polly choked on her coffee.

"Of course."

They settled in the office with Martha at her desk and Polly in the visitor's chair. Polly had difficulty getting comfortable.

"First of all, I want you to know that you're doing a terrific job," Martha said. "The customers can't say enough good things about you. You're easy to work with and I have a good feeling about you."

"Whew!" Polly said, putting her hand on her chest. "I thought you were going to fire me."

Martha laughed.

"Why would I do that?"

"I don't know," Polly said. "You didn't like me."

"I'm sorry if I scared you. I didn't want to say anything at first because I didn't think it was any of my business. But then, I prayed to Jesus for guidance. He showed me that if I truly cared about you, and I do, then I had no choice. I must talk to you about the men you've been spending your evenings with."

"Men? As in more than one?"

"You've been seen dating two men that you really shouldn't be dating."

"At the same time?"

"Well, you would know better than me. One of them is that brown boy who works at the motel."

"Mansoor Amin?"

"Is that his name?" Martha leaned forward and rested her elbows on the desk. "What you need to understand is that there are a lot of patriots and veterans in this town. It doesn't look good to been seen fraternizing with a Muslim."

Polly couldn't believe it. Mansoor was ruining her life again. Of course, in a small Georgia town like Red Fox "patriots and veterans" would perceive any Muslim as an America hating terrorist, even a ladyboy lover like Mansoor. Martha truly thought she was protecting Polly. It would be pointless for Polly to inform Martha that the good people of Red Fox were being racist and xenophobic.

"I let him take me to dinner the first night I was here," Polly said. "He said something rude and I walked out on him. You can ask anyone who was at the Rejoice Diner that night and they'll tell you that I left without him."

Throwing Mansoor under the bus made Polly sick to her stomach, but she felt the need to protect herself. Besides, it was the truth. She did walk out on him.

"Oh my," Martha said. "I didn't know about that. You

should have said something. Do you feel safe staying at his motel?"

"I'm not scared of him. He's all talk and no action. Besides, I like his aunt. She'll keep him in line."

"I certainly hope so, for your sake."

"Um. Who is the other guy that I shouldn't be dating?"

"Skyler Aldridge."

Polly felt like the floor had dropped out beneath her and she was plummeting down a hole. Skyler was white, Christian, and a local law enforcer. She could think of only one reason why she shouldn't go out with him.

"He's married! That's it, isn't it?"

"He didn't tell you?"

"He neglected to mention it," Polly said coldly. "I'm such an idiot."

Martha held her coffee cup in both her hands and took a sip.

"You're not the first woman to be made a fool by a man."

"He seemed so sweet and innocent. Thank God we only went on one date."

Martha narrowed her eyes at Polly.

"You didn't invite him into your motel room, did you?"

"No! Really, no. But to be honest, I was tempted."

Polly sipped her coffee but didn't taste it. Martha glanced at her wristwatch.

"I wanted to talk to you before your first appointment today," she said. "And to warn you."

"Warn me about what?"

Polly imagined the whole town was on their way over with pitchforks and torches to burn her as a witch.

"Skyler's wife, Tracie Aldridge, is coming in today to get her hair done. She asked for you specifically."

"Tracie? Skyler is married to Tracie?"

"How do you know Tracie?"

Polly panicked. How would she know Tracie?

"Isn't she the waitress at Rejoice Diner?"

"No. Tracie stays home and takes care of the kids."

"Skyler has kids?"

"Yes. A boy and a girl."

Polly was stunned. She had been hit with too much startling information to process it all.

"You said Tracie asked me for me specifically. Do you think she knows that I went out with Skyler?"

"She might. That's why I wanted to warn you."

"I don't remember seeing Tracie's name on the appointment book."

"It's in there. I wrote it down as T.A."

Polly thought about the appointment book. Normally, Martha wrote down a name next to the day and time of an appointment. Polly noticed that for one appointment Martha had written down initials instead of a name. Polly assumed that Martha had just been in a hurry, but now Polly realized that Martha had done it on purpose so Polly wouldn't know that Tracie Aldridge was coming in today.

Martha wasn't as innocent and benign as she appeared. This both frustrated and impressed Polly at the same time.

"Wait a minute," Polly said. "T.A. is my first appointment of the day."

The shopkeeper bell rang and was immediately drowned out by the sonic invasion created by shrieking children.

"That would be Tracie," Martha said. "Sounds like she brought Connor and Harper with her."

<h1 style="text-align:center">Chapter Twenty-Six</h1>

Connor and Harper Aldridge burst through the door of Martha's Hair Done Right. The children screamed at the top of their lungs, but their mother, Tracie, didn't seem concerned. However, their shrieks unnerved Polly who wasn't aware that children made that horrifying noise because they were excited and not because someone was ripping their limbs off.

Martha also wasn't concerned. In fact, she was delighted. She welcomed the rambunctious kids with open arms.

"Look at you two," Martha said. "You've gotten so big! Haven't they gotten big, Crystal?"

Running through the store like a chipmunk on speed, Harper stepped on Crystal Beaver's foot as she flew past her.

"Well, they've certainly gotten heavier," Crystal said as she rubbed her toes.

Connor scampered up to Polly, hugged her legs, and pressed his dirty face against her crotch. Polly struggled to keep her balance. She had gotten over her initial shock of their presence and patted the boy on the head.

"Well, hello," Polly said. "What's your name?"

"Tell her your name, Connor," Tracie said.

"You have a pee pee like daddy," Connor said.

Polly paled. The women laughed.

"No, she doesn't," Tracie said. "She has what mommy has."

Connor marched over to his mother. Before he could argue that what he felt inside Polly's pants wasn't anything like his mother's, Martha took a portable DVD player out of the top drawer of the front desk.

"Who wants to watch a cartoon?" Martha asked.

Connor forgot what he was going to say and joined his little sister in the waiting room. Martha put a Disney animated movie into the player and soon the two children were sitting side by side on a couch, completely absorbed by the movie.

"You don't run a salon for as long as I have without learning a few tricks," Martha said, grinning. "That should keep them distracted long enough for Tracie to get her hair done. Polly, this here is Tracie. Tracie, this here is Polly."

Polly nervously shook Tracie's hand. If Tracie was aware that Polly had been on a date with her husband, nothing in her behavior indicated it. Then again, she could be lulling Polly into a false sense of security before she pounced on her.

"Two of my best friends raved about you," Tracie said. "I just had to come and find out for myself."

Polly glanced over at Martha who was beaming at her. Polly had been a hair stylist long enough to know that one of the most important things in this business was word of mouth endorsements.

Polly and Tracie discussed how to style Tracie's hair. Polly listened carefully, asked questions, and made suggestions. Tracie stared in the mirror and turned her head from side to side trying to imagine how the style they settled on would look. Polly stood behind her. Tracie looked up and met Polly's eyes. Polly smiled. Tracie felt a warm feeling in her stomach.

"Okay, let's do it," Tracie said.

Polly took Tracie to the back to wash her hair. When they returned, Martha had Eloise Otey in her chair. Polly had learned that the elderly woman came in to get her hair done once a week. As Polly and Martha worked, snipping here and there, the women in the salon chatted cheerfully.

"Tell me, Polly," Eloise said. "Have you found a husband yet?"

"Not yet," Polly said. "In my defense, I've lived in Red Fox for less than a month."

"That's odd. I'd heard that you'd already found yourself a man."

Polly checked Tracie's reaction. She seemed amused rather than angry. Polly was beginning to think she'd gotten lucky, and no one had told Tracie. Polly was also lucky that she and Skyler had only gone on that one date that resulted in that one kiss. That one very hot kiss.

"Sorry," Polly said. "That was just a rumor. I haven't found me a man yet."

Eloise turned her attention to Martha.

"Have you heard from Brad lately?"

"He emails me at least twice a week," Martha said. "Sends me lots of photos."

"Is he up to his neck in snow?" Crystal asked.

"They don't have snow all year," Martha said. Martha noticed Polly stealing glances at her. "I'm sorry, Polly. You're probably wondering who the heck we're talking about."

"Crystal told me that you have a son named Brad," Polly said. "He lives overseas, right? Is he in the armed forces?"

"He's not in the military, though he would've made a fine soldier. Brad's in Denmark. His job has something to do with computers. He tried to explain it to me, but I can barely use my own computer."

"Why did he have to go all the way to Denmark to get a job?" asked Eloise. "Couldn't he find a computer job here in America?"

"The company he works for is based in Atlanta, but they have offices all over the world. Brad's always loved adventure. He wanted to see what it was like to live in another country."

"It's a good idea," Crystal said. "Once he spends a few years over there, he'll realize how much better it is here in the greatest country on earth. Though I'm surprised he hasn't already gotten homesick for your cooking, Martha."

Martha shook her head.

"Oh, stop it, Crystal."

"That's Brad in the photo there," Crystal said, pointing at a framed photo on the wall of a young man in a football uniform. He was posing with a football in his hand as if he was about to throw a forward pass.

Polly noticed the photo the first time she'd come in the salon for her interview. It made her uncomfortable. She had the creepy feeling that the young athlete with the wavy blonde hair, steely blue eyes, and wide toothy smile was following her with his eyes and that at any moment he would toss his football at her head.

"He was the quarterback at his high school," Martha said. "He led the Fighting Foxes to the AA State Football Championship two years in a row."

Polly noticed the pride in Martha's voice as she talked about her son.

"So, he was a star quarterback?" Polly asked.

"Oh yeah. Our hometown hero. Though, he was one of the top-rated high school players in the country, not too many colleges wanted to recruit him."

"He was too small," Crystal said.

"Brad was the exact same size as Doug Flutie, five-foot-nine and 175 pounds. Flutie won the Heisman Trophy and played in the NFL," Martha said defensively. "Despite his size, Brad got a full ride football scholarship to Stanford."

"That's wonderful," Polly said.

"He was the back-up quarterback and only played a few games. Not enough to catch the interest of the NFL, but he got a great education. Stanford has one of the best computer science programs in the country."

"And now he's in Denmark?"

"That's right." Martha pointed her scissors at Tracie. "Tracie, you and Brad dated back in high school. Do you stay in touch with him?"

Polly was almost done with Tracie's hair. She looked at Tracie in the mirror. There were tears in her eyes and her cheeks were flushed.

"Are you okay, Tracie?" Polly asked. "Do you need a glass of water?"

Tracie bolted out of the salon chair and ran into the bathroom, slamming the door behind her. The women looked at each other with surprise.

"How can she still have feelings for Brad?" Martha said. "She's married and has two beautiful children."

"I'd better go talk to her," Polly said.

Polly stood outside the bathroom door. She could hear Tracie sobbing. She knocked.

"Tracie. It's Polly. Do you mind if I come in?"

"No!" Tracie said firmly.

"Okay, I won't come in. You stay in there as long as you like."

"Wait a minute. You can come in. The door's not locked."

Polly entered the bathroom. The toilet lid was down, and Tracie sat on the lid. She still wore the salon bib. Polly sat on the floor next to her.

"Do you ever feel like everything you've done in your whole life has been a mistake?" Tracie asked.

"All the time," Polly said.

"For me, it's more than a feeling. I have completely screwed up my life."

"You have two lovely children. You can't tell me that you screwed that up."

Tracie buried her face in her hands.

"I love them dearly, but they're a mistake."

"I'm sure you don't mean that."

Tracie grabbed Polly's hand and squeezed it so tightly that Polly winced.

"I know I shouldn't be telling all this," Tracie said "I just met you, but I feel like I've known you for years. I feel like you're someone I can talk to."

Polly held Tracie's hand next to her cheek.

"I'm new here in town. I could use a friend and friends help each other," Polly said. "How can I help you?"

Tracie sat on the bathroom floor next to Polly. Polly put her arm around Tracie's shoulder as Tracie leaned against Polly.

"I never should have married Skyler," Tracie said. "Back in high school, I was Brad's girlfriend. It was never official. I knew girls who prayed every Sunday that Brad would ask them out, but he only asked me out. Skyler used to tag along on all our dates. I didn't mind because Skyler was also on the football team."

"Wait a minute," Polly said. "You dated two football players? At the same time? That must have been interesting."

Tracie nudged Polly.

"It was never like that. They were perfect gentlemen. There were times when I would have preferred to have Brad to myself so that he would have a chance to be a little less of a gentleman if you know what I mean."

"Absolutely! He was the quarterback."

"After Brad went to college, I started seeing Skyler. We were so used to hanging out that it just seemed natural to keep hanging out. But Brad was always the one I wanted. If I could afford it, I would get on a plane tomorrow and fly to Denmark to be with him."

"Why did you marry Skyler if you didn't love him?"

"I liked Skyler and I thought I would learn to love him. I believe we could have been happy together, but over the years he's made it clear that he doesn't love me. I sometimes wonder why I married him, but not as much as I wonder why he married me. I don't think he's ever had feelings for me."

Polly rubbed Tracie's shoulder.

"That can't be true. He must love you."

"He doesn't. He loves Brad. He loves Brad more than I do and I love Brad a lot."

"Skyler's gay?"

"Oh, not that kind of love. More like how teammates love each other. They share a bond that no mere woman can come between."

"God, no wonder you're in the bathroom crying. I feel like crying too."

Tracie laughed, which made Polly laugh.

"I'm pregnant," Tracie blurted out.

Polly swallowed hard.

"Who's the father?"

"Why do you assume that Skyler isn't the father?" Tracie asked defensively.

"Because if he was, you wouldn't be so upset. A third child wouldn't make you feel any more stuck in a loveless marriage than two children."

Tracie closed her eyes and nodded.

"I can't tell you who it is so don't ask me."

"I probably wouldn't know him anyway. Remember, I'm new here in town."

"I don't know what to do."

"Please don't get angry. I'm only saying this because I want to help you. If you decide not to keep the baby and you need money or a ride or anything, just say the word."

"I couldn't let you give me money. I don't know what Martha is paying you, but it can't be that much."

"I have some money saved."

The truth was that Polly had a lot of money in her savings account. It was there to pay for her bottom surgery, but Polly felt that at the moment Tracie needed the money more than she did. Besides, an abortion didn't cost near as much as getting a penis turned into a vagina.

Tracie stood and washed her face in the sink.

"You've already done more than enough," she said. "Just talking to you made me feel a hundred times better."

Polly stood and washed her hands.

"I'm still here for you, whatever you need."

The women hugged and then exited the bathroom. Eloise was gone. Martha and Crystal sat in the salon chairs reading magazines. Connor and Harper napped on the waiting room couch while the movie on the DVD player continued to play.

"About damn time," Crystal said. "I was about to pee in my pants."

She hurried into the bathroom.

"Why didn't she use the other bathroom?" Polly asked.

Martha shrugged.

"She said it was the men's bathroom."

Polly finished Tracie's hair. Tracie was delighted with the results and gave Polly a big tip. She hugged Polly again before she left with her children. Polly watched them get into Tracie's car and drive away.

As Polly was about to sweep up Tracie's hair, Martha put her hand on Polly's arm.

"Can I talk to you in my office?" Martha asked.

Here we go again, Polly thought.

"Of course," she said.

They settled in the office with Martha at her desk and Polly in the visitor's chair.

"I can't tell you what Tracie and I talked about," Polly said. "You understand, don't you?"

Martha held up her hand.

"I don't want to know. I just wanted to tell you how proud I was of you."

Polly blushed.

"I didn't do anything special."

"You gave her comfort. It was the Christian thing to do. Listen, my church has a supper in the fellowship hall after the Wednesday night service. The food's nothing special, but it's a nice way to meet some good people. I was wondering if you weren't doing anything on a Wednesday night, maybe you'd like to come with me."

Polly's eyes widened. Martha was full of surprises today.

"I would love to," Polly said. "Can we do it this Wednesday?"

Martha smiled. "It's a date."

Chapter Twenty-Seven

POLLY DIDN'T THINK it was possible to make tasteless spaghetti with meatballs, but she was proved wrong. Perhaps the cook at Red Fox Baptist Church believed that oregano was the Devil's spice and banned it from the kitchen. The salad was mostly edible, and she avoided the dessert table completely. But then, Polly didn't come to the Wednesday supper for the cuisine.

The average age of the crowd in the fellowship hall ran between fifty and death, though there were some twenty somethings and a few earnest teenagers. The predominately older crowd might have explained why the hall smelled like a nursing home, a combination of cleaning products and burnt coffee. But then, Polly didn't come to the Wednesday supper for the ambience.

She came because Martha invited her. The church members were thrilled to see a new face and Polly did her best to remember their names.

Polly had already met Tammy Baggs. Tammy gave Polly a fierce hug and introduced Polly to her husband, Pastor Simon Baggs. He almost crushed Polly's hand when he shook it.

"Welcome to Red Fox Baptist Church," he said. "We hope this is just the beginning and that you'll come back to join us."

"Martha has really taken a shine to you," Tammy said. "The way she talks about you is more like how a mother talks about her daughter rather than a boss and her employee."

Polly fidgeted with a strand of her hair.

"I like her too. She's the best boss I've ever had."

Tammy smirked. "Did I embarrass you?"

Polly shrugged. "A little bit. I don't want to give the impression that I think I'm something I'm not."

Tammy and Pastor Baggs left Polly to thank members of the church for coming. Polly wandered over to the beverage table and poured herself a cup of coffee from an ancient coffee urn that looked like it had survived both world wars. The coffee was so weak; she could see through it. She took her cup and sat at the table where she'd eaten dinner. She'd gotten a ride to the church with Martha so she couldn't leave until Martha was done socializing with her church friends.

Crystal Beaver and Gloria Medley came by Polly's table.

"Mind if we join you?" Crystal asked.

"Please sit down," Polly said.

They settled in. Crystal leaned across the table.

"Want me to give you the rundown on these here folks?" she asked.

"For God's sakes," Gloria said. "We're in the house of the Lord. I'm sure there's something in the Bible about spreading gossip."

"For or against?"

Gloria rolled her eyes.

"Why do I even try?"

Crystal turned her attention back to Polly.

"Okay. Let's do this. I saw you talking to Tammy and Pastor Baggs. Tammy henpecks the pastor and calls him Simple Simon.

Those two towering Black men are Duane Anderson and his son, Shaun. Shaun is one of the top-rated high school football players in the whole U.S. of A. and a fine young man. Duane's wife left him because he kept cheating on her. You already know Eloise Otley from the beauty shop. She's a widow and couldn't be happier about it. She couldn't stand her husband when he was alive. That young man with the receding hairline with his arm around the woman with strawberry blonde hair who dresses like she's still in high school are Pete and Tiffany Smith. Pete's a deputy in the Red Fox Police department. He and Tiffany are trying to get pregnant. I assume they're trying together, but then you never know. That crusty old codger staring at Tiffany's ass is Graham Rawls. He's retired. Spent forty years working in a carpet factory. Now he spends his days buying scratch off lottery cards and hanging out at strip joints."

"Who is that handsome older gentlemen over there?" Polly said, pointing at a lean man wearing a pressed shirt, pressed jeans, and polished cowboy boots.

"That's Vince Cagle. He's the sheriff of Red Fox."

"What's his story?"

Crystal glanced at Gloria. Gloria shrugged.

"Vince is a widower," Crystal said. "His wife Susan died in a car accident. Vince grew up here in Red Fox. He and Martha were high school sweethearts. Everyone figured they'd eventually get married, but instead he married Susan and Martha married Roy Aldridge. Now that the two of them are single again, it's obvious to anybody who has eyes that Vince would like to reconnect with Martha, but she won't have anything to do with him. Don't ask me why."

Polly studied Vince more closely. He stood in a corner holding a cup of coffee. He kept his attention on the floor except when he stole glances at Martha who was chatting with Pastor

Baggs on the other side of the room. Polly smiled. Martha had a not-so-secret admirer.

"So, what about you, Crystal?" Polly said. "What's your story?"

Crystal harrumphed. "Nobody wants to know about an old spinster like me. If I didn't talk so much, I'd be invisible."

"I don't talk so much," Gloria said. "Are you saying I'm invisible?"

"Not to me."

Crystal and Gloria laughed.

"What about me?" Polly said. "What's my story?"

Crystal narrowed her eyes at Polly.

"You haven't been around long enough for me to know your story. But don't worry. I'll find out what it is."

Chapter Twenty-Eight

IT WAS A rare quiet moment in the Aldridge house. Connor and Harper were on their stomachs on the living room floor drawing with crayons on typing paper. It wouldn't be long before Connor started first grade. As soon as Tracie gave birth to Connor, her friends and family told her to cherish every moment because children grew up quickly. What they didn't tell her was how much time and effort went into raising children leaving her only a few moments in which to cherish them.

She looked forward to sending Connor off to school. Did that make her a bad mother?

Tracie felt a sudden rush of nausea. She raced for the bathroom and vomited into the toilet. She washed her face with cool water and brushed her teeth.

She sat in the living room and watched the children. She put her hand on her stomach. How long before she started to show?

She fantasized what it would be like to tell Skyler that this was what happened when a husband ignored his wife. She had no choice but to find comfort in another man's arms. And not just any man. A man with a bigger dick than his. Then she would have Duane's Black baby and everyone in town would know that Skyler wasn't man enough to satisfy his wife.

Tracie massaged her forehead. The reality was the whole town would condemn her. There was a saying she heard whenever cheating was discovered. *A woman can run faster with her dress up than a man can with his pants down.*

As for Skyler, he probably wouldn't care that Tracie had slept with another man no matter what color his skin was. It would give him an excuse to get rid of her. He would be able to blame their failed marriage on her.

The ones who would suffer the most were Connor and Harper. Other children would whisper about them behind their backs. Tracie doubted Skyler would want custody, but he'd want visitation rights. Connor and Harper would get shuffled from one parent to the other. When they visited Skyler, Tracie would worry that he'd forget to feed them.

"Look, mommy," Harper said. She held up her drawing. It was five stick figures, a house, and some unidentified objects. One stick figure was bigger than the others. "See, it's you and Daddy and Connor and me and Mr. Anderson."

"Mr. Anderson isn't part of our family," Tracie said.

"Yes, he is. See. There's his lawnmower."

"What's this four-legged thing down here?" Tracie pointed at the corner of the drawing.

"It's a doggy."

"But we don't have a dog."

"I'm going to ask Santa Claus to bring me one for Christmas."

Oh joy, Tracie thought. More shit to clean up.

"It's a beautiful drawing," she said. "Let's hang it on the refrigerator."

Harper fidgeted as Tracie placed magnets on the drawing's four corners so that it would stick to the frig, and then Harper ran back to the living room to work on her next masterpiece.

Tracie took down a juice glass and filled it with apple juice and whiskey. If it was good enough for her kids, it was good enough for her. She needed courage for what she was about to do.

She had to get an abortion.

It was nice of Polly to offer to pay, but there was no way Tracie could borrow the money from her. She'd never be able to pay her back. Even though Tracie had taken an immediate liking to Polly, she didn't really know her. Plus, what kind of person offers to pay for a stranger's abortion?

Tracie got herself into this mess and it was up to her to get out of it. She would have to do something terrible to make things right.

She dialed Duane's number.

"Anderson Lawn Service."

"Duane. It's me, Tracie. Where are you?"

"In my truck. I'm on my way home. What do you want?"

"I've been thinking about that suggestion you made about how I can raise money for my you-know-what."

"You ready to sell that sweet booty of yours?"

"That's a crude way of putting it, but yes. Though the whole idea makes me sick, I don't see where I have any other choice."

"I talked to my friend. She wants to meet you before she agrees to set you up. How soon can you come with me to see her?"

Hot anger flared through Tracie.

"You already called her! What made you so damn sure I was going to go through with this?"

"Hey, it's not like you can get a job at Wal-Mart and expect to earn enough money before it's too late. I figured you was smart enough to know that you got a ticking time bomb inside your womb."

Tracie's anger fizzled and she felt hollowed out. She looked in the living room at her lovely children.

"I can meet with her tomorrow."

Chapter Twenty-Nine

THE SUN WAS down but it was still warm. Martha and Polly's shoes crunched on the gravel parking lot as they walked to Martha's red minivan. On the drive to the Fox Creek Falls Inn, they discussed which beauty supplies they needed to order for the shop.

Martha parked outside of Polly's room and kept the motor idling.

"Why are you still living here in the motel?" Martha asked.

"I haven't found an apartment," Polly said. "I've been looking, but I can't seem to find anything decent. I'll find something eventually and meanwhile the rates here are reasonable."

"The reason you haven't found anything is because there are no decent apartments in Red Fox. The town's too small. If you want a place worth renting, you have to know somebody."

"Do you know anybody?"

"Sure do. Me. In my house."

"Martha, you've already done so much for me. I couldn't impose on you."

Martha gave Polly's leg a playful slap.

"It's not like that. It's an actual apartment with its own entrance. I'm not trying to church it up. It has a bathroom, a little kitchen, and a living room. Plenty of space for a single girl like yourself."

"Is it in the basement?"

"I'm not talking about some dingy underground basement. It's on the top floor. When Brad turned sixteen, my ex-husband Roy decided that Brad should have his own place with plenty of privacy. As Roy put it, Brad needed to sow his wild oats. I think Roy tried to live vicariously through Brad."

Polly felt the blood rush to her face, and she had trouble breathing. Everything was working out quicker and easier than she had planned, but this was beyond her wildest imagination. She tried to stay calm. She didn't want to blow this opportunity. She was too nervous to form words, but Martha came to her rescue.

"How about this," Martha said. "Before you make up your mind, come over and take a look at the place."

"That sounds like a good plan to me."

Polly almost reached over and hugged Martha but caught herself in time. They said their good nights and Polly watched Martha drive away. She was about to go into her room when she decided to go to the motel office instead.

Mansoor was at the front desk, his elbows on the table, his head resting in his hands, and his eyes closed. He snored softly. Polly rang the call bell and Mansoor jerked awake. He blinked a few times and then focused on Polly standing before him with her hands on her hips.

"Is there something I can help you with?" Mansoor asked.

"I just wanted to inform you that I will be checking out soon," Polly said.

"I believe I speak for our entire staff when I say that Fox Creek Falls Inn will be sorry to see you go. You were a most excellent customer. We would be eternally grateful if you would give us a favorable Yelp review."

"You won't be able to spy on me anymore. Can you handle that?"

Mansoor crossed his arms.

"That's quite an accusation. I have never spied on you."

"What about the other night?"

"Which night are you referring to?"

"You damn well know which night. The night I kissed Skyler. And just to set the record straight, I had no idea at the time that he was married."

"I was not spying on you. If you had been in your room and I had been peeking in the window, then that would have been spying. You and Skyler were standing out in the open for all the world to see."

"You stood there and watched us. That's not normal behavior."

"I had no choice. I was waiting on a customer to answer his door."

Polly pulled a strand of hair behind her ear.

"It really doesn't matter. I'm checking out soon."

"You already said that," Mansoor said.

"And you won't be able to spy on me again."

"Then what will you do?"

Polly's eyes widened.

"What the hell is that supposed to mean?"

"You want me to pay attention to you. That's why you came in here to accuse me of spying. You want me to think about you because you're thinking about me."

Polly blushed.

"I do not!"

Mansoor shrugged.

"Suit yourself. When you're ready to admit that you're interested in me, you'll know where you can find me."

Polly was flabbergasted. She'd met her share of arrogant pricks in her time, but this guy was something else. She didn't waste her time on a comeback and stormed out of the office.

Once Polly was in her room with the door locked, she caught a glimpse of herself in the mirror. She laughed at herself for looking flustered. To get so hung up over a man she was never going to hook up with was just ridiculous.

Polly sat down at her computer. She didn't have time to think about handsome ladyboy lovers. She had photos to download and emails to send.

Chapter Thirty

Anita Cox was walking home after her shift at the Rejoice Diner when Sheriff Vince Cagle passed her in his car. He parked next to the sidewalk, rolled down the passenger window, and waited for her. Except for the two of them, the street was deserted.

Anita unbuttoned the top two buttons on her shirt before resting her elbows on the open window. She leaned in, giving Vince an excellent view of her cleavage. The interior smelled of Vince's aftershave lotion.

"Evening, Sheriff," Anita said. "Nice night."

"It certainly is," Vince said. "You need a ride home?"

She licked her lips.

"That depends. We talking my home or yours?"

Vince studied Anita's cleavage.

"Mine?"

Anita opened the door and got into the passenger seat.

"Let's go."

"Put on your seatbelt first."

Anita rolled her eyes as she put on her seatbelt.

"You're such a cop."

"Just concerned for your safety."

They were both comfortable with silence and didn't talk during the drive. Vince lived ten miles from town in a cabin in the woods that was anything but rustic. It had a wraparound porch and floor to ceiling windows that afforded an excellent view of Red Fox Mountain.

The interior smelled of wood polish and bacon. Vince wasn't a great housekeeper, but he kept his home cleaner and neater than most single men Anita knew. She wasn't afraid to sit on the toilet seat in his bathroom.

"You want something to drink?" Vince asked.

Anita knew he didn't mean alcohol. Everybody in town knew Vince hadn't touched a drop in years.

"You got any Mountain Dew?" Anita asked.

"Sorry. I got Perrier."

"God, you would, Vince, wouldn't you? Yeah, I'll have that."

Vince went to the kitchen, got two glasses, filled them with ice, and poured sparkling water into the glasses. When he came out of the kitchen, holding the glasses in his hands, Anita was nowhere in sight. Maybe she'd gone to the bathroom. He walked into the living room and spotted her sneakers at the bottom of the stairwell to the second floor.

Her shirt was a few steps higher, and her skirt was at the top of the stairs. He found her bra in the hallway and her panties at the entrance to his bedroom. He entered the bedroom and there was Anita, reclining naked on his bed.

"I was wondering if you'd learn enough in police school to follow my clues," she said.

"The only time I've seen a woman leave a trail of clothes like that was in the movies," Vince said.

"That's where I got the idea, though I can't remember which movie I saw it in."

Vince took a moment to admire her young, supple body

and her perfect breasts with rose-colored nipples. He was damn lucky to have this gorgeous nymphomaniac waiting for him in his bed, but her flawless body reminded him that his body was wrinkled, and his stamina wasn't what it used to be.

Vince handed Anita a glass. She took a sip, put it on the nightstand, and then climbed under the covers. He put his glass next to hers. As Vince took off his clothes, he noticed Anita watching him with a devilish grin.

"I appreciate the ego boost, but it's really not necessary," he said.

"I was just wondering if you'll ever come looking for me on any day other than a Wednesday."

Vince sat on the edge of the bed and pulled off his socks.

"What are you talking about?"

Anita ran her fingers down Vince's back. It caused a shiver in him that went all the way to his testicles.

"We only hook up on Wednesdays. Never a Monday or a Friday and definitely never on a Sunday. There must be something in the food at the church's Wednesday night supper that makes you horny."

"Or somebody you want but can't get your hands on," thought Anita.

Vince got under the covers before he took off his boxer shorts. He pulled them off and tossed them on the floor. He reached for Anita, and she curled into his arms. Her warm body pressed against his.

Vince wasn't like the other men in Red Fox that Anita slept with on a regular basis. He wasn't a disgusting pig like Henry Nix or only available for jittery quickies like Pepe Martinez. Vince was a gentleman and a superior lover compared to the high school boys.

Anita reached down between Vince's legs. She wasn't worried

that he was only semi-erect. At his age, he needed a little extra coaxing. She pulled the covers down, exposing their bodies.

"Lay on your back," Anita said. "Close your eyes."

Vince did as she instructed.

Anita took her time stroking and kissing different parts of his body. He responded best when she traced her finger along the scars on his chest and abdomen, the leftovers from years of dealing with drunks, crooks, and marital disputes. When Anita decided that she'd played this game long enough, she put him in her mouth.

"Thank you," Vince said.

She would have said you're welcome, but her mouth was full. She stopped when she felt he was close.

"I want you to ride me hard and put me away wet," Anita said.

They changed positions and Vince got on top of Anita. His lovemaking was raw and forceful. Anita held onto his skinny ass before throwing her arms back, letting him have complete control of her. Vince lasted a good five minutes before his stamina started to wane. Knowing he was tiring out; he doubled his efforts. When he came, he groaned like a wounded animal.

He rolled off her, his chest heaving as he struggled to catch his breath. Anita curled up next to him.

"I had a nice orgasm," she said. "But I want another one. How soon can you get hard again?"

Vince put her arm around her shoulder and kissed her forehead.

"At my age, I'm lucky to get hard once a night."

Anita playfully slapped his cheek.

"You're not that old and you have no problem getting it up."

"True. But it's not like when I was younger. Back then, I could get it up two or three times a night."

Anita nuzzled in tighter under Vince's arm. The window

shades were open, and they could see the half moon over the mountain.

"You can drive me back into town whenever you want," Anita said.

"You say that every time," Vince said. "I would like for you to stay the night. What do you say to that?"

Anita answered Vince by kissing him.

They almost dozed off when Anita sat up, drank her Perrier, and went to the bathroom. When she came out, Vince went in. While he was in the shower, she wandered naked from room to room.

She gazed at the framed photos on the walls and on bookshelves. There were pictures of Vince's wife, Susan, by herself and with Vince. There was a picture of Vince with his fellow soldiers in the National Guard, a picture of Vince with his fellow deputies when he started out in the Red Fox Police Department, and a picture of Vince with his deputies after he was elected Sheriff. She went into the room at the end of the hallway that Vince used as his home office. She sat in his leather executive chair and propped her feet on his desk.

"There you are," Vince said as he entered the room. He was wearing a Navy-blue terry cloth bathrobe. His bare feet padded on the hard wood floor.

Anita got up, opened Vince's robe, and pressed her naked body against his. He sat in his chair, and she sat in his lap with her arm around his shoulder and his arm around her waist. He nuzzled the space between her breasts.

"What do you know about that vegetarian restaurant up in the hills just off the mountain road?" Anita asked.

"Kitsune?" Vince said. "It's not for me. A meal's not a meal without some kind of meat on the plate."

"Yeah, but what do you know about the folks that run the place? I've heard some weird rumors."

"What kind of rumors?"

"Oh, I don't know. That their employees don't get paid. They're treated like slaves."

Vince made a face.

"I've never heard anything like that."

"Then tell me what you do know about Kitsune," Anita said.

"Some rich city folk built a fancy restaurant on the mountain. They're no different than those rich city folk who built that gated retirement community with expensive homes and a fancy golf course near Jasper. The only thing I don't like about Kitsune is that their customers drive right by Red Fox without stopping. Maybe somebody will stop to fill up their tank at Kemp's Garage, but we don't make any revenue off having them on the mountain."

"Owen bitches about that all the time. He thinks Kitsune is taking customers away from Rejoice Diner. I keep telling him that their customers and our customers are from two different worlds."

Vince ran his hand over Anita's smooth belly.

"I've met the man who owns Kitsune," he said. "Name's Terrence Grigsby. As much as I hate that his place isn't helping our economy, Terrence did us all a big favor buying up the old Payne property."

Anita ran her fingers through Vince's short gray hair.

"Somebody owned that land before this Grigsby fellow?" she asked.

"The twelve acres Grigsby bought belonged to the Payne clan for generations. They lived mostly off the land, but let me tell you, they were nothing but trouble. They may have been hillbillies, but they had a history of selling illegal substances. First it was moonshine, then weed, followed by meth, but their specialty was magic mushrooms. I'm surprised you've never heard of them. They sold most of the weed to the local teenagers around the same time you were in high school."

Anita shook her head.

"I've never done drugs and I never will. A hard dick is the only thing I've ever wanted to inject into my system."

Vince hugged her.

"Amen for that."

"If you know so much about the Payne clan, then how come they aren't in jail?"

"Some of them are locked up. Some drank themselves to death or smoked enough meth that they might as well be dead. The Red Fox police department raided them so many times that we got to be on friendly terms with them.

"One of my first assignments as a rookie deputy was to go with the sheriff to their place to bust up a moonshine still. This was back when Sam Copeland was sheriff. The Paynes didn't even try to hide the damn thing. After we busted the hell out of the old metal contraption, Mamma Payne asked me and the sheriff if we was hungry after all that physical activity. Sheriff Copeland said that was right neighborly of her.

"We sat at the table with the two Payne boys responsible for the still while Mamma Payne served us squirrel stew and a mess of vegetables. It was some of the best eating I've ever had. Say what you will about the Payne clan, but they knew how to cook. After we ate our fill, we put the Payne boys in the squad car and took them to jail."

Anita squirmed in Vince's lap so that she was sitting directly on his crotch. She leaned forward and rested her arms on his desk. She thought about what he'd just told her. It was like looking at a puzzle, but there were some pieces missing.

"When this Grigsby fellow bought the Payne property, who did he buy it from?" Anita asked.

Her backside rubbing on Vince was having more effect on him than he thought possible.

"Um, I don't know," Vince said. "Like I said, most of the Payne clan are either in jail or dead. We didn't catch all of them. Some ran off into the woods and were never heard from again. I supposed the state of Georgia reclaimed the property and then sold it to Terrence."

"If like you said, the Payne's were good cooks, it's a shame their way of cooking is dead and gone."

Vince grabbed the armrests of his chair.

"I wouldn't say that. Recipes get passed down from generation to generation. They got to be around someplace. You should ask your boss about that."

Anita looked over her shoulder.

"What the hell would Owen Tew know about the Payne clan's family recipes?"

"His grandmother was Agnes Payne before she married Albert Tew. Albert and Agnes opened the Rejoice Diner. I'm sure Agnes used some Payne recipes at the diner."

"Now that's really interesting. Hey! I feel something poking me."

Anita hopped off Vince's lap and faced him. She grinned at his erection.

"You said you'd be lucky to get hard once a night," Anita said. "But it looks like I'm the one about to get lucky."

Chapter Thirty-One

"I'm here for my appointment," Anita said.

Martha sat at the front desk. Crystal was on the waiting room couch. Martha ran her finger down the page of the appointment book until she found Anita's name.

"I'll let Polly know you're here," Martha said. She leaned toward the open salon and shouted. "Hey, Polly! You're one o'clock is here!"

"Be right there," Polly called back.

"What's in the bag?" Crystal asked.

Anita swiveled around to face Crystal. She figured Crystal had to be talking to her since she was the only one carrying a paper sack.

"Clothes," Anita said. "I'm donating them to the thrift store."

"That's very kind of you," Martha said.

"I like to think so."

Polly joined them.

"Hey, Anita. Let's go on back and get you started."

Anita followed Polly back to Polly's salon chair. Polly had Anita sit down and stood behind her as they peered into the mirror.

"So, what would you like me to do to your hair?" Polly asked.

Anita gazed at Polly.

"Make it look like yours," Anita said.

"My style does fit your face, but what if we layered it a bit more?"

Polly found an example of what she meant in a style book.

"You really think that would look good on me?" Anita asked. "You don't think my face is too round?"

"Actually, this is the best style for the shape of your face. It helps bring out your best features."

Anita scowled.

"What you mean is that I've got a cute face. It's so hard to be taken seriously when you look like a baby doll."

Polly grinned.

"You do not look like a baby doll. You're an attractive woman. And all women have trouble being taken seriously regardless of their looks."

"Ain't that the goddamn truth!"

They high fived.

Polly got to work on Anita's hair. The two women had a great time talking. Anita had a million questions about Atlanta and Polly asked an equal number about Red Fox. Anita was disappointed when Polly announced that she had finished Anita's hair. She was having too much fun hanging out with Polly. But then, she looked at her hair and her disappointment turned to delight.

"Oh my God," Anita said, turning her head left and right. "I look so fucking hot!"

Anita took a wad of bills out of her purse to pay Polly. This was from her tip money. She peeled out the amount she owed and was horrified that she didn't have enough to give Polly a tip.

"I can come by tomorrow," Anita said.

"Don't worry about it," Polly said, waving her hand.

"But I look so freaking hot because of you. I really want to give you something."

"You can tip me the next time you come in. This way you have to come back."

"Oh, I'm coming back. No doubt about it. Wait."

Anita dug into her bag and pulled out a shirt. She handed it to Polly.

"Here. Take this," Anita said. "Don't worry. I ran it through the wash."

Polly held up Dani's Kitsune polo shirt. She glanced over at Martha and Crystal. Martha shrugged and Crystal rolled her eyes. Polly didn't want a shirt with a restaurant logo, she thought it was tacky, but she didn't want to insult Anita by turning it down. She held it up to her chin.

"It's my size," Polly said. "This is great, Anita. Thank you so much."

Anita hugged Polly before she left. Polly watched her walk down the street. Martha came over and stood beside her.

"Anita doesn't know enough to realize that giving you that shirt was inappropriate," Martha said. "It was very nice of you to accept it."

"Has she done this before?" Polly asked.

"This is the first time she's ever come to my shop. I think before now she cut her own hair."

"Then that makes the shirt even more special. I've known girls like Anita. They're tough because they have to be tough, but deep down they're very sweet."

"For Pete's sake!" Crystal said. "That girl's a slut!"

Martha shook her head.

"Don't talk that way," Martha said. "It's not nice."

"I just call 'em as I see 'em."

Polly folded up the Kitsune shirt and stuffed it into her purse. She could always use another jogging shirt.

Chapter Thirty-Two

Duane drove his pick-up truck on the access road next to Interstate 75 to the outskirts of Ringgold, Georgia. It was a cloudy day which matched Tracie's mood. She watched the shiny cars on the highway speeding toward their destinations. She was sure they all were going someplace better than where Duane was taking her.

Suddenly, Tracie ducked down. Duane did a double take.

"What the hell are you doing?" he asked.

"Are we past it?" Tracie said.

"Past what?"

"Cracker Barrel."

Duane laughed. "Yeah. You can come up now. You worried the rednecks were going to come after us?"

Tracie sat up and craned her neck to see the restaurant receding into the distance behind them.

"Skyler and I used to take the kids there on Sunday after church. Then we stopped going to church because Skyler couldn't get up on time because he was too hungover, but we still went to the Cracker Barrel. And then we stopped going anywhere on Sunday."

"You could have taken the kids to church yourself. Me and my boy go every Sunday."

"It's different when you have two kids. Especially when they're wild like mine."

Duane was going to say that maybe her kids wouldn't be so wild if she made them go to church, but decided it wasn't worth the effort. There were things you just couldn't teach a white woman.

He turned off the access road into a land of dreary businesses. There were no trees or vegetation of any kind. Dull buildings sat in the middle of empty parking lots with splintered asphalt. The road they were on came to a dead end. On the left was a company that sold used heavy-duty trucks. Trucks in a rainbow of colors lined the entrance. On the right was a rectangular building with corrugated metal walls and a flat roof.

All but one of the storefronts were empty with banners indicating they were available for lease. Only Xtra Special TLC Massage had their name on a sign above the awning and a flashing Open sign in the window. A heavy curtain kept anyone from looking inside. A single car with bald tires sat in the parking lot.

Duane parked, got out of the truck, and walked to the front door. He looked back. Tracie was still in the truck. He waved at her angrily. Tracie reluctantly climbed out of the truck. Duane opened the door for her. She could smell the sweet scent of hand lotion. She hesitated in the doorway. Duane nudged her inside.

The waiting room was frigid. Tracie folded her arms under her breasts for warmth and to calm her nerves. Meditation music played softly. The couches were red vinyl, and the carpeting was yellow. A turquoise ceramic Buddha statue sat on a glass coffee table next to a glass bowl full of peppermint candy, wrapped white disks with red stripes.

The receptionist window had frosted glass so Tracie couldn't tell if anyone knew they had arrived. But then, she noticed the security camera bolted to the ceiling. Someone knew they were here. She didn't want to stare at the camera, so she looked down at the floor and noticed cigarette burns in the carpet.

The receptionist window slid open revealing a petite Asian woman. She had streaks of pink in her black hair and acne scars on her cheeks. She smiled warmly at Duane.

"Mr. Anderson," she said. "You're right on time. Is this the young lady you were telling us about?"

Duane put his hand on the small of Tracie's back, making Tracie feel like he was claiming her as his property.

"This is her," he said. "Ain't she everything I said she was?"

"She is very pretty, but I leave it up to the boss to make the decisions." The Asian woman looked at Tracie. "So, you're Tracie?"

"Yes," Tracie said.

"I'm Candy. Welcome to Xtra Special TLC Massage."

Tracie was about to say it was nice to meet her too, though she wasn't sure if that was true, when Candy slid the window shut with a bang. A moment later, Candy opened the door that led from the reception area to inside the massage parlor.

"Come on in," Candy said, holding the door open. Tracie came toward her with Duane close behind. Candy held up her hand. "Just Tracie. You wait here."

Duane reached for his wallet.

"Well in that case, let me see Sally."

"Sally is busy with a customer," Candy said. "Sit down. Have a peppermint."

Tracie joined Candy in the hallway. Candy shut the door. The click of the lock made Tracie shiver. Tracie got a full look at Candy. She wore a white low cut halter top that was so loose that Tracie could see the dark brown nipples on her small breasts. She had on pink hot pants that hugged her cute little ass. Tracie remembered when her ass was that cute. Candy was barefoot and her toenails were painted the same mint green as her fingernails.

Candy led the way down a dimly lit hallway past a row of doorways. Candy walked briskly and Tracie hurried to keep up with her. Tracie only got quick glances inside the rooms. There was a shower room, rooms with massage tables, and a break room where two bored Asian women smoked cigarettes and watched TV.

At the end of the hallway was another door. It had a combination lock. Candy punched the numbers on the keypad to unlock it, and then held the door open for Tracie. Candy closed the door behind them. Again, the click of a lock made Tracie shiver. The sound made her feel that as she got deeper into this place, the harder it was going to be to escape. The hallway took a left turn and they walked past another set of doorways. Instead of massage tables, these rooms had beds and thick carpeting. All of them were empty except for one room.

In that room, a naked man was sprawled spread eagle on the bed. A woman with short brunette hair wearing frilly bra and panties stood next to the bed. She unhooked her bra revealing pancake breasts. As she began to peel off her panties, Candy pulled the door shut. Neither she nor Tracie commented on what they had seen.

The hallway turned right and ended at a door with a sign that read OFFICE. Candy knocked.

"Come in," said a woman's voice inside.

Candy opened the door and held it for Tracie. Tracie went in, but Candy didn't join her. She shut the door, leaving Tracie alone with the woman in the office.

The woman stood next to a filing cabinet. She smoked a cigarette while watering a dying plant. She looked to be in her late forties. Her blonde hair was piled on top of her head. Her blood red lipstick and heavy black eyeliner were in sharp contrast to her pale skin. She had an amazing body with large breasts and luscious curves. She wore a tight tomato red shirt with a plunging neckline and a pair of torn jeans. Her earrings were gold hoops.

"Sit down," she ordered.

Tracie sat in a visitor's chair.

She finished watering her plant and plopped down behind her messy desk. She tapped the ashes of her cigarette into an overflowing ashtray. Tracie recognized the brand. More cigarettes. They were supposedly for women only. They were wrapped in brown paper instead of white and were longer and thinner than regular cigarettes. All the butts in the ashtray had red lipstick on them.

She looked Tracie over as if she were a used car.

"You must be Tracie," she said.

Tracie couldn't identify the woman's heavy accent.

"Yes, ma'am," Tracie said.

"I am Ivanna Cox, but everyone calls me Ivy. I own this dump." She took a long drag of her cigarette and then stabbed it out in the ashtray as she blew out the smoke. "Duane tells me you're pregnant and you need money for an abortion."

"Yes, ma'am." Tracie stared at her lap.

"You're not the first girl to use sex to solve a problem caused by sex. Stand up and take off your clothes."

Tracie's head snapped up. "What? Now?"

"I need to see the product before I offer it to my customers."

The office suddenly felt very small and stuffy. A haze of cigarette smoke hung in the air. Tracie could feel sweat trickling from her underarms as she got out of the chair. She peeled off her Lady Antebellum T-shirt, kicked off her sandals, unbuckled her belt, and slipped off her Wrangler jeans. She unhooked her bra and removed it. Finally, she pulled down her panties and stepped out of them. Her cheeks burned with humiliation as she stood naked in front of Ivy.

"Turn around," Ivy said.

Tracie turned around. She put her hands over her crotch. Ivy came from behind her desk and put her hands on her hips as she examined Tracie. She moved Tracie's hands away from her pussy. Tracie let her hands hang by her side. Ivy cupped Tracie's breasts and ran her thumbs over the nipples. Tracie gasped. The air conditioner had made her nipples stiffen and Ivy's thumbs made them even harder.

"I bet you had tiny tits before you had a baby," Ivy said.

"That's true," Tracie stammered.

"I can read a woman's body better than a gynecologist."

Ivy let go of Tracie's breasts, grabbed her right butt cheek, and squeezed it. Tracie yelped, which made Ivy laugh. Tracie could smell Ivy's perfume, a sweet flowery scent.

"Nice ass," Ivy said.

"Thank you," Tracie said before she could stop herself.

Ivy moved behind Tracie. She pressed herself against Tracie as she reached around and slipped her hand between Tracie's thighs.

"Please don't do that," Tracie said.

Ivy cupped Tracie's pussy. Tingles spread through Tracie's body.

"Have you ever been with a woman?" Ivy asked.

"No. I like men."

"I like men too. But sometimes it's nice to be with a woman because a woman knows exactly where and how to touch you."

Ivy slipped a finger inside Tracie. With her other hand, she cupped Tracie's breast. Tracie resisted the urge to push Ivy's hands away. She had come to this place on her own free will with the express purpose to sell her body. She deserved to be treated like a piece of meat.

Ivy slipped a second finger inside Tracie. She pushed Tracie's hair aside and kissed the nape of her neck. Tracie leaned back into Ivy's arms. The earthy scent of Tracie's body responding filled the room. Ivy certainly knew exactly where and how to touch a woman. Very quickly, Tracie could feel an orgasm building inside her. Her breathing grew ragged.

"If you keep doing that," Tracie said. "I'm going to come."

Ivy pulled her hands away.

"Don't have orgasm in my office. Save it for the paying customers."

Tracie felt a mixture of humiliation and frustration. Her body yearned for completion.

Ivy sat at her desk. She squirted hand sanitizer on her palm, yanked three tissues from a tissue box, and cleaned her hands. She tossed the soiled tissues in a trashcan and lit a cigarette.

"You can put your clothes back on," Ivy said.

Tracie got dressed and then sank into her chair. Though her head was still fuzzy from stimulation, the message from Ivy was crystal clear. When Tracie was in this building, Ivy was in charge.

"Here's how things work here," Ivy said. "I have Asian girls and white girls. The white men only want Asian girls. They still think an Asian girl's pussy is sideways. They pay for a massage and then pay extra for a happy ending. You know what happy ending is?"

"It's when the girl jerks a guy off."

"Sometimes. It depends on how much he tips her. Fifty dollars buys him a hand job. Two hundred minimum for pussy." Ivy stamped out her cigarette and lit another one. "That's how we take care of the white men. The Black men don't care about massages. They just want to fuck. Especially white girls with big asses like you."

"How much do they pay?"

Ivy puffed on her cigarette and tapped the ashes into the ashtray.

"Three hundred for a one-hour session. The house takes a hundred and you get two hundred."

Tracie rubbed her neck.

"I can't do it."

Ivy narrowed her eyes at Tracie.

"How can you not like Black men? You got a Black baby in your belly."

"It's not that. My husband can never find out about this. He just can't. If I only get two hundred for each guy, there's no way of knowing how long it would take me to make enough money for the abortion. I can't be away from home that long. My husband would wonder where I was." Tracie stood. "I should've known this wouldn't work. I'm sorry I wasted your time."

"Wait, wait, wait," Ivy said. "Sit down. Maybe we can work something out."

Tracie slumped in the chair. Ivy put out her cigarette, leaned back, and made a tent with her fingers.

"I don't normally let a new girl do this, but you're a special case. There's way you can make all the money you need not only in one night, but in two hours."

Tracie felt a chill go down her spine. This sounded too good to be true, so there had to be a catch.

"What do I have to do?" she asked.

"Have you ever had sex with more than one man? Maybe once when you had too much to drink, you went to bed with two men at the same time?"

Tracie had, but she didn't remember much about it. She had gotten really drunk with Brad and Skyler in Brad's apartment. The boys made a competition of who was the better kisser. They took turns kissing her and then the kissing developed into petting. Eventually, they were wearing only their underwear. She passed out and the next morning she woke up in bed with the boys. They were naked but she was still in her underwear. She never asked them what they did to her that night.

"No," Tracie said. "I've never been with more than one man."

"Here's your chance to find out what it's like. Sometimes men want to have a gangbang. You know gangbang?"

"Yes. When a bunch of guys do one girl."

Ivy laughed until she had a coughing fit. She took a Coke Zero out of a mini-frig behind her, popped it open, and took a sip.

"You should see your face right now. It's not like we bring in whole football team to pass you around. It will only be two or three at most."

"I don't know. It sounds dangerous."

"What dangerous? There are women who would pay to be in your shoes. But here's best part. Each man pays full price and instead of getting two from each man, you get two fifty. That's how we do gangbangs here at Xtra Special TLC Massage."

Tracie scratched her elbow as she thought it over. If she waited too long to get the money, she'd be too far along and wouldn't be able to get the abortion. Plus, she'd make more money than she needed, and she only had to do it once. She didn't see where she had any choice.

"Okay, I'll do it."

"Good. We have deal. I'll make the arrangements."

"Any idea how long that will take?"

"Few days. Week at most. Give your contact information to Candy."

Chapter Thirty-Three

POLLY TRIED TO look surprised, but she already knew the apartment was perfect. The price was more than reasonable, in fact, it was lower than what Polly expected to pay. She loved the house, a three-story colonial on a big lot with plenty of oak trees in a suburban neighborhood. She liked that the apartment was on the third floor with its own entrance via a staircase on the side of the house.

Martha took Polly on a tour of all the rooms, stopping at each one to tell a story about when her son Brad lived here.

"Brad cooked some decent meals in this kitchen. He only burned a few things before he got the hang of it. I told him I would cook for him, but he said he needed to learn for when he was on his own."

Martha opened cabinets and drawers, revealing plates and bowls, pots and pans, and utensils.

"I didn't expect it to be a furnished apartment," Polly said.

"Unless you've got furniture hidden in the trunk of your car, I knew you wouldn't have any. You can either keep what's here or replace it. If you decide to get new furniture, let me know and I'll have the thrift store come haul this stuff away."

"Can I paint the walls?"

"I wish you would," Martha said. "I meant to do it myself but somehow never got around to it."

Polly couldn't hold in her excitement any longer. She spun around and giggled.

"It's perfect! How soon can I move in?"

"Today if you want to," Martha said.

"Do you prefer the rent paid on the first day of the month or the last?"

"Actually, I was thinking I'd just deduct it from your pay once a month. That makes it easier for both of us."

"I'm so happy, I could hug you. May I hug you?"

"Well, yes, you can hug me."

Polly threw her arms around Martha. While clinging to each other, Martha felt a warmth and familiarity that surprised her.

"Polly?" Martha said. "Are you crying?"

Polly unlatched herself from Martha. She rubbed away her tears.

"I'm sorry. You've been so good to me, and I don't deserve it."

Martha crossed her arms.

"I sense that you're carrying a heavy burden. Jesus can lift that weight off your shoulders. You just need to ask Him."

"Thank you, Martha. I will."

"I don't want to pry into your personal affairs, but if you ever feel the need for girl talk or to pray, just knock on my door."

"You can count on it, Martha."

Martha turned to leave but paused and snapped her fingers.

"Before I forget, there is one more thing." She opened the door to the hallway closet. Inside was a large cardboard box sealed shut with packing tape. "I would have dealt with this sooner, but the box is too heavy for me to carry. I can have somebody come over this week to lug it downstairs."

"What's in it?" Polly asked.

"Some of Brad's things. His sports trophies, school yearbooks, things like that. I boxed them up so that when he finally settles down somewhere more permanent than Denmark, I can send them to him."

"You can leave the box in the closet if you'd like. It won't be in my way."

"Thanks. That makes things much easier. But if you change your mind, I'll have it moved."

Polly and Martha walked to the front door and stood on the small porch at the top of the stairs. Martha handed Polly the apartment keys and went downstairs to her home. The apartment smelled musty from being unoccupied for so long. Polly opened all the windows. The sounds of birds chirping and a car speeding without a muffler drifted into the apartment, the typical sounds of a lazy Saturday.

Polly spent the afternoon lugging boxes into the apartment and unpacking. She decided that she would go to the corner store later for a few things to tide her over.

When she was done and the apartment looked like somebody lived in it, Polly went to the hallway closet, lifted the cardboard box, and carried it into the living room. Placing it in the middle of the room, she used a kitchen knife to slice through the packing tape and opened the box.

She took out the trophies and the yearbooks and put them aside. She pulled out Brad's high school letter jacket. His name was embroidered in cursive letters on the chest and football patches lined the left sleeve. Polly held it close to her face and breathed in the smell of old wool and vinyl. She slipped it on.

Next, she took out an old metal lunchbox. On the front lid was an image of the cartoon character, Underdog, literally kicking a villain's ass so hard that the villain was airborne. Inside the rusty metal box was a thermos. She turned the thermos around, going past the image of Underdog to Underdog's girlfriend, Polly Purebred. She wore a red blouse, a black skirt, and a stylish yellow scarf. Her hair was white blonde.

Polly twisted the cap off and carefully extracted a rolled plastic baggie from inside the thermos. She unrolled the baggie. There was enough marijuana in the baggie for at least one or two joints.

She felt around the interior lining of the letter jacket until she found where it had been cut open and then resealed with a strip of Velcro. She peeled back the Velcro and reached inside the lining for the pack of rolling papers and lighter hidden in there. She put the baggie, lighter, and papers on the wood desk that Brad had used to do his homework.

She opened the baggie and sniffed the contents inside. The pot didn't smell of mildew, but it was over ten years old. It would likely taste like shit and give her a headache, but Polly rolled a joint anyway. She licked the paper to seal the joint.

She put the joint and the lighter in the pocket of the jacket. Two of the apartment's windows were built into the slope of the roof. When Polly had first come to Red Fox, she had slipped into the apartment through one of these windows. Martha didn't know Polly had done this and Polly intended to keep it that way. Polly used the same window to get on the roof. She walked across the roof and sat under the branches of the oak tree next to the house. From this position, no one could see Polly unless they were on the roof with her.

Polly lit the joint. It sputtered before catching fire and a thin plume of smoke rose into the branches. Polly sucked in the smoke and held it until it burned her lungs. She coughed it out. She was right. The pot tasted like shit, but she did get a slight buzz. She hugged her knees and gazed up into the branches.

She remembered when Dad gave Brad the Underdog lunch-box. She had never heard of the cartoon. Dad had watched it when he was a kid, but that still didn't explain why he bought the lunchbox at a flea market and presented it to Brad as if it were a sacred artifact.

"No one in your division thinks your team can win. Everybody in town says you're not big enough to be quarterback. That makes you the underdog quarterback," Dad said. "The other teams underestimate your power and your drive to succeed. You're going to prove them wrong and take your team all the way to the championship. You're going to beat the odds, just like Underdog."

Polly cherished the love behind the gift, but she wished she could have explained to her father that Brad never wanted to be Underdog. Brad wanted to be Underdog's girlfriend, fashionable career gal Polly Purebred.

Later, Brad took her first name.

Polly Swift took another toke of the joint. A squirrel watched her from a nearby branch. Polly asked the squirrel a question.

"Now that I'm back home, how do I tell Mom the truth?

Chapter Thirty-Four

Anita stuck around until the rest of the staff had gone home before she approached Owen. She lurked in the doorway of his office. He was at his messy desk going over the day's receipts.

"What do you want Anita?" Owen said without looking up from the strips of paper spread out in front of him. "It better not be about a raise. Didn't I give you one not too long ago?"

"Yes, you did, Owen," Anita said. "But that's not what I want to talk to you about."

"Have a seat and spit it out."

Owen didn't have visitor chairs, but he did have produce crates. Anita sat on a stack of crates.

Considering how much lard went into the food served at the Rejoice Diner, Owen was not fat. He was quite the opposite, thin to the point of emaciated. He had a long face and sunken cheeks. His skin was pale, and his large hands were scarred and ruddy from years spent working in a hot kitchen. On the plus side, he still had a head full of sandy brown hair.

"I want to ask you about Agnes," Anita said. "Your grandmother."

"What about her?"

"She was a Payne before she married your granddaddy."

Owen stopped studying the receipts and squinted at Anita.

"Why this sudden interest in my family history?"

Anita shifted her butt on the crates, which caused them to wobble. Fearful that they might topple, she held still.

"I heard that the Payne clan, other than being no good moonshiners and drug dealers, were mighty fine cooks."

Anita froze. She hadn't meant to insult his relatives and especially didn't mean to imply anything bad about his grandma. To her relief, Owen laughed and slapped his desk.

"The Paynes, God almighty," Owen said. "Never seen a bunch more allergic to hard work and earning an honest dollar. But they're family so I love 'em."

"Did the Payne clan pass down their recipes to your grandma Agnes?"

"Now I see where you're going with this. You want to know if my secret recipes are Payne family recipes. The answer is no."

Anita was disappointed. She thought she was onto something, though she wasn't sure what that something was.

"I'd go broke if I used their recipes," Owen continued. "Don't get me wrong. There's not a damn thing wrong with them, but that style of cooking is for dirt poor people. There was a time when everybody on Red Fox Mountain was poor. They grew their own food and few of them could afford to feed both livestock and their kinfolk. They supplemented their crops with plants that grew wild in the forest."

"My daddy talked about how during the depression people around here ate clay," Anita said.

"There's a few folks way up in the hills that still do. Life got better and people could afford to eat decent. They got to where they felt a meal wasn't a meal unless it had some meat on the plate."

"But those old Payne recipes. Was the food any good?"

Owen leaned back in his chair and stared at the ceiling.

"Once in a blue moon Grandma Agnes would whip up some of them dishes. Any good? They were real good. The Paynes figured if they had to eat dirt, they might as well find a way to make it tasty."

Anita leaned forward, almost toppling over the crates again.

"Damn, Owen. The way you talk about it is making me hungry. Would you dig up some of Agnes' old recipes so I can try some?"

Owen stroked his chin.

"I don't know. Seems like a lot of trouble."

"Please, Owen. For me?"

For all his gruffness and constant threats to fire her, Anita knew that Owen would do anything in the world for her. Unlike most men in Red Fox, his attraction for her wasn't sexual. He was fond of her the same way he was fond of all his long-time employees. They were his family.

"Okay, okay, I'll do it," he said. "I'll need some time to prepare but I should have something whipped up by the end of the day tomorrow. And then we'll have some good eating."

"Thank you, Owen."

"Now get the hell out of my office. I'm trying to run a business here."

Chapter Thirty-Five

HALF-TRUTHS. THAT THING where you don't want to lie but you can't tell the whole truth. When Polly told Mansoor that she'd come to Red Fox so that she could experience life as a woman, that was a half-truth. The whole truth was that she also wanted to experience life as a daughter.

Martha Aldridge was a good woman and a loving mother, but Polly knew without question that Martha would never be able to accept her beloved son, Brad, as her daughter, Polly. So, Polly came up with a plan. If she couldn't tell Martha the truth about her transition, then she would do the next best thing. She would move to Red Fox and become Martha's friend. Not quite mother and daughter, but better than nothing.

Polly had no illusions. She knew that someday Martha would learn the whole truth. Someday Martha would finally see her son in Polly's eyes. And there would be hell to pay that day. But until then, Polly was going to cherish every moment with her mother.

Today, Polly was forced to tell another half-truth.

Martha claimed to hate gossip, but she was dying to know what Polly and Tracie talked about when Tracie came in to get her hair done. Polly was cutting Tracie's hair when Tracie suddenly started crying and ran to the bathroom. Polly joined Tracie and the two of them talked for ten minutes before they came out. They acted like nothing had happened.

At first, Martha had accepted that Polly couldn't tell her what they talked about out of respect to Tracie. But as the days rolled by, Martha's curiosity had eroded her respect for Tracie's privacy.

"Did she find out about Skyler?" Martha asked. "Does she know that he's been cheating on her? Does she know that you're the one he's been seeing on the side?"

"We only went out that one time," Polly said. "And I swear I didn't know he was married."

Since Polly had come to work for Martha, business had doubled. Customers raved about Polly and word of mouth recommendations led to a full appointment book. Still, there were days when the salon chairs sat empty. There were only so many heads in Red Fox. Today was a slow day, which meant Martha had nothing better to occupy her time than to interrogate Polly.

"You're sure Tracie doesn't know about you?" Martha said.

"Not to my knowledge," Polly said.

"Then what the H E double hockey sticks was she crying about?"

Martha seemed almost disappointed that Tracie didn't know about Polly. Being a good Christian woman, it probably bothered her that Polly might escape her sin without punishment.

Seeing that she had to tell Martha something if she was to experience any peace this day, Polly was forced to tell a half-truth.

"It's like you said," Polly said. "Tracie still has feelings for Brad."

"But that was years ago," Martha said.

Polly could tell that as much as Martha wanted to convey

sympathy for Tracie, she was swelling with pride that Tracie still carried the torch for Brad, Martha's pride and joy. Polly felt pity and shame. Pity that poor Tracie was still in love with a boy who selfishly used her. Shame that she used to be that boy.

As for the half-truth. Yes, it was true that Tracie was still in love with Brad. But that wasn't why she locked herself in the bathroom. Marrying Skyler because she couldn't have Brad was the beginning of the twisted trail that led to Tracie getting pregnant with her yard man's baby. Tracie had told Polly the whole truth in confidence. The very least Polly could do for Tracie was to protect her secret. Or at least, the worst part of her secret.

"So, what exactly did Tracie say about Brad?" Martha asked.

"Just that she wished she'd married him instead of Skyler," Polly said.

"Come on. She must have talked about him in detail."

Polly didn't want to talk about Brad. She had worked very hard to leave him behind. Luckily, the phone rang. Martha reluctantly went to answer it. Polly retreated to the break room for a glass of cold water.

Martha poked her head in.

"Tracie's on the phone," Martha said in a loud whisper. "She wants to talk to you."

Polly drank her water quickly. She went to the front desk and picked up the receiver.

"Hey, Tracie" Polly said, trying not to sound nervous and failing miserably. She felt like Tracie somehow knew that she and Martha had been talking about her. "Wasn't expecting to hear from you so soon. Do you want to come in for a trim?"

"Actually, I was wondering if you would do me a huge favor. I shouldn't ask you, but you're the only friend I can turn to."

"Whatever you need, just ask."

"Will you babysit my kids this Friday?"

Polly was gobsmacked. She didn't know what she expected from Tracie, but this wasn't it.

"If you don't want to do it, I understand," Tracie said.

"No, it's not that," Polly said. "I was just trying to remember if I had any plans for Friday and now that I've had a chance to think about it, I know I'm free. I would be happy to babysit Connor and Trixie."

"Harper."

"Sorry. Harper."

"I can't tell you how much I appreciate this."

"It's no problem. So, do you and Skyler have a hot date?"

"Shit, no! He'll be out drinking with his buddies. I'll be lucky if he makes it home at all."

Polly was relieved to hear that. She wanted to avoid Skyler as much as possible.

"What time should I come over?"

"Around seven."

"I'll see you then."

Polly hung up the phone. She went back to the break room for another glass of cold water. After downing a glass, her dry throat felt a little less parched. Martha joined her.

"So?" Martha said. "What did she want?"

"She asked me to babysit her kids."

"How much is she paying you?"

"I'm doing it as a favor."

Martha started a fresh pot of coffee. As she poured the water and took a coffee filter out of the cabinet, she kept grinning at Polly.

"What?" Polly asked.

"You know what's going to happen, don't you?" Martha said. "Once you spend quality time around her children, you're going to want to have some of your own."

"Really?" Polly asked.

"Those precious angels are going to make your womb throb. We'll have to get you married to a good Christian man so you can bless him with perfect Christian babies."

"My womb is going to throb? Is that some kind of a medical condition? Should I see a doctor about it?"

"Only if he's handsome and Christian. Doctors make great husbands."

Martha brewed the coffee, and they had a cup while reclining in their salon chairs. The conversation about babies, throbbing wombs, and Tracie's timeless crush on Brad petered out and they talked about the weather and what they loved best about Fall.

While they talked, Martha's comment about a throbbing womb kept coming back to Polly. She had female breasts and female hormones, but no pill and no surgical procedure in the world could ever give her a womb. She could never get pregnant and give birth to her very own baby. The longing sometimes made her cry.

She would always be a half-woman and that was the whole truth.

Chapter Thirty-Six

Dani was sitting on the couch reading a mystery novel when Anita came home from work.

"Oh good," Anita said. "You're awake."

Dani didn't look up from the page she was reading.

"I made spaghetti with zucchini if you're hungry."

"Actually, I brought you something special."

Anita took a plastic container out of a bag and handed it to Dani. Dani pried off the lid and sniffed the contents. The cooked vegetables inside looked and smelled familiar.

"What is it?" Dani asked.

"Taste it," Anita said.

Dani reached inside the container with her fingers and pulled out a Brussels sprout. After a few bites, she couldn't swallow anymore. She felt like her throat was on fire, not because the food was spicy but from the rage and fear the food created inside her. She threw the container against the wall. Cooked vegetables splattered and dripped to the carpet.

"This is one of Kitsune's signature dishes!" Dani shouted.

"Have you been working for them all along? Are they coming to get me?"

Anita looked at green lumps on her wall and carpet. She didn't know what felt worse, that she had frightened Dani or that Dani doubted her.

"Do you really think I'm working for those freaks?" Anita asked.

"What else am I supposed to think?" Dani said.

"My boss, Owen Tew, cooked those vegetables from an old family recipe."

Dani's fear quickly subsided, and she felt a prickling between her shoulder blades that told her that something awesome was about to happen.

"Maybe you'd better tell me the whole story."

Anita told Dani about Owen's grandmother and the Payne clan that used to live up in the mountains where Kitsune was now. Mr. Kite's secret was that he was making the Payne family's poor folks' food and selling it as special vegan cuisine.

"But how did Mr. Kite and Mr. Grigsby get those recipes?" Dani asked.

"When they bought the property, they probably found the recipes lying around," Anita said.

"This is wild. Can you get a copy of those recipes from your boss?"

Anita pulled photocopies out of her purse.

"Got 'em right here."

After all this time in hiding, Dani finally saw a path to freedom from Kitsune.

"Too bad you don't have a computer," Dani said. "If you did, then I could tell the world the truth about Kitsune."

"There's a computer at the library," Anita said. "We're not hillbillies. We got cable TV and internet porn like the rest of the world."

Dani went into the kitchen and got spray cleaner and rags. She came back and began to clean up the mess she'd made.

"I'm sorry," Dani said. "I never should have doubted you."

Anita joined her. Together they cleaned the wall and the carpet.

Chapter Thirty-Seven

THE GREASE SOAKING through the brown paper bag left large translucent spots. Worried that the foiled wrapped burritos inside might rip through the weakened paper, Mansoor held the bag from the bottom. He knocked on the motel door, ignoring the Do Not Disturb sign hanging on the doorknob.

It was a beautiful afternoon with hardly a cloud in the sky. The leaves were beginning to change color and drop from their branches. Soon, people from the valley would drive up the mountain to marvel at the red, yellow, and brown leaves. A few would stop at the diner for lunch or fill their tanks at the gas station. A few would even stay overnight at the motel for a full weekend excursion.

Mansoor wasn't particularly fond of fetching take-out for guests, but on a day like today he cherished any opportunity to escape the front desk and get outside. He knocked on the door again.

The door cracked open and a woman with frizzy hair peeked out at him.

"What do you want?" she demanded.

Mansoor held up the bag.

"Hello, Ginny. I brought you the burritos you ordered from Zorro Deli. One beef and one black bean along with chips and salsa."

Red Fox was too small for a delivery service, but Fox Creek Falls Inn was willing to pick up food from local food establishments for their customers.

"Just a minute," Ginny said. She slammed the door shut.

Mansoor rolled his eyes. For the last five days, either Corey or Ginny had called the front desk and asked the Mansoor to go to the Zorro Deli for a beef burrito and a black bean burrito along with chips and salsa. And every time he delivered the food, Ginny had answered the door and acted like she didn't know why he was there. He had grown quite weary of the routine but did his best not to show his irritation.

Ginny cracked open the door and thrust a handful of bills at Mansoor. She wore a T-shirt with the Kitsune logo on the front and nothing else. Her nipples pressed through the fabric and the tip of her triangle of pubic hair poked below the bottom hem of the shirt. Mansoor didn't take the money and her hand hung in the air.

"The cleaning staff was wondering when they might get a chance to clean your room," Mansoor said.

"We don't want to be disturbed," Ginny said.

"I understand, but it's been quite a few days. Wouldn't you like fresh sheets and towels?"

"We're on our honeymoon. You know how it is when a couple is on their honeymoon."

She was implying that she and Corey had been having intercourse for five days straight. That was even more reason to want the room cleaned. The sheets must be crusty, and the smell of sex would be overpowering. Mansoor wrinkled his nose in disgust but said nothing. If they wanted to live in their filth that was their business. When Corey and Ginny finally did leave, the cleaning staff would have to scrub the room clean from top to bottom.

Mansoor took Ginny's money and handed her the bag. As always, she shut the door before he could check if she'd given him the right amount. As always, she had given him the right amount, but not enough for a tip.

Corey and Ginny sat at the small table next to the kitchenette and ate their burritos. It was a testament to Pepe Martinez's cooking skill that they still craved his burritos after eating them for a week straight.

"It was rape," Corey said.

"It's not rape if you consented," Ginny said. "Nobody forced you to have sex with Mr. Kite. He certainly didn't force me."

"But why would I have sex with him if I'm not gay?"

"Maybe you're bisexual."

Corey shook his head.

"No. I didn't consent. It was mind control. He made me do something against my will."

Ginny took a bite of her burrito and talked with her mouth full.

"I think you just don't want to admit that you were curious to see what it was like to have sex with a man. I've had sex with men and women. Sex is sex. The plumbing doesn't matter."

"You're right. The plumbing doesn't matter, but consent is crucial."

Ginny pushed her hair out of her face.

"You'll feel better once we got back to Kitsune."

Corey put his burrito down.

"I'm never going back. I'm going home to Seattle." He looked her in her eyes. "I'd like for you to come with me."

Ginny took another bite and chewed for a long time before swallowing.

"Okay," she said. "I'll go with you. After we complete our mission."

Corey smacked his forehead.

"Forget about the mission! I don't work for Kitsune anymore."

Ginny didn't argue. Instead, she concentrated on her burrito, but Corey wasn't finished with his tirade.

"I can tell you the exact moment when I knew I was no longer working for those assholes at Kitsune. I was in the Zorro Deli for the first time. This blonde girl came in and said she was buying a burrito for a girl named Dani. I just knew she meant my Dani. I could have followed the blonde girl. I could have found Dani and dragged her back to Kitsune. But I didn't want what happened to me to happen to her. We might not be a couple anymore, but I still care about her. Instead, I decided right then and there to quit and get the hell away from Kitsune's crazy culinary cult!"

Ginny slowly put her burrito down.

"You know where Dani is?" she asked.

"No. But I could have found out. Don't you see? We can't let Kitsune control our lives anymore. We have to escape."

Ginny rubbed her chest.

"God, you make me so hot when you talk like this."

Corey glanced down at his crotch.

"Yeah. I'm getting pretty turned on too."

They left their half-eaten burritos on the table. Ginny took off her T-shirt and Corey removed his briefs and T-shirt. They embraced as he pressed his lips against hers. Corey hurried over to the bed to prepare the restraints they had attached to the four corners of the bed. During their week of constant sex, they had come up with several ways to tie Ginny to the bed. Corey had learned that Ginny also enjoyed a good spanking, so they kept her wooden hairbrush on the nightstand.

"Wait," Ginny said. "You always tie me up. When do I get my turn to tie you up?"

Corey's forehead wrinkled with worry.

"I'm not really into receiving pain. That's why I like being the Dom."

She grabbed him and gently squeezed. Corey gasped.

"I'm not going to hurt you," Ginny said. 'I'm going to drive you crazy with pleasure."

"I like pleasure," Corey said.

Corey lay on the bed and Ginny bound his wrists and ankles. He pulled on the straps. They gave a little, but he couldn't get free. Ginny dug around in her suitcase and pulled out a green scarf. She used it to blindfold Corey.

"Now you're in my control," she whispered in his ear. "I'm going to blow your mind."

Ginny trailed her fingers across his chest. Corey sighed with delight. She pinched his left nipple and he gasped in surprise. She pinched on his right nipple. She brushed her long hair across his stomach. She put him into her warm mouth. Corey strained at the straps. True to her word, Ginny was driving him crazy with pleasure.

"Why didn't we do this before?" Corey asked.

Ginny brought him close to orgasm then pulled back.

"Not yet," she said.

She climbed off the bed and gazed down at her prisoner. Corey grinned as he waited for her next move.

"I could leave," Ginny teased. "You'd have to wait here not knowing when I'd come back and release you."

"Don't," Corey pleaded. "I'm so close. Don't leave me hanging."

Ginny ran her fingernails down his leg and tickled the sole of his foot. He tried to pull away but couldn't.

She kneeled in front of her suitcase. She took out Mr. Grigsby's gun from where she'd hidden it under her clothes. She flipped the safety off and placed it on the nightstand next to her hairbrush.

"Where are you?" Corey asked. "I don't know how much longer I can wait."

"Be patient," Ginny said. "I'm almost ready."

She straddled him and put him inside her.

"God, you're so wet. I don't think you've ever been this wet," Corey said.

"Being in control is really turning me on," she said.

She scratched his chest as she rode him. They moved beyond words to grunts and moans. Sweat dribbled down between her breasts and to her belly.

"I can't last much longer," Corey said. "I'm almost there."

"Me too," Ginny said. "Wait for me."

Ginny pressed her hand against his neck and felt his pulse. His heart was beating quickly. This was his life force. She gritted her teeth. Her buried rage was bubbling to the surface along with her orgasm.

Ginny pulled the pillow out from behind Corey's head.

"This will be the best orgasm of your life," she said.

Ginny placed the pillow over Corey's face. He said something, but his words were inaudible. He tried to shake his head to get the pillow off, but she held it in place. She grabbed the gun from the nightstand and pressed the muzzle against the pillow. She pulled the trigger three times.

The pillow muffled the sound of the gunshots. As the bullets entered Corey's brain, his orgasm triggered Ginny's orgasm and she moaned like an enraged animal. Corey's blood soaked the sheets. Bits of pillow joined the dust floating in the air.

"Did you really think I would leave Mr. Kite for a traitor?" Ginny asked the dead man between her legs.

Ginny got in the shower and washed off Corey's blood and bodily fluids. She put on a fresh T-shirt before finishing her burrito.

Chapter Thirty-Eight

DANI HAD A moment of panic when she and Anita first arrived at the Red Fox Public Library. The red brick building sat alone on a hill. There were only two cars in the parking lot. Dani feared that the only books they had were ten versions of the New Testament and that the library's computer would be some brand she'd never heard of with half the letters missing on the keyboard.

She was relieved to find that the library was clean, brightly lit, and had plenty of books on all subjects. There were current magazines and newspapers, DVDs, and a children's reading room. The computer was the latest Dell desktop.

Dani had to wait twenty minutes before she could use the computer. A woman named Sally Ann wearing a T-shirt that read "This Chick is Packing" over a picture of a baby chick holding a gun was on the computer when they came in. Sally Ann was searching the internet for the perfect Hawaiian SPAM Musubi recipe. She explained to Anita and Dani that she'd fallen in love with the combination of SPAM, rice, and seaweed on a recent vacation to Maui and wanted to try making her own. Dani paced behind Sally Ann, she studied recipe after recipe that were essentially identical because there are only so many ways to make SPAM Musubi.

This was the first time since Dani had escaped Kitsune that she'd been out in the open where someone other than Anita could see her. To say she felt exposed and vulnerable was an understatement. She was certain that at any moment, burly men wearing Kitsune polo shirts were going to bust through the library's front door and drag her back to the compound.

Sensing her friend's discomfort, Anita stood close to Dani and said softly, "It's okay. I got your back." Dani relaxed. Not completely, but enough to keep from jumping out of her own skin.

Unable to make a final decision, Sally Ann printed out four versions of the recipe.

"I'm going straight to the grocery store to get the ingredients. Hope mine comes out as good as what I had in Maui."

"Best of luck," Anita said.

As soon as Sally Ann was gone, Dani jumped into the vacated seat and quickly logged onto the website for her foodie podcast, Tooti Frooti O'Foodie. Considering she hadn't been on the site for four years; Dani was pleased that she had no trouble remembering the password.

Four years. Dani and Corey had been to so excited to begin this new chapter in their lives. They had believed that working for Mr. Kite at Kitsune would improve their understanding of food as something that filled both the body and the soul. What naïve fools they had been.

Anita pulled a chair over and sat next to Dani.

"I've never listened to a podcast," Anita said.

Dani pinched the bridge of her nose.

"I would show you how I record an episode, but I've been podfaded."

"Sounds painful," Anita said. "What does it mean?"

Dani stared at the screen.

"Corey and I didn't do a farewell episode to let followers know we weren't going to do anymore podcasts. That's called podfading. Four years is a long time to be gone. Nobody's listening to Tooti Frooti O'Foodie anymore."

Anita stared at the computer screen.

"Is anybody else doing a podcast like yours? Maybe you could send them the recipes."

Dani's face lit up and she hugged Anita.

"Thank you for having the brain cell today. That's a great idea."

Anita blushed from the hug.

"It is?"

Dani left her website and did a search for other foodie podcasts. She went to the website for the podcast, God Save The Foodie.

"This guy I know, Aiden, does this podcast," Dani said. "He's a fellow foodie and there was friendly competition between our podcasts. He tried to warn me and Corey about Kitsune."

Dani typed this message to Aiden:

Hey, fellow foodie. Been a long time. How would you like to reveal the secrets of Kitsune on GSTF?

"Wait," Dani said. "I can't have him email me. Kitsune security is probably monitoring it."

"Give him my phone number," Anita said.

"You sure?"

"I don't see how Kitsune is going to make a connection between Aiden, you, and me."

Dani added to the message that Aiden should call her at the following number and gave Anita's phone number. Then she hit send.

"No telling when Aiden will see the message," Dani said. "He might not call until tomorrow."

Anita's phone rang.

"Yeah? Hold on. She's right here."

Anita handed the phone to Dani.

"Dani? Is that really you?" Aiden said.

"Hey, Aiden. It's been a long time. I was afraid you wouldn't remember me."

"Of course, I do. How's Corey?"

Dani sighed.

"I'm not sure. I left Kitsune."

"He's still there?"

"As far as I know."

"Dani, I've been hearing some weird rumors about Kitsune."

Dani glanced around the library. Other than the librarian, she and Anita appeared to be the only people here.

"What kind of rumors?" Dani asked.

"That it's become some kind of a cult," Aiden said.

"It has. But I can't go into details"

"Why not?"

"It's not safe for me to talk about it. Not yet."

"Why not call the police?"

"It would be my word against theirs."

"Then why did you contact me if you can't tell me anything?"

Dani sighed.

"I have a bigger secret, one that I think will bring them down."

"Really? What have you got for me?" Aiden asked.

"Kitsune got their recipes from a family that used to live on their property. Seems other families in this area still use those same recipes. Kitsune just gave them fancy names and said they were Mr. Kite's exclusive creations."

"Holy shit! If you could find those recipes, we could destroy Kitsune."

Dani glanced up at Anita and smiled.

"A good friend already tracked them down for me."

For the half hour, Dani carefully read the recipes to Aiden. He promised that this would be the next episode of his podcast.

"Don't mention my name," Dani said.

"You'll only be identified as unknown source," Aiden said. "I'm going to get on this right away. Should be live by tomorrow."

"Thank you, Aiden."

"Are you kidding? This is the best foodie scoop I've ever gotten."

"Bye, Aiden. Hopefully, we can have dinner together again someday."

"You take care of yourself, Dani."

Dani ended the call and handed the phone back to Anita. Before they left the library, Dani peeked out of the front door to make sure the coast was clear.

Anita followed a path only she could see through patches of woods, back yards, and back alleys. Even though they had come this way from Anita's house, Dani didn't recognize a single rock, tree, or house.

"How do you know all these shortcuts?" Dani said as they dashed from the alley behind a hardware store, across a dirt road, and onto a trail in the woods.

"I grew up here," Anita said. "As a kid, I learned to get places without my parents knowing where I was going."

Dani gazed at the mountains in the distance. As a teenager, she might have shared Anita's desire to spread her wings away from her parents' watching eyes, but this was a different world from the urban neighborhood she grew up in.

"What happens now?" Anita asked.

Dani shrugged.

"Hard to tell. God Save The Foodie used to be one of the most popular foodie podcasts around. If it still is, tomorrow all the foodies in the world will know Kitsune's secret. That should damage Kitsune's reputation and make people look at them more closely. Hopefully, there will be enough attention on the restaurant that the world finds out they're abusing their employees."

The trail through the woods ended at Anita's Street. Just as Anita was about to emerge from the dense forest, she froze, and Dani almost ran into her. A gold Lexus was parked in Anita's driveway. The personalized license plate read BBC LVR.

"Oh shit!" Anita said. "What the fuck is she doing here?"

"Who is it?" Dani asked nervously.

"My mother."

Chapter Thirty-Nine

"Your mother?" Dani said. "What do we do?"

Anita scanned the other houses on her street. No one seemed to be home.

"Stay here. I'll get rid of her as fast as I can."

Dani moved deeper into the woods as Anita marched across the street and her front lawn. Her feet crunched early fallen leaves. The stink of cigarette smoke hit her the moment she opened the front door. Once Anita got rid of her mother, she'd have to open all the windows for the rest of the day to air out the house.

Anita found Ivy Cox sitting on the living room couch, smoking a More cigarette and tapping the ashes into Anita's favorite coffee cup. On the coffee table was Anita's last can of beer.

"There's my beautiful daughter," Ivy said. "I was just about to give up on you."

"What do you want, Mom?" Anita asked.

"I need a reason to visit my own flesh and blood? I missed you. I wanted to see you."

"Well, here I am. Take a good look."

Anita held out her arms and spun around.

"Sit down," Ivy said. "Spend some time with your mother."

Anita plopped down on the chair across from the couch.

"Give me your key," she said. "I don't want you coming in here whenever you damn well feel like it."

Ivy crossed her arms.

"This is still my house. You can't order me out into the cold."

"Dad signed the deed over to me and I pay the mortgage. Besides, you haven't lived here in years."

Ivy shrugged.

"I don't care. I'm keeping the key."

"Then I'll change the locks."

"Do whatever you want."

They sat in silence for a minute. Anita stared out the window while Ivy smoked and sipped beer.

"I want to meet him," Ivy said.

"I have no fucking idea what you're talking about. Meet who?"

"Whoever is living with you. That's who."

Anita reacted before she could catch herself. Ivy smirked.

"I don't know what you're smoking, but I want some," Anita said. "There ain't nobody here but me."

Ivy stabbed her cigarette out and walked over to the window. There was a time when she stood at this window and felt like a prisoner looking out of her cell.

Ivy began life as Ivanna Blanarescu in Bucharest, Romania. When she was sixteen, she lied and said she was eighteen on her mail order bride application. She had signed up because she'd heard that America didn't suck like Romania. She almost refused to marry the man who picked her out of a catalog because he was from Georgia and the only Georgia, she knew of was the country and it sucked as bad as Romania. But then, a friend pointed out that Georgia was a state in America that apparently had more peaches than they knew what to do with. Ivy liked peaches.

Her husband, Harry Cox, expected Ivy to be a docile wife who cleaned his house, fulfilled his sexual fantasies, and had no opinions or ambitions of her own. For their honeymoon, he took her on a fishing trip and showed her how to gut a trout. Despite his best efforts to keep her ignorant of the world outside of Red Fox, Georgia, Ivy learned everything she could about her new homeland and decided that it had more to offer than what Harry was willing to allow her to obtain.

Ivy taught herself to read and write in English and audited business classes at the local community college. Harry didn't approve, but she did it anyway and despite her rebellion, she tried to be a good wife. They thought having a baby might smooth over their differences. It didn't.

Ivy let Harry name their daughter. He chose Anita after his great grandmother. Ivy was still learning English at the time, so she didn't realize until later that her little family, Harry Cox, Ivana Cox, and Anita Cox, was one big dick joke. Ivy loved her precious daughter Anita and did her best to teach her child to think for herself. For his part, Harry taught Anita to be as narrow-minded as he was.

Adding to Ivy and Harry's marital discord was their unhappy sex life. During sex, Harry not only refused to consider Ivy's pleasure he couldn't find a woman's clitoris if it were a large-mouth bass dangling on the end of his fishing line. Ivy finally refused to have sex with Harry.

It took years before Harry found out that his not so docile wife was cheating on him, but not because Ivy had been discreet about seeing other men, which she hadn't. At all. When Ivy decided to stop sleeping with one of Harry's friends, he complained to Harry about it. Harry divorced Ivy and because of Ivy's adultery, he got custody of Anita.

To say that Ivy and Anita's relationship had been strained since the divorce would be an understatement. Even though every encounter ended up with them screaming at each other, Ivy hadn't given up hope that somehow someday she would find a way to reconnect with her daughter.

Ivy spun away from the window and faced Anita.

"You say nobody is here but little Anita? Prepare to be dazzled by my amazing detective skills," Ivy said, wiggling her fingers. "In the dish rack there are two plates, two glasses, two forks, and two knives. There are two toothbrushes on the bathroom counter, two razors in the shower, and two towels hanging on the bathroom door."

Each time she said the word two, she flashed two fingers.

"You might have developed a split personality and that's why there are two of everything, but the house is cleaner than I have ever seen it. The only thing that would have gotten you to do that was if there was a special man in your life. Now I want to meet him."

"I don't allow men in my house," Anita said. "Once you let a man inside, they're damn near impossible to get out."

"I don't believe you. Where is he? Is he at work? Tell me the truth or I will come over here every day until I find him."

Anita put her hand on her stomach where it had begun to ache. She had inherited her mother's stubbornness, so she knew very well that Ivy wasn't kidding about stalking the house until she caught Anita's mystery roommate.

She had to tell Ivy about Dani without telling her about Dani. What she needed was a good half-truth that would satisfy Ivy's curiosity. An idea popped into her head.

"It's not what you think," Anita said. "I want to get a car. Not a new one. A good used car that I can drive to Chattanooga when I feel it."

Ivy narrowed her eyes.

"What does that have to do with your new boyfriend."

"Get it through that thick skull of yours. I don't have a

damn boyfriend. I'm renting out my old room so I can save up to buy a car."

"Why didn't you ask me? I would gladly give you money for a car."

"And you know I would gladly spit in your eye if you tried."

Ivy sat on the couch and lit a cigarette. She blew a smoke ring into the space between her and Anita.

"I want to meet this roommate."

"No. You'll scare them away and then I'll have to start looking for a new renter."

"I will stay until this person returns. I have a carton of cigarettes in the car so I can wait a long time."

She inhaled on her cigarette and exhaled a cloud of smoke. Anita waved the air, but only managed to spread the cloud over more space.

"Gawd damnit!" Anita said, jumping to her feet. "I'll get her, but after you see her, you got to get the fuck out of my house."

Ivy was startled. Anita stormed out of the house before she could ask her any questions.

Anita marched across the street and into the woods.

"Dani?" she said.

Dani came out from behind a pine tree.

"Is she gone?" Dani said. "Her car's still in the driveway."

"She won't leave until she meets you."

"I don't understand what's happening."

"She figured out that I wasn't living alone. I told her that you were renting my old room."

Dani put her forefinger on her lower lip.

"That's not a bad story. Is she likely to tell anybody about me?"

"The only people she talks to are whores so unless you're worried about whores talking about you, then you ain't got shit to worry about."

"I take it you and your mother have issues."

"That's a nice way of putting it."

Dani followed Anita to the house. Anita entered the living room while Dani hung back in the hallway.

"Mom," Anita said. "Meet Dani. Dani. Mom."

Dani inched her way into the living room. At the sight of her, Ivy's eyes grew wide. Dani gave her a little wave.

"Hello, Mrs. Cox. Nice to meet you."

Ivy sprang from the couch. Dani retreated, but Ivy caught her and threw her arms around the surprised girl.

"I am so happy to meet you," Ivy said. "After wasting years of her life screwing stupid white men it's so nice to see Anita found herself a black lesbian."

"I'm not a lesbian," Dani said.

"Damn it, Mom!" Anita said. "This is why I didn't want you to meet her."

Ivy released Dani.

"It's nothing to be ashamed of," Ivy said. "I like men too, but sometimes it's nice to be with a woman because a woman knows exactly where and how to touch you."

Anita took the cup Ivy had been using as an ashtray and carried it into the kitchen. She threw out the butts and filled the cup with water before leaving it in the sink. She came back to the living room, leaned against the wall, and crossed her arms.

"You met Dani," Anita said. "You can go now."

"I can't go now," Ivy said. "We need to celebrate."

"There's nothing to celebrate."

Ivy grabbed her purse from where she'd left it next to the couch and rummaged around until she found her silver flask. She unscrewed the top and took a swig of the Rum inside. She held it out for the others, but they didn't accept the offer.

"Come on," Ivy said. "This is tremendous thing that has happened here. My little girl, my little Anita, has finally evolved into a real human being. And I have you to thank Dani. Oh, wonderful Dani! Look at this."

Ivy yanked down the front of her shirt to reveal a tattoo on her left breast of a black spade with the letter Q in the middle.

"You know what that means, don't you?" Ivy said winking. "It means Queen of Spades. I love black cock. The bigger and darker the better. You know what I'm talking about. Or maybe you don't. Have you always been a lesbian?"

"I'm not a lesbian," Dani said.

"You don't have to lie to me. I can tell that you two have been sleeping in the same bed. I think it's so adorable that you chose the smaller bed so that you could be closer together."

Anita felt a rush of embarrassment.

"You don't know what you're talking about, Mom. Will you please leave?"

Dani grabbed Ivy's arm.

"Why did you show me that tattoo?" Dani asked.

"Anita must have told you what a terrible racist she was before you came along," Ivy said. "She hated Black people. She was always saying n-word this and n-word that. When she was in school, she used to beat up the Black kids. Boys and girls. She didn't learn to be that way from me. It's her father's fault."

Dani let go of Ivy's arm and narrowed her eyes at Anita. Anita hung her head and stared at her feet.

"Anita somehow failed to mention that she hated Black people," Dani said. "I guess she didn't want me to worry that she might attack me while I was asleep."

Ivy cocked her head as she studied Dani's top, a blue sports jersey with the Chanel logo on the front.

"I used to have a shirt just like that," she said.

"I have to go now," Dani said. "I no longer feel safe in this house."

Dani left the house, slamming the door behind her. Anita

sunk into a chair and covered her face with her hands. Ivy took another sip from her flask.

"Was it something I said?" Ivy said.

Chapter Forty

Polly double-checked to make sure she had the right address. The house was a split level probably built around 1960. A maple tree with vibrant red leaves dominated the front yard. A blue minivan sat in the driveway. The grass needed mowing and had grown so high that it threatened to devour a swing set.

Polly rang the doorbell. Tracie opened the door so quickly, Polly wondered if she hadn't been waiting on the other side.

"Hey," Tracie said. "Come on in."

The house smelled of baby powder and overcooked vegetables. Tracie led Polly to the kitchen, showed her where she kept snacks if the kids got hungry, informed Polly of the time they positively had to go to bed, and pointed out the list of emergency phone numbers on the refrigerator if God forbid something terrible happened.

"This is for you," Tracie said as she presented Polly with a bottle of white wine.

"You didn't have to give me anything," Polly said.

"You're going to need it after dealing with my little monsters."

"Mom!" shouted Connor from the living room. "I'm thirsty."

"Like I said, little monsters."

Tracie poured apple juice into a sippy cup. She and Polly went into the living room where Connor and Harper were on the couch watching cartoons. Connor took a sip of his juice and grimaced.

"It doesn't taste right," he said. "Something's missing."

"Nothing is missing," Tracie said. "It's the same apple juice you always drink."

The children were in their pajamas. Connor's pajamas were baby blue with footballs and pennants. Harper had a Disney princess on her shirt.

"Connor. Harper," Tracie said. "You remember Polly, don't you? You met her at the beauty shop when Mommy got her hair done."

The children studied Polly's face, but Polly could tell they had no memory of her.

"Polly's going to look after you tonight."

"Where are you going, Mommy?" Harper asked.

"Mommy has to go out, sweetie. But I won't be gone long, and Polly is going to take good care of you while I'm away."

Polly couldn't get over how much Harper looked like her father. Or that she was in Skyler and Tracie's home. She was still having trouble processing the fact that Skyler and Tracie were married and had children.

She always figured that Tracie would settle down with a boring straight man and make babies. But Skyler? She pictured Skyler living in Key West working as an activity director for a clothing optional gay resort hotel.

Polly worried that she might be partly responsible for Skyler and Tracie's marriage. Back in high school, when Polly was still Brad Swafford, she and Skyler used Tracie as their beard. Tracie was so thrilled to date the school's star quarterback and the team's best wide receiver that she willfully blinded herself to the fact that Brad and Skyler were a couple.

When Brad left Red Fox, he said goodbye to Skyler and Tracie. He promised to stay in touch. He made vague plans for Skyler to join him after graduation. Those plans never came to be. By the end of his first year at Stanford, Brad had lost touch with both of them.

"Earth to Polly. Come in, Polly."

Polly snapped out of her thoughts and focused on Tracie.

"Sorry about that. I spaced out there for a minute."

"Don't worry. You'll do fine. All you have to do is keep them alive until I get back."

Polly looked at Connor and Harper.

"I'll do my best."

"Okay, I better get going."

Tracie gathered her purse and her car keys. Polly walked Tracie to the minivan.

"I have to be honest with you," Tracie said. "I've got a job tonight. One that will pay me enough to cover the abortion. And I only have to do it for one night."

"One night?" Polly said.

The only kind of jobs Polly could think of that paid that kind of money involved either prostitution or robbery.

"Don't worry," Tracie said. "I know what I'm doing."

"Listen, Tracie. You don't have to do this. I can lend you the money. You don't even have to pay me back. Please. Let me do this for you."

"I can't accept your money. I have to do this on my own. I got myself into this mess and I'm going to get myself out of it."

Polly felt sick. She was certain that this sweet innocent girl she had taken advantage of in high school was about to do something that would change her forever. As if marrying Skyler hadn't already changed her enough. Polly wanted to drag Tracie back in the house and force her to listen to reason.

Instead, Polly watched Tracie get into her car and drive away.

Polly waited until the car disappeared around a corner before she trudged back into the house. She sat in an overstuffed chair in the living room.

"Are you okay?" Harper said.

"You look like you're going to cry," Connor said.

"Do I?" Polly said. "Maybe I am going to cry. I'm not sure yet."

Polly went into the kitchen and opened the bottle of wine. Tracie probably would have preferred Polly waited until she got home to open it, but she desperately needed a drink.

As Polly sipped the wine, which wasn't very good, she wondered why hadn't she suspected what Tracie was up to? Why else would Tracie have asked Polly to babysit her ankle biters?

Polly returned to the living room. The kids were completely absorbed in the cartoon on the TV. She asked them what they were watching. They told her. She'd never heard of it. She tuned out the funny voices and silly sound effects coming from the TV and with wine glass in hand, she studied the framed photos on the living room walls.

One of the photos was of Tracie's parents. Whenever Brad picked up Tracie for a date, he always had to spend at least ten minutes talking football with Tracie's father before they could leave. Most of photos were of Skyler, Tracie, and the kids in happier times. Or maybe they just pretended to be happy when the photos were taken? There were photos of them at football games, camping in the woods, and posing in their seats after a restaurant meal.

In one of the restaurant photos, it was clear to Polly that the family was at the Cracker Barrel. For some unfathomable reason, Skyler loved Cracker Barrel. He was always trying to get Brad to go there with him. Brad agreed to lunch, but never dinner. More than once, he had to remind Skyler that two dudes having dinner together looked too much like a date.

Polly came upon a photo that stopped her in her tracks. It was of Brad and Skyler in their football uniforms. Skyler was covered in mud. They were smiling and had their arms around each other's shoulder.

Polly felt like she was looking at a ghost and honestly there was no better way to describe it. The boy next to Skyler was dead and gone. Polly was his executioner.

"Polly!" Connor shouted. "Polly! Polly! PA-LEEEEEEE!"

"Why are you shouting?" Polly said. "I'm standing right here."

"Tell us a story."

"That's what the TV is for."

"But we want *you* to tell us a story," Harper said.

Tracie didn't warn Polly about this. She tried to think of a fairy tale, but her mind drew a blank. She sipped her wine and looked around the room for a children's book. She couldn't find one. Apparently, the Aldridge family wasn't into reading.

She looked back at the photo of Brad and Skyler. She remembered when the photo was taken. She was certain that everyone in her class remembered that night.

Polly located the remote and turned off the TV so she wouldn't have to compete with the noise.

"Has your dad ever told you stories about when he played football in high school?" Polly asked. The kids shook their heads. "You mean to tell me that he's never told you about The Slide?"

"We used to have a slide on our swing set," Harper said. "But it fell off."

"Not that kind of slide. The kind where you slide on the ground."

"Can I have some of your wine?" Connor asked holding out his hands.

Polly frowned at Connor.

"No, you cannot. Children are not allowed to drink wine."

"Dad lets me drink his beer all the time."

Polly worried that he might be telling the truth.

"I'm not your father," Polly said. "If you want wine, ask him. Now do you want to hear about The Slide or not?"

The kids shouted that they did indeed want to hear about The Slide. Polly stood in front of them as if she were on a stage.

"It happened during a regular season game between the Red Fox Fighting Foxes and the Putnam County War Eagles. The weather forecast called for slight precipitation. That was a joke. Buckets of rain poured down. Everybody was soaked to the skin and the field turned into a giant mud puddle."

Polly finished her wine and put the glass on the coffee table. Immediately, Connor grabbed the glass and put it to his lips. He scowled when he realized the glass was empty.

"Are you thirsty, Connor?" Polly said. "I can get you some more apple juice."

"No thank you," Connor said. "I want to hear the rest of the story."

"Okay, where was I? The football field had turned to mud. Every time the Foxes had a chance to score, the runner would slip and drop the ball. I mean, it was ridiculous. Even the field goal kicker kept falling on his butt."

The kids giggled at the word "butt."

"Luckily, the Eagles were having the same problem. At half time the score was tied six to six. Everyone hoped that the rain would let up, but instead it started coming down harder. Both teams went to their running game because the heavy rain made it impossible to throw a pass."

Polly paused. She had to admit that the Tracie and Skyler's kids were pretty darn cute. She put that thought aside and continued her story.

"The fourth quarter started with the score still tied at six to six. But then late in the quarter an Eagle running back got the ball, broke through the Foxes' defensive line, and ran all the way to the fifth yard line before he was tackled. The Eagles made three attempts to score a touchdown, and three times the Foxes' defense held them back. The Eagles had to settle for a field goal. But now the clock was running out. The Foxes had three minutes and change to drive down the field and either get a field goal to tie the game and send it into overtime or score a touchdown and win the game."

"What about Daddy?" Connor said. "I thought this story was about him."

"I was just getting to him. The Foxes worked their way down the field thanks to their talented quarterback. But then, they were stopped at the fifteen-yard line. After three attempts to run the ball, they were on their last down. The coach called a time out. He gathered the team together and said he wanted to kick a field goal. But the quarterback wanted to throw the ball. Do you know why he wanted to throw the ball?"

"Because he liked to throw the ball?" Harper asked.

"You're almost right. He did like to throw the ball, but here's what happened. The quarterback told the coach that he was certain that the defensive line was tired and wouldn't be able to cover their man. But the truth was, the quarterback was tired of being wet and muddy and wanted to get out of the rain. The coach called for a ten-yard pass so that they could get a first down. Can you guess who the quarterback wanted to throw the ball to?"

"Daddy?" Connor asked.

"Yes. Daddy. I mean, Skyler. The quarterback told Skyler to forget about running for the ten-yard pass. Run toward the end zone and he would throw him the ball. So, the Foxes snapped the ball, Skyler hauled butt down the field, and the quarterback threw a perfect pass that sliced through the rain and landed perfectly in Skyler's hands. But then, Skyler slipped on the wet grass. Because he'd been running so fast, he slid through the mud and into the end zone. Nobody is sure how many yards he slid, but since none of the Eagles touched him before he crossed the goal line, the officials called it a touchdown. Skyler won the football game."

Harper raised her arms and cheered. Connor picked his nose.

"You made that story up," Connor said.

"No, it's true," Polly said. She took the photo of Brad and Skyler from the wall and sat between the kids. "In fact, there's Skyler and the quarterback after that game. As you can see, Skyler is covered in mud from The Slide. He's holding the game ball."

Connor and Harper leaned into Polly and scrutinized the photo. They asked Polly to repeat the story and she said she would the next time she babysat for them, which she hoped would be never. She hung the photo back on the wall and turned on the TV. She surfed the channels until she found a Falcons pre-season game. She entertained the kids by explaining to them why the Falcons were going to break her heart this season.

When it came time for the kids to go to bed, Polly made them brush their teeth before they crawled under the covers. Harper hugged Polly goodnight and almost choked her to death in the process. Polly adored every agonizing second.

"Your daddy doesn't know how lucky he is," Polly said as she brushed a stray hair off Harper's forehead. "To have a beautiful little girl like you."

"I know," Harper said and then closed her eyes. She was asleep before Polly left her room.

Polly went back to the game. At half time, the Falcons were ahead, but Polly was certain they would find a way to lose. She checked on the kids. They were both asleep. Now she just had to wait for Tracie to get home.

With time to kill, Polly couldn't resist snooping. Skyler and Tracie's bedroom gave her chills. She opened closets until she found Skyler's clothes. She breathed in his scent and felt a guilty stirring in her loins. Looking at the unmade bed, Polly thought back to the nights when Skyler stayed over at Brad's apartment. After vigorous lovemaking, Skyler would hold Brad in his arms as they shared each other's deepest secrets.

Tears welled up in Polly's eyes and she hurried out of the bedroom.

She found Skyler's man cave in the basement. She resisted the urge to get on his computer and look through his files. His scent was stronger in this room than anywhere else. This was where Skyler did most of his living inside this house. Instead of feeling aroused, Polly felt embarrassment. She was intruding on his personal space without his approval.

Polly retreated to the living room. It was the only room she felt safe in. The second half of the game was starting. Polly poured herself another glass of wine.

Chapter Forty-One

It was just a room with four walls, a ceiling, and a floor. And a bed. A bed big enough for three people to sleep side by side. Or more if they squeezed in together. There was a mini-frig in the corner and a nightstand next to the bed. On the stand was a clock, a CD player, a box of condoms, and a lamp with a red velvet lampshade. The room smelled heavily of lemon-scented cleaning fluid. The sheets on the bed smelled freshly laundered.

As Tracie entered the room, she felt like she was entering an arena for battle, which wasn't entirely untrue. She didn't feel ready for this fight, but then she didn't think she'd ever feel ready. She glanced down at the box of condoms and noticed that like the bed, they were size extra-large.

"Don't be nervous," Candy said. "You'll be fine."

"Should I take off my clothes?" Tracie asked.

"Wait until the men arrive. They'll probably want you to undress the same time they do. Or they may want to take your clothes off. Go with the flow. Have fun."

"Right. Have fun."

Candy took Tracie's hand.

"I understand. The first time is scary. I was petrified my first time and I only dealt with one man."

"Why did I agree to do this?"

"You can figure that out later. They'll be here soon. Let's go over a few things. There is plenty of bottled water in the frig in case anybody gets thirsty. We don't serve alcohol and if they offer you any, say no. You'll want to stay sharp. Drink the water. You need to stay hydrated. If you need to use the bathroom, it's across the hall."

"What if..." Tracie wasn't sure how to put her fear into words. "What if something goes wrong?"

"If for any reason you decide you can't handle the situation, leave the room. It's happened before. One girl got so freaked out when she saw a man's penis she ran screaming out of the room. And she had children. It's not like she hadn't seen one before. Just not one that big."

Tracie squeezed Candy's hand.

"But what if they won't let me leave?"

Candy pointed at a small vent in the wall near the ceiling.

"There's a hidden camera up there. We'll be watching the entire time. If a customer does something he's not supposed to or tries to manhandle our girls, we bust in the room and take him out. If you feel you have to get out, you can wave at the camera. We'll come get you."

Tracie stared at the vent.

"You're going to watch me?"

"It's not like we're taping it and selling it on the internet. Unless you want us to?"

"Hell no!"

"Sorry. Bad joke. Would you rather we didn't watch and left you on your own?"

"No! I understand."

Ivy appeared in the doorway.

"Your guests are here, Tracie. Shall I bring them in?"

Goosebumps popped up on Tracie's arms.

"Yeah, I guess."

Candy followed Ivy out of the room. A minute dragged by before Ivy appeared again.

"Gentlemen," she said, "I would like you to meet Tracie. She is eager to make you happy."

Three Black men entered the room. Their skin was as dark as midnight. They wore hoodies on top of oversized T-shirts. Their jeans sagged so low, Tracie could see their boxer shorts and they waddled like penguins. Their body odor indicated they hadn't bathed today. They slouched against the wall and scowled at Tracie as if she were a bad piece of meat.

These men were nothing like Duane Anderson. Duane ran a landscaping business and raised his son on his own. These guys looked like gang members and were probably on drugs. These were the Black men she had been taught to fear and despise. These were not the type of men Tracie had expected Ivy to find for her. Yet, here she was, dependent on their money to get her out of trouble.

"Perhaps you should break the ice by introducing your-selves?" Ivy said.

The men mumbled their names. Tracie wasn't completely certain, but she thought they said their names were Deon, Tyshawn, and Reggie.

"Okay," Ivy said. "That wasn't so bad, was it? I will go now."

Ivy left the room, closing the door behind her. Tracie was trapped in the room with three thugs. Panic rose inside her throat and threatened to burst out in a scream.

They surrounded Tracie and sniffed her like dogs checking to see if a bitch was in heat. Moving in closely, they rubbed their bodies against her. Not a word was spoken.

Deon tugged at Tracie's shirt.

She figured he wanted her to take it off, so she reached for the hem of the shirt, but Tyshawn slapped her hands. The slap hurt. Tracie rubbed her hand and glanced at the vent near the ceiling. Should she leave?

No. She needed the money too much. Tracie dropped her hands by her side. Deon pulled her shirt up. Tracie raised her arms. Once her shirt was off, Deon tossed it aside. Tyshawn unhooked her bra and removed it. Tracie resisted the urge to cover her bare breasts. The air felt cool on her skin.

The three men laid Tracie on the bed and pulled off her pants and panties. She watched as they removed their clothes. They had beautifully sculpted bodies, almost as magnificent as Duane's. After so many years being ignored and untouched, having all this youth and desire directed at her was intoxicating. Tracie thought about Candy's advice. Go with the flow. Have fun.

As three men used her, Tracie went with the flow. Tracie had fun.

When they were finally sated, Tracie was too worn out to move on the bed. She was reminded of an old sex joke about comparing strenuous sex with riding horses: she had been ridden hard and put away wet. She lay on her side, her body cooling as she watched the three men slip off their condoms and drop them in the waste basket.

Deon opened the mini-frig and took out plastic bottles of water. He tossed a bottle to Tyshawn and one to Reggie. They twisted off the caps and guzzled the water, their Adam's apples bobbing. Deon twisted the cap off a third bottle and sat on the bed next to Tracie.

"Would you like some water?" he asked.

It was the first words spoken since the session began.

Tracie struggled to sit up and took the bottle. She pressed the cool bottle next to her face before taking a long drink. Cool water had never tasted so good. She handed the bottle to Deon, and he took a sip.

"That was amazing," Deon said. "I hope we weren't too rough on you."

After the silent treatment and being used like a sex toy, it was astounding to hear the tenderness in his voice. Tracie smiled.

"I'm not as delicate as I look."

Deon chuckled.

"You are definitely not a delicate flower."

Deon located his jeans, dug into his pockets until he found a roll of bills, and peeled off a small stack. Tyshawn and Reggie did the same. They combined the bills and placed them on the nightstand.

"Didn't you guys pay before you came in?" Tracie asked.

"Yes, we did," Deon said.

"If this is a tip, it's more than generous."

"It's not a tip," Reggie said.

"Then what's this money for?"

"It's for another session," Tyshawn said. "We want to get off again."

"We want to get you off again," Deon added.

Tracie had forgotten the magic trick all young men could perform. It didn't take them long before they were ready to go again.

"I don't know, guys," Tracie said. "I think I'll get sick if I have another orgasm. Besides, I have to be somewhere."

"Come on, baby," Deon said. "Cancel your plans and stay with us."

Tracie looked at the clock on the nightstand. If she wanted to get home before Skyler, she'd have to leave soon.

But then, she looked at the three beautiful men. She wondered if this was what drug addicts felt, a desperate stirring for more.

No. She couldn't stay. She did what she had to do, and she earned the money she needed. Besides, she was afraid if she didn't leave now, she might stay forever.

"I'm sorry, guys, but I have to go."

Deon sat on the bed next to her. He ran his hand along the curve of her side. Tracie shivered with pleasure. He leaned down and pressed his lips against hers. She felt his warm breath.

"Please stay," Deon said.

"I can't," Tracie said. "Besides, I don't think my body can handle any more sex."

"You won't know unless you try."

Chapter Forty-Two

Polly entered the lobby of the Kunakorn Plastic Surgery Center. The air conditioning was a welcome relief after the soupy humidity of Bangkok's busy streets. The crowded buildings, dirty sidewalks, and tangled powerlines were in sharp contrast to the elegant serenity of the center's lobby. A middle-aged woman in a plain dress sat behind a reception desk. With her overnight bag hanging on her shoulder, Polly walked to the desk. The receptionist looked up and smiled.

"Hello," she said. "How may I help you?"

"Hi, I'm Polly Swift."

The receptionist flipped through the appointment book.

"Yes, Ms. Swift. You are here for SRS?"

"That's me. Finally getting my bottom surgery."

The receptionist located Polly's file and looked it over. Everything she needed, blood tests, receipt for final payment, and signed waivers, was in there.

"You will meet with the Dr. Kunakorn this afternoon," the receptionist said. "I will have someone show you to your room."

"Wait," Polly said. "I have someone with me. She's here for emotional support."

Martha walked into the lobby carrying her own overnight bag.

"The people on those little scooters drive like maniacs," Martha said.

Polly put her arm around Martha's shoulder.

"So, Mom. How do you like Thailand?"

Martha grimaced.

"I'd rather be in Denmark."

Polly laughed. She and Martha were escorted to Polly's room, which reminded them of a Days Inn motel room. They freshened up after the long plane ride. Martha took a nap while Polly watched the traffic outside her window.

Dr. Kunakorn came to the room in the late afternoon and discussed the procedure he would be performing on Polly in the morning. He looked to be in his late sixties. He wore a dark blue suit. His movements were precise. His manner was calm and confident. Martha asked good questions and managed not to cry. After the consultation, Dr. Kunakorn left them alone.

"Are you sure about this, Polly?" Martha asked. "Once you go through with this, there's no going back."

"Yes, Mom. I'm sure."

"You must have had doubts. Why else would you have waited so long?"

"All my life I felt like God made a mistake and put me in the wrong body. There were times when I really hated my penis. But I thought my penis was the last link to the people who love Brad Swafford, and the surgery would literally sever that link. I would lose those people forever. That scared me, but what scared me the most was losing you, Mom. Having you here with me means I won't lose you and I can finally be free of Brad. I can finally begin living."

Neither Polly nor Martha slept well that night.

The next morning, the nurses prepped Polly for surgery. They took her on a gurney down to the operating room. They scooted her from the gurney to an operating table covered with clean white sheets. The big glaring lights made Polly feel exposed. Dr. Kunakorn entered, wearing his surgical gown, mask, and gloves. On a metal table, his surgical tools awaited him.

Suddenly, Skyler Aldridge burst into the room and shoved Dr. Kunakorn aside. The doctor fell to the floor. Skyler loomed over Polly.

"What are you doing here?" he demanded.

"What did you do to Dr. Kunakorn?" Polly said. "Where's Mom?"

"Why are you in my house?"

"Your house?"

Polly snapped out of her dream. Her head hurt from the cheap wine and her mouth was dry. She was in the Aldridge's living room. The TV was on, but the game was over.

"That's right. This is my house," Skyler said. "Where's my wife and why are you sleeping in my living room?"

Polly looked around the room as if she expected Tracie to jump out from behind a chair and shout olly olly oxen free. She faced Skyler. She had forgotten how cute he was when he was upset.

"I honestly don't know where Tracie is," Polly said. "She didn't tell me where she was going."

Skyler paced back and forth. Polly glanced at her wristwatch. It was almost one in the morning.

"This isn't like Tracie," Skyler said. "Where the hell is she?"

Polly wondered the same thing. Where the hell was Tracie?

Chapter Forty-Three

POLLY GATHERED UP the empty wine bottle and wine glass and took them to the kitchen. She put the glass in the sink and threw the bottle in the trash bin. She went to get her purse. Skyler dogged her every move.

"You can't leave," he said. "Not until we know where Tracie is."

"Call the police and the hospital and make sure she didn't have an accident on her way home," Polly said.

"Will you call them?"

Polly rolled her eyes.

"You're the husband. You need to make the call."

Skyler looked at the phone in the kitchen but didn't go near it.

"Did you tell Tracie about us?"

As much as Polly adored Skyler's pretty face, she really wanted to punch it with her fist.

"I didn't tell her about our date, though God knows I should have. Why didn't you tell me you were married and had children?"

Skyler ran his fingers through his thick hair.

"I'm sorry. My bad."

"You need to talk to Tracie. She needs you. Your children need you. You keep asking where she is. Where were you tonight?"

"I was watching the game with the guys. I told Tracie I was going out. She didn't say a word to me about going out."

They heard a child crying. Skyler looked in the direction of the child's room but didn't move. Polly cursed, put her purse on the couch, and followed the cries to Harper's room. The little girl was sitting up in bed, rubbing tears from her eyes. Polly sat next to Harper, and she threw her arms around Polly's neck.

"I had a bad dream," Harper said.

"It's okay," Polly said. "It was just a dream. Everything's okay now."

Polly rubbed Harper's back until the child calmed down. She peered over her shoulder. Skyler stood in the doorway with his hands in his pockets.

"Did you watch the Falcon's game on my TV?" Skyler asked.

"Yes," Polly admitted. "I watched the game. Do you have a problem with me watching your TV?"

"I can't believe the Falcons already suck."

"It's pre-season. Some of those guys won't be on the final roster."

"The defense is still letting passes get completed up the middle. It must be some sort of rule that Atlanta has to start on their own goal line after every punt!"

"Watch your language." Polly nodded at Harper. "I agree with you on that one. The Falcons must have the worst starting position average after punts in the entire NFL. The offense looked solid, but they need to stop forcing the ball to Julio when he's double covered."

"Wow!"

"What?"

"I've never had this kind of conversation about sports with a woman before."

"You don't know enough women."

Skyler kneeled next to the bed. Harper switched from hugging Polly to hugging Skyler.

"Time for you to go back to sleep," Skyler said. "Dream about something nice."

"Okay, Daddy," Harper said.

Harper let go of Skyler and lay her head on the pillow. Skyler pulled the covers up to her shoulders and kissed her forehead. He and Polly left Harper's room.

Polly retrieved her purse. Skyler was home. There was no reason for her to stick around. Skyler stood in front of the door and blocked her from leaving.

"I'm tired, I have a splitting headache, and I want to go home," Polly said. "Tracie asked me to do her a favor. I did it because I like her, and I care about her."

"I'm not a bad guy," Skyler said. "There's a lot about Tracie you don't know about."

"Like what?"

"Just leave it at that. She's not as sweet and innocent as she seems."

The front door opened and banged into Skyler's back. He stumbled forward as Tracie entered the house. She pushed past Skyler and grabbed Polly's hands.

"Where the hell have you been?" Skyler said.

Tracie acted as is Skyler wasn't there even though he was standing right next to her.

"I'm sorry I'm late," Tracie said to Polly. "Thank you for staying. I wouldn't have blamed you if you had left."

"I would never do that," Polly said. "I'm just glad to see you made it home safe and sound."

"Aren't you going to answer my question?" Skyler asked.

"Did Connor and Harper give you any trouble?" Tracie said.

"They were no trouble at all," Polly said. "Your kids are great."

"Tracie, you're my wife and I demand that you answer me!" Skyler said.

Tracie hugged Polly. Polly noticed that Tracie's hair was damp and though she had tried to wash it off, a man's scent still clung to her. They parted.

"I'll talk to you later," Polly said.

Polly left the house and sprinted to the Purple Beast. She felt like she was escaping a hungry animal and if she didn't hurry it would reach out and drag her back inside. She got into her car and locked the door. She looked back at the house.

He knew! Skyler knew Tracie was cheating on him. Polly was certain that he knew. Did he also know she was pregnant?

After Polly left, Tracie went directly to the bedroom. Skyler stormed after her.

"What the hell is going on?" he said. "I come home to find you've left our children alone with a stranger and then you show up and act like nothing happened."

"You mean I'm acting like you?" Tracie asked.

"What's that supposed to mean?"

"You never tell me where you're going or when you'll be home. You expect me to stay here and look after the kids while you do whatever the hell you want."

"I work hard all day. Sometimes I need to get away and unwind."

Tracie glared at Skyler. He'd seen that look in her eyes too often. He was about to catch hell.

"Did you ever think for one minute that maybe I might need

to get away and unwind? I'd like to see you take care of the kids by yourself for one day! You couldn't handle it."

"I never said you weren't a good mom."

Skyler's lame attempt to appease Tracie only made her angrier.

"I never get to take a break. I went out for one night to do something for me, and you have the nerve to give me shit about it! How dare you!"

Skyler was a far cry from the smartest or the most sensitive husband in the world, but he knew when the battle was lost. Though he was burning to find out, he didn't dare ask her again where she had been all night.

He was certain that Duane Anderson was somehow involved. Wasn't it enough the yard man screwed Skyler's wife in his bed, was he now making Tracie abandon her children to screw him at night? Skyler didn't love Tracie, but she was still his wife. There was only so much his pride could tolerate.

Tracie took a pillow off the bed and threw it at Skyler. He caught it before it hit his face. She took a blanket out of the closet and tossed that at him as well.

"What's this for?" Skyler asked.

"You're sleeping on the couch tonight."

"Why? What the hell did I do?

"You embarrassed me in front of Polly."

Skyler didn't want to sleep next to Tracie anyway but mentioning Polly's name just seemed unfair. He left the bedroom with the pillow and blanket under his arm. Tracie locked the bedroom door behind him, went into the bathroom, and locked the bathroom door. She dug into her jeans' pocket and pulled out a roll of bills. She had counted the money before she left Xtra Special TLC Massage, but she wanted to count it again. The amount was the same, fifteen hundred dollars. She had never had this much money that was hers and hers alone.

She rolled up the bills and put a hair tie around them. She

would have to find a place to hide the money that Skyler would never look. The answer was obvious. She took tampons out of their box and stuffed the roll into the empty box.

With her money safely hidden, Tracie undressed and examined her body. Bruises were blossoming on her arms and thighs. Her body ached as if she had worked out for hours. Tracie chuckled. She had been through a very strenuous workout.

The sorest part of her body was her pussy, though her ass was a close second. When she and Skyler had first married, there were times when he'd left her pussy sore, but never like this.

Tracie studied her face in the bathroom mirror. She had done what she had to do. She could afford the abortion. Skyler would never find out. Connor and Harper would never find out. But most important, Red Fox would never find out. Her secret was safe.

She swore that she would never have sex for money again. Even though she'd had the best sex of her life tonight, and even though a hunger gnawed inside her to return to that room with three men like Deon, Tyshawn, and Reggie, it was far too dangerous to ever do it again.

Chapter Forty-Four

MANSOOR ENJOYED WATCHING Aunty Lata cook. She moved about the kitchen with absolute confidence. There were no wasted movements in her preparation. She knew precisely when a pot needed stirring and another needed an extra sprinkling of spices.

Aunty Lata made traditional Indian family dishes. Mansoor loved the smell of her cooking even if it reminded him of the country he was forced to leave. He missed the hustle and bustle of Mumbai. Most of all he missed his beautiful Riya. Surely, she had found another man by now.

Tonight, Aunty Lata was preparing red lentil curry, rice, raita, naan, and kheer. A wonderful family meal, but it wasn't for her family. It was for the mystery guest in room nine. When the dinner was ready, she transferred it to a series of plastic containers. She stacked them inside a grocery sack and handed the sack to Mansoor.

"I will call her room and let her know you're coming," she said.

"Did she pay you to make her dinner?" Mansoor said.

"I offered to do it. It was no trouble."

Mansoor carried the sack to room nine. The Do Not Disturb sign hung from the door. Two doors down, room eleven also had the Do Not Disturb sign on the doorknob. Mansoor knocked on room nine's door. No one answered. There were no lights on inside. He leaned close to the door.

"It's Mansoor," he said. "I brought you something to eat."

The door opened and Mansoor entered the dark room. The door closed and the light came on.

An attractive African American woman wearing skinny jeans and a blue sports jersey with a Chanel logo on the front watched him warily. Mansoor carried the grocery sack over to the table in the kitchenette and took out the stack of plastic containers.

"It's only fair that I warn you that my Aunty Lata's cooking is addictive as hell," he said.

"I know a thing or two about addictive food," the woman said. "Tell your aunt that I appreciate this very much."

"I will leave now so you can enjoy your meal."

Mansoor headed for the door.

"Wait. There's more here than I can eat. Would you care to join me?"

Mansoor needed to get back to the front desk, but he sensed that she needed the company more.

"I would be delighted," he said.

There were cheap plates in the cabinets. They set the table and spooned out the food. The only thing available to drink was tap water, but neither of them complained about it.

"By the way, my name's Dani," she said. "Sorry about all the secrecy. I know this must seem very weird."

"There's a difference between weird and cautious," Mansoor said. "Now I've seen some weird guests. In fact, just a few doors down from you there is a couple on their honeymoon who haven't left their room for a week."

"Oh, my Gawd. Their room must stink something awful."

"The cleaning staff agrees with your assessment. They have been complaining to me, but there is nothing I can do about it."

Dani swallowed a spoonful of raita and closed her eyes.

"This is amazeballs!"

Mansoor tore off a chunk of naan and used it to scoop up some red lentil curry.

"May I ask you something?"

"You can ask. I may not answer."

"Fair enough. Did you fall in with a bad crowd and that's how you came to be in such dire circumstances?"

"That's a good way to put it. Yes. I got involved with some very bad people. They can't know I'm here."

"Why haven't you gone to the police?"

Dani chewed on hunk of naan.

"Can I trust you? I mean really really trust you?"

"Did you do something illegal?"

"No. You can't repeat any of this. Not even to your aunt."

"Yes. You can trust me. I'm very good with secrets."

Dani told him about Kitsune, the mysterious Mr. Kite's mind control over his employees, and the unpaid employees' stoned orgies under the moonlight. He was sorry that he had agreed to keep Dani's story a secret. Aunty Lata would have loved to hear about a culinary cult that was just a few miles away.

"Now that is amazeballs!" Mansoor said.

"So, you believe me?"

"Completely. But tell me, if you ran away from Kitsune with nothing but the clothes on your back, how did you manage to get a room here at the motel?"

"I went to the library. I borrowed their phone and made a collect call to my mother. She called the motel and made all the arrangements."

"The library. I will remember that the next time I'm on the run from a cult."

"I wish I'd thought of it when I first came to Red Fox."

"I don't understand. How long have you been in town?"

Dani ignored his question. She got up from the table and went to the window. She peeked out of the curtain for a second and then pulled it shut. She sat back down at the table and stared at her food.

"You think you know someone, but then they turn out to be the exact opposite," she said. "Why do people do that? Is it some kind of sick game just to mess with your head? I went through enough crap at Kitsune without having to deal with somebody's fucked up agenda."

Riya used to have tirades like this where she railed against India's oppression of transgender women. Listening to Dani rant made Mansoor miss Riya even more than he already did.

"I can't wait to get to hell out of Red Fox," Dani continued. "It's full of two-faced racist rednecks. You live here. Am I wrong?"

"The way I see it," Mansoor said, "they are good people who believe bad things."

"That's very generous of you. If I feel like an outsider here, then you really must feel like this is some kind of alien world."

Mansoor drank some water to loosen the knot in his throat.

"It was very hard when I first came here. I was afraid they were going to hang me from a lamppost because I'm a Muslim and my skin is darker than theirs. But after some time, the fear was replaced with loneliness. I have my aunt and uncle and I get along with most of the staff, but really, I haven't been able to make any real friends."

Dani nodded.

"Friends are important."

"Whoever he was, he really broke your heart," Mansoor said.

"Yes. She did."

Chapter Forty-Five

No matter which position he tried, Skyler couldn't get comfortable. He'd slept through dozens of ballgames on this couch, but he wasn't getting any sleep tonight. There was too much buzzing in his head. Tracie and Polly. They both hated him.

The fight with Tracie didn't bother him so much. It was just one more skirmish in the life of a marriage that never should have happened. She could cheat on him all she wanted as long as she didn't do it in their bed. And since she was cheating on him, shouldn't he be allowed to cheat? It was only fair. But the woman he wanted to cheat with wanted nothing to do with him.

Polly. What was it about that woman? He barely knew her, but he couldn't stop thinking about her. It didn't help that her perfume lingered on the cushions of the couch.

It was clear to Skyler that he wasn't going to get any sleep, so he kicked off the blanket and padded on bare feet to his man cave. He felt under his desk for the magnetic key hider. He took out the key inside and unlocked his filing cabinet. In the bottom drawer, under a stack of old instruction manuals, was a photo album.

Skyler sat in his office chair with the album in his lap. The photos in the album had been taken on a Polaroid instant camera. Skyler had found the black bulky device in his parents' basement. He was thrilled when he discovered that he could get film for it on eBay. The camera appealed to him because the photos came right out of the camera. This was even better than a digital camera. There was no record of the photos he took other than what he held in his hand.

Skyler turned the pages slowly. Here was the only evidence he had of his real relationship with Brad Swafford. There were photos of them on camping trips and in Brad's apartment. There were photos of them posing for each other. They ranged from fully clothed to no shirt to just underwear to nothing at all, their peach-colored skin shining with the vigor of youth.

There were no sex photos in the album. They were always too involved having sex to grab the camera.

For a long time, Skyler had managed to not think about Brad. He couldn't remember when he finally stopped hating him. He thought looking at these photos would get his mind off Polly, but they were just another testament to how his relationships always turned to shit.

As if to punish himself, Skyler kept turning the pages. Toward the end of the album, he saw something that made him slam it shut. His heart raced as he went back to the page and looked again at what jolted him. Photos of Brad dressed as a woman.

At first, Skyler couldn't remember when he had taken these photos. But then, it came back to him. Brad sometimes insisted that he wasn't gay. He claimed he was a straight woman in a man's body. Skyler tried not to laugh. He figured that since Brad grew up in a strict Christian home, he needed a way to justify his homosexuality.

Then one weekend Brad's mother went to visit some cousins, leaving him alone in the house. When Skyler came over, Brad greeted him at the door in full drag. He had on one of his mother's dresses along with a pearl necklace, earrings, stockings, high heels, make-up, and a blonde wig that matched Brad's natural blond hair. Later, Skyler discovered that underneath the dress, Brad wore a bra, panties, and a garter belt.

Brad made an attractive if mannish woman. Skyler took out his camera and Brad posed as if it were a fashion shoot. He'd never seen Brad so happy. That night, they had the best sex ever, even though it annoyed Skyler that Brad refused to take off the wig.

A week later, Brad made Skyler promise that he would burn the photos he took that night, but of course, he didn't.

Skyler looked at the photos more closely. He was shocked when he first saw them because he thought they were pictures of Polly and that was impossible. Now it made sense. He'd been thinking of Polly and then saw a photo of an attractive blonde who slightly resembled her. But it wasn't Polly. It was Brad in his mother's clothes. Skyler had made the connection because he wanted to be as close to Polly as he had been with Brad. Wishful thinking.

"Daddy. I can't sleep."

Skyler quickly shut the album as if he'd been caught looking at pornography. Connor stood in the doorway.

"Connor," Skyler said. "What are you doing up?"

"I told you. I can't sleep."

"Let's see what we can do about that."

Skyler locked away the album, picked up Connor, and carried him to his bedroom. He put his son in bed and pulled the covers over him. Skyler sat in a rocking chair.

"So, why can't you sleep?" Skyler asked.

"I don't know. I just can't. Tell me a story."

"A story? Will that help you sleep?"

"Yeah."

"Okay. Let me think of a good bedtime story."

"Tell the one about The Slide?"

"A slide? I don't know any stories about slides."

"Yes, you do. You slide on your butt into the end zone. You beat the eagles."

Skyler racked his brain to figure out what the hell Connor was talking about.

"You don't mean the time we won against the Putnam County War Eagles? I slid in the mud but still made the winning touchdown."

"That's the story. Tell it again."

"I never told you that story.

Skyler had never told his children stories about his high school football games. He didn't want to be one of those has beens always bragging about their glory days.

"Polly told us the story," Connor said. "It was funny."

"Polly? Told you about The Slide?" Skyler asked.

"Daddy, tell me the story!"

"Okay, okay. Calm down, you little monster."

Skyler told Connor the story about the The Slide. Connor corrected Skyler whenever his version deviated from Polly's. It almost seemed like Polly remembered the play more clearly than Skyler. Connor fell asleep before Skyler got to the best part where Skyler caught the ball, slide across the goal line, and won the game.

As Skyler watched Connor sleep, he wondered how Polly Swift knew about The Slide. She had to have been at that football game. She remembered too many details. Maybe she went to Putnam County High School and was there to see her War Eagles lose to the Fighting Foxes. That was a plausible explanation, but it still didn't make sense. Why would Polly tell his kids about the time her school lost a football game to Skyler's school?

There was another possible explanation, but it didn't make a lick of sense. Skyler felt stupid even thinking it. Polly Swift was Brad Swafford. That was why that photo of Brad in drag reminded Skyler of Polly. Skyler shook his head. That couldn't be true. Skyler would have known in his bones if Polly and Brad were the same person. And more importantly, Brad would have told Skyler. He wouldn't have lied to Skyler about a thing like that.

Chapter Forty-Six

Polly woke up before her alarm went off. Her headache was gone but not her heartache. She went into the kitchen and made coffee. Sitting in the living room with a steaming cup, she sipped the black liquid and continued to think about the things that had prevented her from getting a good night's sleep.

Skyler and Tracie. What a mess. Intellectually, Polly knew she wasn't responsible for the decisions they made. She didn't make them get married. And it certainly wasn't her fault they were cheating on each other. But she still felt guilty.

Mostly, she felt guilty about her feelings for Skyler. She remembered every inch of his body, especially the inches that counted the most. She ached to explore them again just to make sure they were still the same.

But she wasn't going to be a bad girl. She was going to keep her hands to herself. When Skyler got married, he took a vow to love and cherish Tracie, and Polly was going to honor that vow even if Skyler wouldn't.

Polly finished her coffee and put the cup in the sink. She went into the bedroom to change. She would go on her morning jog earlier than usual. It would give her more time to clear her head.

She stripped, stood in front of the mirror, and examined her body. As always, her inspection led down to her penis. She didn't hate it. She looked at it was if she'd been born with an outie bellybutton when it was supposed to have been an innie, a physical defect that could be corrected with surgery.

If her penis could talk, oh the stories it would tell. Once she had escaped the strict conservative world of Red Fox, she had acted out by engaging in a wide variety of sexual activity with men and women. Not that she'd been all that innocent and pure in Red Fox but living in San Francisco and then Atlanta gave her endless opportunities for carnal adventures.

There had been so much confusion in her life back then. She kept finding ways to avoid facing herself. She'd done more than her share of drugs and alcohol. She had lost endless career opportunities. Her decadent path led through bathhouses and penthouses, gay bars and straight bars, dark alleys, and intimate bedrooms.

But at the end of that decadent path, she realized that she wanted to come home and be the person she should have been. So, she got rid of Brad and became Polly.

Polly put on her sweatpants and her sports bra. She hadn't gotten around to doing her laundry so the tops she wore for jogging were smelly.

She remembered the polo shirt that Anita Cox had given her. Polly found it in the back of a drawer and held it up. Anita was smaller than Polly so she had her doubts that it would fit, but to her surprise, it fit perfectly. Polly had to admit that the fox head on the Kitsune logo was kind of cute.

Polly put on her sneakers and laced them up. She stretched her muscles and then left the apartment. When she reached the bottom of the stairs, she saw that there were no lights on in the main house. Martha was an early riser. Polly felt an odd pride that she had gotten up before Martha.

Polly breathed in the cool mountain air. She started off slow, before increasing her speed to a steady jog. The sun hadn't yet broken the horizon. The world was soft yellow and purple. A mist hovered a few inches above the ground and the grass was wet with dew. Other than a few birds calling out to each other, it was completely quiet.

Polly could tell it was going to be a beautiful day. After the sour drama in Skyler and Tracie's home the night before, Polly needed a bright, sunny day. Certainly, nothing bad could happen on a day like this.

Chapter Forty-Seven

GINNY PACED THE short distance between the bedroom and the kitchenette. After spending days wearing little to nothing, she now wore layers of clothes. She had turned the air conditioning up as high as it would go, and the room was freezing cold. As she walked back and forth, she held her gun in her hand and tapped the barrel against her thigh.

"How could you betray Mr. Kite?" Ginny asked. "Has he not given us everything? Has he not shown us that food is more than mere fuel for the body? Have his divine dishes not given us a glimpse of the cosmos that mere mortals such as we could never hope to see?"

Ginny paused to glare at Corey's corpse. He was still bound to the bed with the pillow over his face, or rather what remained of his face. Ginny had covered his body with a bedsheet.

Ginny fanned away the flies that buzzed around the dried blood near Corey's head.

"How did these stupid flies get in here? I put up the Do Not Disturb sign."

She put the gun on the dresser next to the tablet computer

and began to pack her things. And then she unpacked them. She had repeated this routine many times since the murder.

"I only had sex with you so that you'd come to your senses and realize that nothing was more important than the mission. But instead, I find out that you sabotaged the mission. You knew how to find Dani and you didn't tell me. How could you do that to Mr. Kite? How could you do that to me? I let you put your penis in my mouth. The same place I put Mr. Kite's food!"

Ginny sat on the edge of the bed with her back to Corey.

"And now I'll have to waste time getting rid of your body when I could be looking for Dani. Mr. Grigsby is going to want to know what happened to you. I'll tell him the truth. I'll tell him how you betrayed Mr. Kite. You tried to leave, but I couldn't let you leave. Mr. Grigsby knows that better than anybody. Nobody leaves Kitsune. That's why we were looking for Dani."

Ginny brushed her hair out of her face. The smell of death should have repulsed her but instead it made her ravenous. She had devoured every edible item in the room except for the half of Corey's beef burrito that he'd never gotten a chance to finish. Finally, she gave in and ate the rest of his burrito. It gurgled in her stomach and gave her flatulence.

"Who are we kidding?" Ginny said. "I'm never going to find Dani. I'm going to go to jail for killing you. And the worst part, I let Mr. Kite down. I can't go back to Kitsune. I would rather die than see the disappointment in Mr. Kite's face."

Ginny went to the dresser and picked up the gun. She put the barrel in her mouth and wrapped her finger around the trigger. She knew what her mother would tell if she were here right now. She'd tell her to stop being a baby and get on with it.

The tablet computer screen lit up. Ginny pulled the gun out of her mouth and stared at the screen. A blue dot pulsed as it moved across the screen. Ginny held the tablet in one hand and pointed at the screen with her other hand.

"You see that! Dani's crawled out of whatever hole she'd been hiding in. I told you it was just a matter of time, but you wouldn't listen to me. I'm going to get that bitch and drag her ass back home."

Ginny gathered the car keys, her wallet, her cellphone, the tablet, the room key, and the gun. When she got to the door, she stopped and looked back at the corpse tied to the bed.

"Wait here. I'll come back to deal with you later."

She left the room, slamming the door behind her with such force that it caused the Do Not Disturb sign to fall off the doorknob.

Ginny got into her car and started the engine, completely oblivious to the fact that the sign had fallen to the ground. Her attention was focused on Dani's GPS signal as she roared out of the parking lot.

Chapter Forty-Eight

THE SKY WAS orange, and the mountain was a dark green. The mist was melting away. Polly savored the burn in her leg muscles as she jogged past wood fences and grazing cows. Other than the occasional early riser driving past her, she had the road to herself.

Instead of dwelling on Skyler and Tracie, Polly decided to focus on the things in Red Fox that made her happy. Sunrises. Fresh mountain air. The smell of wildflowers. Martha.

Before the divorce, Brad had been closer to his father than his mother. Their separation had happened without warning or reason. Brad's father left town, cutting off all ties to his wife and son. It was if he had vanished into thin air. Then there was the mystery of how his father managed to get out of paying child support. As Martha struggled to keep her home and her business, Brad had done his part to earn money to pay the bills. He did odd jobs and whatever he could to help Martha both at home and at the beauty salon.

They learned to work as a team and as a result, Brad grew closer to his mother than he had even been to his father. Brad admired how hard Martha worked and respected how her faith helped her through her darkest days. Martha let Brad know how proud she was that he never complained and managed to work after school and still make good grades and play football.

And now Polly was working together with her mother again, even if it was under false pretenses. Someday she would tell Martha the truth. But not now. Until then, she was going to enjoy this time with her.

A BMW drove past Polly, screeched to a stop, turned around, and drove back. It stopped a few feet in front of Polly. A woman with frizzy red hair, dark circles under her eyes, and way too many clothes jumped out of the car and pointed a gun at Polly.

Polly froze in her tracks. A chill enveloped her body. The woman didn't look familiar, but Polly had seen those insane eyes before. They were the eyes of the strung-out junkie, the jilted lover, and the normally reasonable person transformed into a homicidal maniac by road rage.

"Where's Dani?" the woman shouted.

"I don't know anyone named Danny," Polly said. "Is he your boyfriend? If he's cheating on you, he's not doing it with me."

"Don't play games with me. If you don't know who Dani is, then why are you wearing her shirt?"

Polly glanced down at her Kitsune shirt. If she survived this, she was going to have a long talk with Anita Cox about the proper way to tip a hairdresser. On the other hand, there was no way in hell that Polly was going to tell this crazy bitch how she got the shirt. Polly barely knew Anita, but she didn't strike Polly as the type to put an innocent person in harm's way on purpose.

"I found it at a thrift store," Polly said.

"Liar!"

Polly checked her surroundings. The nearest shelter was a barn a quarter mile away in the middle of an open field. Unless the crazy woman was incapable of hitting anything she shot at, Polly literally had nowhere to run.

Polly swallowed the lump in her throat and clenched her fists. She could feel the wind on her skin and the colors of the flowers that grew wild along the side of the road seemed to vibrate. The idea of dying a useless death made her incredibly sad.

"I'm telling the truth. I don't know anyone named Danny. I got this shirt at a thrift store. Please don't kill me."

A car appeared in the distance. It was just a blur at the end of a long ribbon of road, but it was headed their way. Its motor echoed in the distance.

"What's your name?" Polly asked.

"Ginny," the crazy bitch said.

"Listen to me, Ginny. Whoever that is coming our way is going to see you pointing a gun at me. They're going to call the police. If you don't want to go to jail, then you'd best get in your car and drive away."

Ginny ran her hand though her unruly hair.

"I don't care if they see me. If they stop, I'll shoot them. If they call the police, then I'll shoot the police. I've already killed one person who got in my way. A few more won't make any difference."

The small bit of hope Polly had felt when she saw the car coming evaporated and she peed a little bit.

"Can we please get in the car?" Polly asked.

Ginny tilted her head to side.

"What are you trying to pull?"

"I don't want them to see us." Polly nodded in the direction of the car. It was close enough now that she could see that it wasn't a car. It was a pick-up truck.

Ginny grinned.

"You're afraid they'll stop. You're afraid I'll kill them. Do you recognize that truck?"

The truck was approaching quickly. Polly could make out two people in the cab.

"Never seen it before in my life."

"You're trying to save a stranger's life. How very noble of you."

"Didn't realize I was until this moment. Can't say I'm particularly happy about it."

The sound of the engine grew louder and louder as the truck got closer and closer.

"Here's how you can save their life. Take me to Dani."

"I would if I could, but I don't know where he is."

Ginny looked at the truck and then back at Polly.

"Get in the car," Ginny said.

Polly climbed into passenger seat. Ginny slid in behind the wheel. Ginny kept the gun pointed at Polly as the pick-up truck rumbled past them. As it went by, Polly saw that an old man was driving. An old woman was seated next to him. The woman locked eyes with Polly for a second before they continued on their way. Polly breathed a sigh of relief. She checked out the BMW.

"Nice car."

"Belongs to my boss," Ginny said.

"I told you the truth. I don't know this person you're looking for. I found the shirt at a thrift store."

Ginny pressed the muzzle of the gun against Polly's ribs.

"I am sick and tired of your lying!" she screamed.

Polly closed her eyes and waited for death. The only consolation was that she would die protecting someone else. Why did being noble suck so much?

Instead of the sound of a gunshot, Polly heard the engine starting. She opened her eyes. Ginny pulled onto the road. She had one hand on the steering wheel and the other on her gun which she kept pointed at Polly.

"Where are we going?" Polly asked.

"I'm taking you to Mr. Kite," Ginny said. "He'll make you talk. Nobody can lie to him."

Even though it was a pleasantly cool morning, Ginny had the air conditioning on high. Polly's Kitsune shirt was drenched with her nervous sweat. She shivered from the cold and fear.

"Did you really kill somebody?" Polly asked.

"Shot him while we were having sex," Ginny said. "Best orgasm I've ever had."

Chapter Forty-Nine

DURING HIS MANY years as sheriff of Red Fox, Georgia, Vince Cagle had seen the number of murders drop to a measly five a year. He felt this had more to do with the dwindling population than to a possible growing pacifism among the remaining residents. But now it looked as if tourists were coming to Red Fox to keep the town's murder rate from falling any lower.

Teresa Martinez had discovered the body. She was a maid at Fox Creek Falls Inn. She entered room eleven around 10:30 a.m. Teresa pointed out to Vince that the guests hadn't allowed the cleaning staff to enter the room for over a week and she was expecting a horrible mess. What she found was certainly horrible.

To her credit, when Teresa realized that the man strapped to the bed wasn't breathing, she didn't become hysterical and run screaming from the room. She carefully exited the room. locked the door and told the motel's manager to contact the police.

"I've seen enough CSI episodes to know you shouldn't contaminate the crime scene," Teresa said.

Vince ducked under the yellow tape strung across the doorway and entered room eleven. A man wearing khakis, a brown sports coat, and medical gloves moved slowly around the bed. He lifted the victim's arm turned it from side to side as he examined the wrist.

"How's it going, Mike?" Vince asked.

Mike Thurston was the medical examiner for Rabin County. Mike was blander than mayonnaise, which is why Cagle liked him so much. He did his job with as little fuss as possible.

"The victim is male, somewhere in his mid-thirties. He was shot twice in the face at close range. Once we retrieve the bullets, I'll be able to tell exactly what gun was used, but judging from the entrance and exit wounds, I'd say it was 9MM handgun. The ligature marks on the wrists and ankles are minor suggesting he didn't struggle to free himself."

"Which suggests that he let her tie him up," Vince said.

Mike placed the victim's arm back where it had been on the bed.

"You know for certain that the murderer was a female?"

"No. But right now, our leading person of interest is Virginia Spencer," Vince said. "The room is registered under her name and paid for with her American Express card. The victim is a thirty-two-year-old male. His name is Corey Chan. His Seattle driver's license expired last year. We're looking for a next of kin. Neither Chan nor Spencer has a criminal record, not even speeding tickets."

Mike pointed at Corey's groin.

"There's dried sperm on the sheets. You figure this is one of those kinky sex affairs gone bad?"

Vince pushed his cowboy hat back on his head.

"From a certain angle it looks that way. But I have a funny feeling that it's not that simple."

Mike took a step away from the bed so he could look at the entire body.

"The pillow is the part that bothers me the most."

"Me too. Let's see if it's for the same reason," Vince said.

"The killer put the pillow over Chan's face to muffle the sound of the gunshots. That suggests this wasn't a crime of passion and that it was premediated."

"Yep. This could be cold blooded murder. Spencer told the motel manager that she and Chan were on their honeymoon. For a week, they didn't come out of the room because they were supposedly too busy consummating their marriage. At the end of the week, the bride shoots the groom in the head."

"I guess the honeymoon was over."

Chapter Fifty

"Hello, thank you for joining God Save the Foodie. I'm your host, Aiden Belcher. This week's episode is about the mysterious Kitsune Restaurant and its secret debt to poor white trash.

"For years, Mr. Kite the head chef of Kitsune has been delighting gastronomes with his haute cuisine. No one else cooks like Mr. Kite. He didn't work his way up in someone else's kitchen. He invented his unique dishes without any outside influence. His amazing dishes are divinely inspired and magically appeared in his kitchen just like Athena sprang from the head of Zeus, fully grown and in a full set of armor. That is the myth of Mr. Kite. But here is the reality. There is no such thing as a self-educated chef. Mr. Kite's dishes were taken from the Payne family.

"The Payne family lived on Red Fox Mountain for generations. Dirt poor and notorious for their illegal activities that ran from bootlegging to dealing meth, they were also known to be excellent cooks. Owen Tew is owner of the Rejoice Diner in Red Fox, Georgia, and a descendent of the Payne family. He remembers sharing delicious vegetarian meals with his cousins. The Paynes weren't vegetarian by choice. They could rarely afford to buy meat, so on the days when they failed to kill a rabbit, squirrel, or possum, they ate only vegetables. As Mr. Tew put it, the Payne family figured if they had to eat dirt, they might as well find a way to make it tasty.

"The Payne family no longer lives on Red Fox Mountain, but their cabin still stands. At least, some of it still stands. It has been added onto and modernized. Mr. Kite lives in it now. Did he buy the Payne family recipes along with their land or did he steal them? Either way, Mr. Kite built his reputation on their cooking. The least he can do is honor their contribution.

"Owen Tew doesn't hide his family roots. He has graciously provided two Payne family recipes which are posted on the God Save the Foodie website. Try them at home. If you close your eyes, you'll swear you were eating dinner at Kitsune."

The podcast was an hour long. Terrence Grigsby listened to it three times. More secrets were revealed but not once does this Belcher asshole reveal where he got his information.

Terrance downloaded the recipes from the website and compared them to Mr. Kite's recipes. They were identical. He still couldn't believe it. Kitsune's reputation rested on the groundbreaking vegan masterpieces invented by their genius chef, Mr. Kite. Dani Lewis had single-handedly destroyed that carefully created myth. Terrance couldn't prove it was Lewis who talked to Aiden Belcher, but who else could it have been?

The recipes proved nothing. Lewis could have stolen them from the Kitsune kitchen and then claimed they were from the Payne family. But she had caused enough doubt that people were now questioning everything about their operation.

Terrence found out about the podcast that morning when he sat down with a cup of coffee at his computer in his home office to check his emails. He had a dozen interview requests from reporters. The list included Town & Country, Food & Wine, Bloomberg, Reuters, and The New Yorker. Every email had a link to the podcast, which had gone viral in the foodie universe. The reporters wanted to know if there was any truth to the claim that there was a link between Kitsune and this family from Red Fox Mountain.

As the list of interview requests grew, so did the list of reservation cancellations. Former diners emailed to express their outrage that Kitsune had bamboozled them. Terrence knew that this was just the beginning of the shit storm Kitsune would have to weather.

Terrence closed his computer. He was desperate to be in his beloved restaurant before the world took it away from him. But his cellphone started ringing before he made it out the door. He figured it was another reporter, but then saw it was from Scott, the head security guard.

"What's the problem now?"

"I don't know if this is a problem, sir," Scott said. "But it definitely requires your attention."

Terrence waited, but Scott said nothing.

"Spit it out," Terrence said. "What requires my attention?"

"We just opened the gate for Ginny Spencer."

Terrence's heart skipped a beat.

"Is she alone?"

"No, sir. She has a female with her."

"Where is she now?"

"Ginny and the female are waiting in your office in the restaurant."

Terrence hung up and flew out the door. He covered the short distance between his house and the restaurant in less than thirty seconds. Scott stood outside his office door. Terrence paused to catch his breath before going in.

Two women sat in his visitors' chairs. They turned their

heads when he entered the room and watched him as he walked to his desk. Terrence sat and stared at them.

When Scott said Ginny was with a female, Terrence had hoped the female was Dani. A bud of hope had blossomed in Terrence's mind that he could convince Dani to tell the world that the podcast was a hoax, that she had provided false information to Belcher to get Mr. Kite's attention. He would assure her that Mr. Kite would forgive her, and she would be welcomed her back into the happy Kitsune family.

But this female wasn't Dani. She wasn't even close.

"Who are you?" Terrence asked.

"Polly Swift. Who are you?"

"I'm Terrence Grigsby, owner of Kitsune restaurant."

"I've had friends who have eaten here. They say it's as good as the Inn of the Seventh Ray. I've been to the Seventh Ray, but I've never been here."

"You're not Dani."

"Never said I was. Could we have this conversation without her pointing a gun at me? It's not like I'm going anywhere."

Polly nodded at Ginny. Terrence looked at the gun in Ginny's hand.

"Is that the gun I gave you?" Terrence asked.

"Yes sir," Ginny said.

"This isn't Dani. You know that don't you?"

"She's wearing Dani's shirt."

"That doesn't make her Dani. How do you know it's Dani's shirt?"

"GPS tracker."

Terrence narrowed his eyes at Polly. Polly did her best to look sweet and innocent.

"Why are you wearing Dani's shirt?"

"She's going to say she found it at a thrift store," Ginny said. "She's lying. She got it from Dani. She knows where Dani is."

Terrence held up his hand and Ginny shut up. Terrence turned to Polly.

"Why are you wearing Dani's shirt?" he repeated.

"You do know that kidnapping is a crime," Polly said.

"Answer my question."

"There's a thrift store in Red Fox called Faith Inc. Thrift Store. A lovely woman named Rosalyn runs the place. I bought the shirt from her for two dollars and fifty cents. If you don't believe me, you can ask her yourself."

Polly hadn't stepped foot inside the store in over a decade so she no idea if Rosalyn still ran the place or if the price of shirts had gone up.

Terrence turned to Ginny.

"Where's Corey?"

"He's at the motel," Ginny said.

"What the hell is he doing there? Why isn't he here with you?"

Ginny gnawed on her knuckle. Terrence had a bad feeling about Corey, but he had enough on his plate and would deal with Corey later.

"Ms. Swift, I agree with Ginny," Terrence said. "I think you're lying. I think you do know where Dani is and you're not telling us out of a false sense of loyalty. It's very important that you tell me how I can reach her. She's in trouble and she needs our help."

"Is this how you help people?" Polly asked. "By kidnapping them at gunpoint?"

Terrence pinched the bridge of his nose.

"I don't have time for this shit."

"Mr. Kite will make her talk," Ginny said. "Nobody can hide the truth from him. He sees into our souls and exposes our lies."

That bud of hope in Terrence stopped withering and began to blossom again.

"That's not a bad idea."

Terrence stood and left the two women in his office. Scott was still standing guard.

"The blonde's name is Polly Swift," Terrence said. "Take her to Mr. Kite. She can be his problem. I have other fires to put out that need my immediate attention."

"What should I tell Mr. Kite?" Scott asked.

"Ms. Swift refuses to tell us where Dani Lewis is hiding. She thinks she's protecting Dani. Mr. Kite needs to gain her trust so that we can find Dani and bring her home."

Scott scratched his balding head.

"How is Mr. Kite supposed to do that?"

"Oh, come on, Scott. You're familiar with Mr. Kite's powers of persuasion."

Scott took a step back.

"Are you suggesting that Mr. Kite indoctrinate her into the Kitsune culinary clan? He can't do that. She hasn't proven herself worthy of his enlightenment."

Terrence grabbed Scott's arm.

"We don't have time for that. Ginny took it upon herself to kidnap this woman. Once we get the information we need, we can't exactly send her home with our heartfelt thanks. We either make her part of the family or we bury her where her body will never be found. Which one do you think we should do?"

Scott scratched his head.

"I would do anything for Mr. Kite, but I'd rather we didn't kill anybody if we don't absolutely have to."

"Good man. Now take Ms. Swift to Mr. Kite. I'll keep Ginny here. She has some explaining to do."

Chapter Fifty-One

SHERIFF VINCE CAGLE stood outside room eleven and watched the ambulance take Corey Chan's body to the morgue for an autopsy. Meanwhile, Vince and his men had plenty of work to do at Fox Creek Falls Inn. Vince hated murder investigations. They were always messy, and the killer's motive never justified cutting someone's life short.

Vince's cellphone rang. He checked the number and was shocked to see who was calling him. It was someone he thought would never speak to him again.

"Martha?"

"Vince," Martha Swafford said. "I need your help."

Her voice tottered between worried and frantic.

"What seems to be the trouble?" he asked.

"Polly's missing."

"Polly? That the girl who took over for Susie at your shop?"

"Yes. Polly Swift. She's missing and I'm worried sick."

"Are you sure she's missing? It's a beautiful day. Could be she decided not to come to work."

"If she just didn't show up for work, I wouldn't be calling

you," Martha said impatiently. "Polly is renting my upstairs apartment. When I left for work, her car was in the driveway. I figured she was running late, so I went on to the shop. When she didn't show up by noon, I called her phone, but she didn't answer. I had a feeling something wasn't right, so I went back to the house. Her car was still in the driveway. I used my key to look inside the apartment. She wasn't there either."

The mention of noon reminded Vince that it was almost lunchtime, and he was getting mighty hungry.

"Maybe a friend picked her up."

"You don't understand, Vince. Polly is a very responsible girl. She wouldn't take the day off without telling me. Something in my bones tells me the girl's in danger."

Vince asked Martha questions that would help his men begin their search for Polly.

"Don't worry, Martha," he said. "We'll find your girl."

"Thank you, Vince."

Martha hung up.

Normally, Vince would have assumed that Martha was being overprotective, and that this girl Polly would show up by the end of the day. But there was a murderer on the loose. This girl might be in danger.

Deputy Pete Smith and Deputy Skyler Aldridge approached Sheriff Cagle from opposite directions.

"The motel manager was able to give us a description of the suspect's car as well as the license plate number," Pete said. "It's a midnight blue BMW and it's registered to Terrence Grigsby."

"The same Terrence Grigsby that owns Kitsune restaurant?" Vince asked.

"One and the same, sir. I put an APB out for the car."

"Good man. What do you have for me, Skyler?"

"I just finished questioning the guest staying in room nine," Skyler said. "I think you're going to want to talk to you. Her name is Danielle Lewis. Ms. Lewis knew Corey Chan and Virginia Spencer. Until recently, the three of them worked at the same place."

"Let me guess. Kitsune?"

"Yes, sir."

"Come with me Pete. I want to talk to Ms. Lewis and then we're going to go pay Terrence Grigsby a visit."

"What about me, Sheriff?" Skyler said. "I was the one who questioned Ms. Lewis."

"I need you to handle a missing person case that just came in."

"What? Now?"

"Yes. Now. The missing person's name is Polly Swift."

Skyler paled.

"Polly's missing?"

Vince cocked his head.

"You know this, Polly Swift?"

"Not really," Skyler sputtered. "She's a friend of my wife."

Vince put his hand on Skyler's shoulder.

"Martha Swafford reported her missing. She said Swift jogs every morning. Check the roads near the Swafford house."

"Yes, sir."

Skyler waited until Vince and Pete entered room nine, and then he hurried to the motel lobby. Mansoor was seated at the front desk.

"Mr. Amin," Skyler said. "Is there somewhere we can talk privately?"

"Certainly, officer," Mansoor said. "Come this way."

Mansoor led Skyler to his small office. Once they were inside, Skyler closed the door and locked it. Mansoor's eyes widened.

"Is that necessary?" Mansoor asked.

Skyler moved toward Mansoor with his fists clenched.

"Where's Polly?" Skyler said. "What have you done to her?"

Mansoor stepped back and slumped into a chair.

"Has something happened to Polly?"

"Don't play games with me. She was reported missing and I'm going to find her."

"And you think I abducted her because I'm a Muslim and that's what Muslims do."

"No," Skyler said. "You being Muslim ain't got nothing to do with it."

"Typical racist cop. Accuse the Muslim."

"Damn it, Mansoor. I thought of you first because I know you like her. I could tell from the way you were looking at her the other night."

Mansoor took deep breaths to calm himself.

"You're a fucking asshole. You know that don't you?"

"Yeah," Skyler said. "You're an asshole too."

"I do like Polly. I would never hurt her."

Skyler could tell Mansoor was telling the truth. He leaned against the wall.

"I guess I did come on strong," Skyler said. "I'm sorry, Mansoor."

"You could make it up to me by letting me come with you."

"Come with me? Where?"

"To look for Polly, of course."

Skyler was about to refuse, but then figured it would be good to have a second set of eyes when he searched the country roads.

"Aren't you working the front desk?"

"I'm on a break," Mansoor said as he unlocked the door.

Chapter Fifty-Two

Polly waited on the screened-in front porch of Mr. Kite's home with her wrist handcuffed to the chair she was sitting in. She was surrounded by foxes. The oldest fox sniffed Polly's hand, licked her fingers, and then rubbed his snout against her knee. Polly reached over with her free hand and scratched the fox behind the ear.

"Hey, Butterbean," Polly said. "Been a long time. Glad to see you're still around."

The lodge had been so heavily renovated that Polly didn't recognize it at first, but then she saw the foxes and felt there was a slim chance she might get out of this mess alive.

She could hear Scott inside the cabin talking to someone. Scott was explaining why Polly needed something called culinary enlightenment. The other foxes came over and rubbed against Polly's legs.

"Hey, I can only pet one of you at a time," she said.

An hour passed before Scott came out and unlocked the handcuff. He grabbed Polly's arm and pulled her inside the cabin. A hairy man wearing a fake fox fur loincloth, leggings, and hat stood behind a table laden with freshly cooked food. A middle-aged woman stood behind him. Polly looked up and down the hairy man and stifled a laugh.

"I'll be outside," Scott said. "So, don't try to run."

"I wouldn't dream of it," Polly said.

Scott left the room. The man in the fox furs held out his arms.

"They call me Mr. Kite," he said. "I am the Fox God."

"The Fox God?"

"Yes. I am the Fox God. I am the head chef of Kitsune. Kitsune is more than the best restaurant in the world." Mr. Kite walked around the table. "It's a religion. It's a way of life." He dropped a cushion on the floor in front of Polly. "Kneel and accept this sacred offering."

Polly put her hand on her stomach.

"Sorry. I'm not hungry. I had a huge breakfast."

Polly was lying. She hadn't eaten anything since the night before and the wonderful smell of the food made her stomach grumble.

Mr. Kite ran his forefinger over Polly's lips.

"I can have Scott come in here and force you to eat," Mr. Kite said. "He was in the Marines."

Polly peered at the dishes lined up on the table. They looked innocent enough, but Polly was certain that some of the ingredients in them weren't so innocent.

"I hate to eat alone," Polly said. "I'll partake of your sacred offering, but only if you and your lady friend join me."

"Lady friend?" Mr. Kite said. "Forgive me. I didn't introduce you. That's Cheryl."

"Hey, Cheryl," Polly said.

"Hey," Cheryl said.

"But about this sharing," Mr. Kite said. "That's not part of the ritual. You're the inductee. You must consume the offering alone."

Polly put her hands on her hips.

"You won't eat your own cooking? That's not very encouraging."

Cheryl stepped forward and stared daggers at Polly.

"Mr. Kite's cooking is the best in the world!"

"Then why won't you join me?" Polly pointed at the table. "What's wrong with this food?"

Mr. Kite stroked his bushy beard.

"Cheryl. Get some plates and utensils. Then, let's eat."

Chapter Fifty-Three

Ginny moaned as if she was having an orgasm. Terrence wasn't sure that she wasn't. They'd been talking in Terrence's office for over an hour when Terrence had the kitchen bring them something to eat. Ginny tore into her food with a ferocious intensity.

"I haven't had Kitsune food for weeks," Ginny said between mouthfuls. "I missed it so much."

"Explain it to me again," Terrence said. "Why did you kill Corey?"

Ginny crunched on the maple glazed carrots.

"I had to. Besides, you told me to."

Terrence coughed and took a sip of sparkling water to clear his throat.

"When did I ever tell you to kill anybody?"

"When you gave me your gun, you told me that my job was to step in if Dani refused to listen to reason. Just like Dani, Corey betrayed Mr. Kite. He was going to leave Kitsune. I tried to get him to listen to reason, he wouldn't listen. I had no choice. I had to eliminate the threat to Mr. Kite."

Terrence took a bottle of Johnnie Walker Blue Label Whisky

from the bottom drawer of his desk and poured the amber liquid into his glass of water. He took a long sip and waited for the burn in his throat to pass.

"When I gave you the gun, I meant for you to use it to scare Dani into coming back. I never said you should use it to kill anybody."

"If you only wanted me to use the gun for show, then why did you give me a box of shells to go with it?"

"I thought you might have to fire a warning shot."

"You can't shoot a warning shot in a motel room. The other guests would hear it. It's not that I wanted to kill Corey. I did everything I could to convince him to stay and complete the mission."

"Screwing Corey was your way of convincing him to stay?" Ginny smirked.

"Are you telling me that no one ever used sex to talk you into doing something?"

"Sure. That's how I ended up getting married. Are you sure Corey's body is safe?"

"I left him in the motel room with a Do Not Disturb sign on the door. I'll go back tonight and get him."

"Better leave that to Scott. He and his men are more experienced at handling delicate situations like this."

Ginny shrugged. She dipped her finger into a smear of maple syrup on her plate and sucked on her finger before popping it out of her mouth.

"You're the boss. What about the gun?"

"Give it to me. I'll have Scott take care of it too."

Ginny placed the handgun on Terrence's desk. Terrence drained the rest of his drink and poured more whisky into his glass. He didn't bother adding water.

"I hope you realize the danger you've put me in. If the police were to find Corey's body, they would eventually find out that you drove my car and used my gun. I already have enough to deal with without adding a murder investigation."

"There's nothing to worry about. I put the Do Not Disturb sign on the door."

There was a knock on the door and a security guard whose name Terrence couldn't remember entered the room.

"What is it now?" Terrence asked.

"The police are at the front gate," he said. "They want to see you."

Terrence rose to his feet and shouted at Ginny.

"I thought you said there was nothing to worry about!"

"I guess the Do Not Disturb sign fell off the doorknob," she said.

"Take the BMW and go out the back road."

"Where do I go?"

"As far away from here as you can get. If the police catch you, tell them anything you like as long as Kitsune has nothing to do with it."

Ginny hurried out the door, taking her food with her. Terrence turned to the security guard.

"Don't let the police in until Ginny has a chance to get away."

The security guard left. Terrence plopped down in his chair. He ignored his glass and drank whisky directly from the bottle. He dialed his lawyer's number, but then hung up. Calling him now might make Terrence look guilty.

Terrence wished Cheryl was here. She was always good in a crisis. After this shit storm passed, he was going to give her an ultimatum. She had to choose between him and Mr. Kite.

His phone rang.

"Hello?"

"I let police in," the security guard said. "Should I take them to your office?"

Terrence was shocked. It felt like Ginny had just left. Did the security guard wait long enough for her to escape? He glanced at his desk. It was messy, but he was a busy businessman. Of course, it was messy. But then, he noticed the gun he'd lent Ginny sitting on the edge of the desk.

It was the murder weapon, and it was sitting in plain sight on his desk. He quickly stashed the gun in his desk drawer.

"Yes," Terrence said as he wiped sweat off his brow. "Show them in."

The two policemen introduced themselves as Sheriff Vince Cagle and Deputy Pete Smith. The sheriff sat in the chair that Ginny had sat in. Terrence did his best to pay attention to the sheriff's questions and not be distracted by the gun hidden in his desk.

"Yes, sheriff," Terrence said. "Danielle Lewis, Corey Chan, and Virginia Spencer were employees here."

"Were?" Vince said. "As in past tense?"

"That's correct. I'll have to check my employee records, but I believe Dani quit back in June. Corey and Ginny left around the beginning of the month."

"Chan and Spencer quit on the same day?"

"Again, I'll have to check the records, but I pretty sure they did. You have to understand. In the restaurant business, not only do people come and go all the time, they sometimes leave in groups."

"Why would they do that?"

"A new restaurant opens and steals half your staff. Or two employees are dating. One of them gets another job and they leave together."

"Sounds like a tough business."

"It's no place for pussies."

"What do you remember about Lewis, Chan, and Spencer?"

Terrence pulled a handkerchief out of his back pocket and mopped his sweaty face.

"Why all these questions about these ex-employees? Are they in some kind of trouble?"

Vince and Pete glanced at each other.

"Corey Chan has been murdered. We have reason to believe that Virginia Spencer was somehow involved. Ms. Spencer is missing and anything you can tell us that would help us locate her would be greatly appreciated."

It suddenly dawned on Terrence that they could probably smell the whisky on his breath.

"I'm afraid there isn't much I can tell you other than what's in their employee records. As I said before, restaurants have a high turnover rate. They weren't here long enough for me to get to know them."

"Is it in your employee records that Ms. Spencer is driving your car?" Vince asked.

Terrence mopped a fresh wave of sweat off his face.

"Ginny took one of my cars? I had no idea."

Vince and Pete glanced at each other again.

"Are you telling me that one of your employees stole your car and you weren't aware of it?" Vince said.

Terrence chuckled nervously.

"Kitsune is a very successful restaurant and has given me an embarrassment of riches. I have several cars, but little time to drive them. I'm not surprised that I didn't notice that one of them was missing. Which one did Ginny take?"

Vince took off his cowboy hat and held it in his hands.

"You stated that Virginia Spencer and Danielle Lewis weren't employed here long enough for you to know them, yet you call them by their nicknames, Ginny and Dani. Why is that?"

Terrence opened his mouth to speak, but no words came out. He swallowed and tried again.

"I guess I just picked up their nicknames from the rest of the staff."

"I see."

"I can understand why you're questioning me about Corey and Ginny, but what does Dani have to do with all this?"

"Ms. Lewis was questioned as part of our investigation. Tell me, do you know a woman named Polly Swift?"

Terrence was caught off-guard. He recovered quickly, but not before Vince saw the look of panic in his face.

"I'll have to check the employee records, but I don't recall anyone by that name," Terrence said.

Vince and Pete stood. Vince put on his cowboy hat.

"We'd like to take a look around your premises," Vince said.

"Do you have a warrant?" Terrence asked.

"No, I do not, but I can get one soon enough. Are you hiding something, Mr. Grigsby?"

"Not at all, but a lot of our competitors would love to get an inside look at our operation."

"We're not your competitors. We're officers of the law."

"I'm sorry, but I won't have anyone traipsing through my kitchen without a court issued warrant."

"One of your employees was brutally murdered and you're standing in the way of our investigation to bring his killer to justice," Vince said grimly. "If I find out you're hiding evidence, you'll go to jail along with Ms. Spencer."

Terrence and Vince stared at each other. Pete stood to the side and watched them stare at each other. Finally, Vince shook his head.

"Okay, we'll do it your way, Mr. Grigsby. We're going now, but we'll be back soon. In the meantime, explain to your security guards that when we return if they don't open that fucking gate of yours immediately, then I'll arrest them for obstructing a law enforcement officer."

Vince and Pete stormed out of the office. Terrence laughed, not because anything was funny but to release the tight coil of tension in his chest. He didn't have much time. He had to get rid of the murder weapon and Polly Swift before that hick sheriff and his deputy returned.

There was a knock on the door and Terrence dived under the desk. Scott entered the room.

"Sir?" he said. "You in here?"

Terrence got to his feet and brushed dirt off his knees.

"I thought you were at Mr. Kite's cabin," Terrence said.

"Mr. Kite told me to leave. He said he had the situation under control."

Terrence brightened.

"That's good news. The only good news I've heard today."

"I wouldn't start celebrating just yet, sir."

Terrence gave Scott the stink eye.

"Why? What's wrong now?"

Scott leaned in close as if he were sharing a secret.

"I stayed around after Mr. Kite told me to go. Normally, I would never question a direct order from the Fox God, but I had an odd feeling that something wasn't kosher."

"Did you spy on them?" Terrence asked.

Scott blushed.

"Yes, sir. I did. Mr. Kite and Mrs. Grigsby consumed the special tasting menu with the prisoner."

Terrence wished Scott wouldn't refer to Swift as "the prisoner," but didn't ask him to use a different word.

"Go on," Terrence said.

"After a while, it was obvious that Mr. Kite and Mrs. Grigsby had become quite intoxicated. But the prisoner only seemed to be slightly affected and showed no sign of being under Mr. Kite's control."

Terrence slammed his fist on the table.

"Damn it! Do I have to do everything myself around here? Not only do I have to save the restaurant from a podcast's fake expose, I have to clean up Ginny's mess. I can't count on anybody to help me."

"I could take care of the prisoner," Scott said.

"No! I'll do it!"

Terrence yanked open the desk drawer. He took his gun and carried it into the kitchen. Scott followed him. Terrence took one of the cardboard food containers that the restaurant used for guests' leftovers and put the gun inside.

"Sir?" Scott said. "Are you sure you should be carrying that gun?"

Terrence looked over his shoulder at Scott.

"I might have to fire a warning shot," he said.

Chapter Fifty-Four

THE BOTTLE OF Dom Pérignon passed from Mr. Kite to Cheryl to Polly. The champagne tickled their noses. A warm breeze blew through the mesh of the screened-in front porch and tickled their skin. Polly sat in a chair while Mr. Kite and Cheryl snuggled together on a sofa. Cheryl's hand was nestled inside Mr. Kite's loincloth. Mr. Kite's foxes napped in various places on the porch except for the old fox curled up in Polly's lap.

"Butterbean has really taken a shine to you," Mr. Kite said as he passed the bottle to Polly.

In the open field beyond the porch, Polly watched people leave makeshift cabins and wave at Mr. Kite as they climbed into golf carts. They drove toward the path through the woods that had brought Polly here. Occasionally, Mr. Kite waved back.

"He remembers me," Polly said as she stroked the fox's red fur.

Mr. Kite and Cheryl laughed. An hour earlier, they had eaten Mr. Kite's special tasting menu of raw cannabis and kale salad, psilocybin mushroom risotto, and chocolate moonshine cake. Before they broke into Mr. Kite's wine cellar, they had smoked some of Mr. Kite's excellent weed. At this point, the three of them were extremely high and getting along quite splendidly.

"I'm serious," Polly said. "Butterbean and I are old friends."

"Stop trying to mess with my head," Mr. Kite said. "It's already messed up enough."

Polly took a sip of champagne and passed it to Mr. Kite. He handed the bottle to Cheryl.

"It's been over ten years, but he remembers my scent," Polly said. "Back then, you weren't Mr. Kite, the Fox God. You were Eldon Payne, the drug dealer."

If Mr. Kite was shocked that Polly knew his real name, he didn't show it. He squinted at Polly.

"I don't remember you and there ain't enough drugs in the world to make me forget someone as pretty as you."

"Back then, I wasn't Polly Swift. I was Brad Swafford."

Mr. Kite pulled Cheryl's hand out of his loincloth and struggled to his feet. He stumbled about until he was facing Polly. He stared directly into her eyes for a full minute before he grinned.

"Damn, Brad. It is you!"

Polly smiled.

"Good to see you again, Eldon. But please, call me Polly."

Mr. Kite hopped up and down.

"Wait here. I've got something to show you."

He dashed into the house. Cheryl leaned toward Polly so far that if she leaned any more, she'd fall out of her chair.

"You used to be a guy?"

"Inside I was always a girl," Polly said.

"What did your parents say when you told them?"

"I haven't seen my dad in years. I haven't told my mom yet."

A brown object sailed toward Polly's head. Instinctively, she put up her hands and caught it. Butterbean was unperturbed by the sudden movement.

"Once a quarterback, always a quarterback," Mr. Kite said. "Do you recognize it?"

"It's a football," Polly said.

"Yeah, but do you know which football it is?"

Polly turned it around in her hand, enjoying the nubby surface. She lined her fingers over the laces and her forefinger over a seam. She turned it from side to side.

"Sorry. I have no idea."

"It's the game ball from the second time the Fighting Foxes won the AA State Football Championship. I was at that game. You were fucking amazing! You won most valuable player and they gave you the game ball. You brought it to the cabin to show it to me, but you got so hammered you forgot to take it with you. It's been here ever since."

Polly tossed the ball in the air and caught it. It felt good in her hands.

"You used to play football?" Cheryl asked.

"He was the star quarterback," Mr. Kite said. "I mean she was."

"I was raised in a very religious family," Polly said. "A boy who wanted to be a girl. That was against God's plan and an outright sin. I did everything I could to deny what I was. I went in the opposite direction and became a macho athlete."

"But didn't you have a boyfriend?" Mr. Kite asked.

Polly licked her lips. "Skyler. He was my secret boyfriend. I couldn't completely deny my true feelings."

"You're blowing my mind," Cheryl said and then she drank the rest of the bottle of Dom Pérignon and belched. "I'm going to need another bottle of this."

Cheryl went inside the cabin and got another bottle from the wine cellar, popped it open, and took a healthy swig. She and Mr. Kite cuddled together on the couch. He put his hand inside her shirt and fondled her breast.

"Did you two go to high school together?" Cheryl asked.

"I didn't go to high school," Mr. Kite said. "After eighth grade, my folks had me stay home and help 'em with the family business."

"The Payne clan sold the best drugs in the county," Polly said. "I came up here to score weed and shrooms."

"You did more than that," Mr. Kite said. "You used to sell pot to your high school buddies. I was your supplier."

Mr. Kite handed the bottle to Polly. She balanced the football on Butterbean's back and lifted the bottle to her lips. Some of the bubbles trickled down her chin.

"After my dad left, it was just me and Mom," Polly said. "I did odd jobs to help pay the bills. Mom would be beyond upset if she ever found out that one of those odd jobs was dealing pot. I paid our heating bill with the money I made."

"Damn, girl," Cheryl said. "You were full of secrets. Your mother had no idea who you were."

Polly lifted the bottle again.

"Martha Swafford is a good woman and a wonderful mother. She can't help the way she was raised. I love her and never wanted to hurt her, so I did everything I could to maintain the fantasy she had of me." Tears rolled down Polly's face. "I'm still doing it. This college buddy of mine who got an IT job in Copenhagen. He's constantly posting updates and photos on Facebook. I have an old email account that's in Brad's name. I've convinced Mom that Brad got that job in Denmark. I email her twice a week. I just make sure my buddy isn't in any of the photos I send her. Last month my friend got a promotion, so Brad did too."

Cheryl wiped away her own tears.

"Congratulations to Brad."

"Yes. Congratulations to Brad."

Polly took a sip before handing the bottle to Mr. Kite.

"But there's something I don't understand," Cheryl said. "How do you know Dani?"

"Danny who?" Polly asked.

"Yeah, who's Danny?" Mr. Kite said.

Cheryl punched Mr. Kite's forearm.

"You know. Dani Lewis. We're supposed to get Polly to tell us where she's hiding."

"Danny's a girl?" Polly asked.

Cheryl and Mr. Kite laughed.

"Yes, silly," Cheryl said. "She ran away."

"I feel like I knew that," Polly said. "But now I can't remember."

The three of them laughed.

Polly put Butterbean on the floor and got to her feet. She put the football in the chair and wobbled a bit before getting her balance.

"Oh no," Cheryl said. "Polly is running away."

"Just to the bathroom," Polly said. "After all that champagne, I have to piss like a racehorse."

Chapter Fifty-Five

Skyler and Mansoor stood side by side and urinated into the weeds. They had been driving for hours on the outskirts of Red Fox and finally had to pull over to answer nature's call.

Skyler knew this was no way to conduct a search for a missing person. Before they started driving around, Skyler had stopped by the station and sent a description of Polly Swift to the state police. He alerted the hospital and told the other Red Fox Police Department deputies to let him know if they located her. There was no reason for him to be roaming back roads looking for her. Especially with a civilian. But Skyler was too wound up with worry to sit idly by and wait for someone to call in.

After Skyler and Mansoor had emptied their bladders, they got back into Skyler's patrol car and continued on their way. They were on a two-lane winding road that climbed its way up the mountain. The guard rail was the only thing preventing a careless driver from rolling to the bottom.

"We've established that Polly doesn't want anything to do with either one of us," Mansoor said. "Yet here we are looking for her. Why is that?"

Skyler shrugged.

"She can't stay mad at us forever."

"And yet, I will be the only one who can ask her out because I'm the only one who isn't married with children."

"Damn, Mansoor! That was cold. I was just getting to where I liked you."

Mansoor grinned.

"What can I say, my friend? The truth hurts."

"Speaking of truth, you pointed out why Polly's avoiding me, but what did you do to make her hate you?"

"Can you keep a secret?"

"Sure."

"So, can I. Which is why I can't tell you."

Skyler concentrated on the road while Mansoor scanned the woods.

"She has the prettiest blue eyes," Skyler said.

"They are quite beautiful," Mansoor agreed.

"I wish I'd met her before I made the mistake of asking Tracie to marry me."

"Did you know that a baby's eyes are the same size as an adult's eyes?" Mansoor said, hoping to change the subject.

"Yeah. Your eyeballs stay the same size from birth. That's why babies' eyes look so big."

"Well, whoever told you that was wrong. The eyes do grow. Otherwise, a baby's eyes would be so big they would look like aliens."

"I don't know, Mansoor. I've seen some babies that definitely looked like aliens."

"I've seen them too. They're called ugly babies."

Skyler chuckled but his mind was still on Polly's blue eyes. They were as blue as a cloudless day.

"Is Polly really in danger?" Mansoor asked.

Skyler tightened his grip on the steering wheel.

"You know what happened at your motel. The killer could still be in this area driving a midnight blue BMW. Until we find her, nobody is safe."

As they rounded another curve in the road, a midnight blue BMW passed them going in the opposite direction.

"Is that the car you were just talking about?" Mansoor asked.

Skyler slammed on the brakes and made a U turn. He switched on the flashing blue lights and the siren wailed as he sped after the car. He pressed the transmit button on his radio.

"Delta 4 to dispatch. Radio clear?"

The tinny voice of the dispatcher responded that the line was clear.

"Delta 4 to dispatch. In pursuit of a dark blue BMW." Skyler was close enough to the car to read the license plate to the dispatcher.

"Way to be, Skyler," the dispatcher replied. "We've been looking for that one. What's your location?"

Skyler told the dispatcher, and he alerted all the patrol cars in the vicinity to head toward that location. As Skyler got closer to the BMW, it increased speed. The luxury car's wheels squealed as it navigated the road's hairpin turns. Skyler sped up, but almost lost control on a steep curve. He decreased his speed.

"What are you doing?" Mansoor said. "You're letting them get away."

"This is the only road until you reach the bottom of the mountain," Skyler said. "When the car gets there, the other deputies will be waiting on it. I just need to keep it in sight."

"But Polly might be in that car!"

"And I have a civilian in my car whose safety is my responsibility. Besides, what do you expect me to do? Run the car off the road?"

The BMW took a sharp curve too quickly and the driver lost control. The car spun into a guard rail, bounced over it, and rolled down a rocky ravine before landing upright. Smoke rose from the engine.

Skyler parked next to the guard rail, called the dispatcher, informed him of the accident, and requested an ambulance. Mansoor sprang out of the car and hopped over the rail.

"Wait up," Skyler said. "The driver might have a gun."

"Who cares?" Mansoor said. "They're in no condition to use it."

"You don't know that."

Mansoor slowed down and let Skyler take the lead. They followed a trial of broken car parts. The twisted remains of the front bumper sat in a clump of juniper bushes. The smell of burnt rubber hung in the air.

"Let me see your hands," Skyler called out. He received no response. "Let me see your hands. Now!"

Still no response.

Skyler took his gun out of the holster and pointed it at the battered car. As he inched closer, he repeated his demand to see the driver's hands.

"I think they might be dead," Mansoor said.

Mansoor circled around to the other side of the car and peered inside. Skyler opened the car door. The driver fit the description he had of Virginia Spencer. The airbag had deflated after doing its job. Virginia's eyes were closed, and her nose was bloody. Skyler pressed his finger against her neck. She had a pulse. He did a visual check for any injuries. It appeared she had been badly shaken up, but otherwise was okay. If this proved to be true, then she was a very lucky woman.

Virginia stirred and looked around.

"Where am I?" she asked.

"In a world of trouble, ma'am," Skyler said. "Stay right where you are. An ambulance is on its way."

"Where's Polly?" Mansoor asked. "What have you done to her?"

Skyler made a face at Mansoor. He didn't need civilians doing his job.

"You heard the man," Skyler said. "Where's Polly Swift?"

"Check the car," Ginny said. "Nobody here but me."

Skyler spat on the ground. He put his gun back in the holster.

"Are you Virginia Spencer?" Skyler asked.

She squinted at Skyler.

"Yes. I'm Virginia Spencer but everybody calls me Ginny."

"I'm placing you under arrest for the murder of Corey Chan."

Skyler recited her Miranda rights, but Ginny shook her head.

"I know my rights," she said. "I admit it. I killed Corey Chan."

Skyler and Mansoor glanced at each other.

The ambulance arrived and parked next to Skyler's patrol car. Skyler handcuffed Ginny to the steering wheel and then went to talk to the EMTs. Ginny leaned her head back and closed her eyes. Her face was caked with dirt. Mansoor glared at her.

"I don't believe you," he said.

Ginny didn't open her eyes.

"I really did kill Corey."

"That I believe. I think you know where Polly Swift is, but you're protecting someone. The police will find her eventually and then you will be in even more trouble."

Ginny opened one eye.

"More trouble than committing first degree murder?"

Mansoor clenched his fists. He wanted to punch her stupid face, but he would never hit a woman.

"Corey Chan was a nice guy. Why did you kill him?"

Ginny closed her eye and licked the dirt off her lips. The texture reminded her of the spice Mr. Kite used on his grilled asparagus.

"I did it for the benefit of Mr. Kite," she said.

Mansoor couldn't help but reply, "And of course Henry the Horse dances the waltz."

Chapter Fifty-Six

TERRENCE PARKED HIS golf cart in front of Mr. Kite's cabin. He grabbed the take-out container on the seat next to him and dashed onto the porch where he was greeted by the sight of Cheryl and Mr. Kite half-naked and kissing. The way they were sucking face with mouths stretched wide open and slobbering, it looked like they were trying to eat each other's face. Neither of them noticed Terrence's arrival.

"What the hell is going on here?" Terrence asked.

Cheryl and Mr. Kite gazed up at Terrence. Mr. Kite greeted him with a goofy grin.

"Terry, my main man," Mr. Kite said. "There's some leftover mushroom risotto and moonshine cake in the frig. Get you some and join the party. It'll be just like old times."

"He already has some leftovers," Cheryl said, pointing at the box in Terrence's hand. "Did you bring us a snack?"

"No, I didn't bring a snack," Terrence said. "I can't believe this. We're losing customers, the employees are turning on us, and the police are on their way. I'm doing everything I can to save Kitsune while you two sit here getting stoned out of your minds."

"Stop being so negative," Mr. Kite said. "You're starting to harsh my mellow, man."

"Screw your mellow! You were supposed to get that girl to tell you where Dani was hiding. But instead, I come here, and the girl is gone. You had one job to do, and you failed miserably."

"Who's Dani?"

Terrence's face turned red.

"Where is the girl?

Mr. Kite looked at the chair Polly had been sitting in. A football was sitting in it now.

"She's around here somewhere," Mr. Kite said.

"You let her escape? What do you think is going to happen when she gets back to Red Fox? The police already suspect we're involved in Corey's murder, now that girl's going to tell them that we kidnapped her."

"Polly wouldn't do that," Cheryl said. "She's cool."

"Yeah," Mr. Kite agreed. "Polly is super cool."

Butterbean rubbed his snout against Terrence's leg. Terrence pushed him away with his foot. Butterbean scampered to the other side of the porch and hid under a chair.

"Face it, Eldon," Terrence said. "Your mind control doesn't work anymore. First you lost control of Dani and Corey, and now this girl, Polly."

"That's Mr. Kite to you, Terry."

"My name isn't Terry. It's Terrence."

Mr. Kite pulled up his loincloth and struggled to his feet.

"Watch it, *Terrence*," he said, jabbing his forefinger into Terrence's chest. "If it weren't for me, you'd still be a real estate agent in Charlotte."

"Give me a break," Terrence said. "If it weren't for me, you'd still be a fugitive meth dealer hiding in the woods."

Mr. Kite straightened his spine and gave Terrence his most indignant stare.

"Hey! I never sold meth. I sold weed, shrooms, and corn liquor. I never dirtied my hands with crap like meth."

Terrence took the gun out of the box and pressed the muzzle against Mr. Kite's chest. Cheryl jumped to her feet.

"You ruined my life," Terrence said. "I built you a restaurant. I made you world famous. I got you all the ass any man could ask for. But that wasn't enough for you. You had to take my wife and my employees. And what did you give me in return? You treated me like I was shit on the bottom of your shoe."

Mr. Kite peered down at the gun aimed at his heart.

"You ain't gonna shoot me. You ain't got the balls. That's the problem with you, Terry. You could have had the same things I have, but you were too much of a pussy to grab 'em. You know why I took Cheryl? That woman is the sexiest thing in the southeast United States, but you were always too full of my cooking to get it up."

"Shut up!" Terrence shouted.

"Make me!"

"Shut up! Shut up! Shut up!"

Terrence pulled the trigger and blew a hole in Mr. Kite's chest. Mr. Kite's blood sprayed on Terrence's face and the Kitsune shirt he was wearing. Mr. Kite was dead before he hit the floor.

Cheryl screamed. Employees on their way to the restaurant to begin their shift heard the gunshot and the scream. They ran toward the cabin to investigate.

"What have you done?" Cheryl asked. "Are you insane?"

"I did what I should have done a long time ago," Terrence said.

He aimed the gun at Cheryl. She didn't wait to find out if he had the balls to shoot her. She bolted off the porch and ran toward the employee cabins on the other side of the open field. She waved at the employees coming toward her.

"Run!" Cheryl shouted. "He's got a gun!"

Terrence fired the gun at Cheryl as he chased her across the field. His first shot grazed the tall grass a few inches to her right. She yelped and kept going. The next shot put a hole in an employee's arm. The other employees retreated quickly.

Polly came out of the cabin to see what all the commotion was about. Mr. Kite's foxes surrounded his body and licked his face. The sight of her dead friend got her adrenaline pumping, counteracting the effects of the mind-altering substances she had taken earlier. She saw Terrence chasing Cheryl and realized the poor woman's life was in danger.

Polly picked up the football Mr. Kite had given her earlier. Tucking the football under her arm, she ran after Terrence and Cheryl.

Cheryl tripped on a rock and scraped her hands. She got back up, but the fall gave Terrence time to close the gap between them. The closer he got, the less chance there was that his next shot would miss her.

Polly stopped and positioned herself in the throwing stance. She lined her fingers over the laces and her index finger over a seam. Terrence was running a basic go route making him an easy target. It had been ten years since she'd thrown a football, but as Eldon said, once a quarterback, always a quarterback.

Polly threw the football.

It sliced through the air in a perfect spiral and slammed into the back of Terrence's head. He pitched forward and landed on his face. The impact caused the gun to fly out of his hand. Once on the ground, he didn't move.

Polly fist pumped and then ran to Terrence. She stood over him and gloated.

"That's why the Flying Foxes won the AA State Football Championship two years in a row!"

Polly assumed Terrence was unconscious, but her assumption proved to be false. He grabbed her leg. She lost her balance and fell on her back. He climbed on top of her and wrapped his hands around her throat.

"You bitch!" Terrance roared. "I don't know who you are, but I hate you and I want you to die!"

Polly tried to push him off, but he was too heavy. She scratched his arms and face, but his blind rage made him oblivious to the pain. She fought for her life, but he was winning the battle. Yellow spots blossomed in front of her eyes as she struggled for air. She couldn't believe this was how she was going to die.

The police would discover her true identity. They would inform Martha. Polly should have been the one to tell her. She should have told her mother the truth a long time ago.

From far away, Polly heard someone call Terrence's name. He looked up. A gun fired close to Polly and echoed in her ears. A hole appeared in Terrence's forehead. Thick red blood dripped onto Polly's face. Terrence's grip on her neck loosened and Polly sucked in mouthfuls of air. Terrence collapsed on top of her, his weight knocking the air out of her again. With her last ounce of strength, Polly pushed his body off her.

Polly's chest ached and there was a ringing in her ears. Cheryl helped Polly to her feet.

"You?" Polly said, her throat raw and her voice barely above a whisper.

Cheryl held the gun Terrence had dropped.

"Yes. I found it in the grass."

"Thank you."

They looked down at Terrence's body.

"Running a restaurant is very stressful," Cheryl said.

Chapter Fifty-Seven

MORE PEOPLE THAN usual attended Red Fox Baptist Church's Wednesday night supper. A month had passed since the triple murder case. The Red Fox Police Department had spearheaded the investigation and Sheriff Vince Cagle had appeared on national TV answering reporters' questions. The reporters and the TV trucks had moved on to the next salacious crime scene, but to the folks of Red Fox Vince was still a celebrity. The best place to get up close and personal with him was at the Wednesday night supper.

Everybody crowded around his table. White paper plates stained red from the tasteless spaghetti and meatballs sat in front of each person. Vince sat at the head of the table. He leaned back in his chair and sipped weak coffee.

"It's funny how one random thing leads to another," Vince said. "About seven years ago, Terrence and Cheryl Grigsby went on a weekend camping trip on Red Fox Mountain. On their first day, they went hiking in the woods and got lost. It was getting late, and they were getting mighty worried when they stumbled upon the Payne cabin. They knocked on the door and Eldon Payne answered."

"I thought Eldon was in jail at that time," Crystal Beaver said.

"He was supposed to be. He was wanted for dealing drugs, but when we went to arrest him, he was nowhere to be found. We searched everywhere, but never found him. The Paynes have family in Florida, so we figured that was where he was holed up. Turned out, he'd never left the mountain."

"Enough about Eldon's disappearance act," Gloria Medley said. "You left off at the part where the Grigsbys show up at Eldon's door."

"That's right," Vince said. He sipped his coffee before continuing. "The Payne clan might have more than their share of criminals in their family, but none of them would ever turn away a person in need. Eldon took the Grigsbys into his cabin, had them warm up by his fire, cooked them dinner, and shared his homegrown weed with them. Later that evening, he had sexual intercourse with Cheryl and Terrence. At the same time."

"Good heavens!" Tammy Baggs said.

A few people giggled which brought a stern look from Pastor Baggs.

"The Grigsbys spent the rest of the weekend in Eldon's cabin," Vince said. "Using the vegetables he grew in his garden, and the spices he gathered from the forest, Eldon made all their meals. Terrence was so impressed by Eldon's cooking that he suggested they open a restaurant together. Eldon was keen to do it, but there was a problem. Eldon was a fugitive. If Johnny Law found out he was still on Red Fox Mountain, he'd go straight to jail.

"Terrence came up with Eldon's new identity. Since Eldon kept tame foxes as pets, Terrence decided he would be Mr. Kite, the mysterious Fox God who invented his own unique style of vegetarian cooking. The restaurant was a big success, but it must have been tough on Eldon. He was a world-famous chef, but he couldn't leave the mountain without being recognized and arrested. So, Eldon took the Fox God idea and ran with it. He created a cult of personality and his employees worshipped him as if he really was some kind of god."

"Blasphemy!" said Pastor Baggs.

His outburst caused more giggling and the pastor blushed.

"It was crazy town up there," Vince said. "The people who joined the Kitsune cult weren't allowed to quit. A brave young lady escaped. She should have come straight to the police, but eventually she provided important information that helped us solve a murder case. Sadly, we didn't make it to Kitsune in time to prevent two more murders."

"What's going to happen now?" Crystal asked.

"Virginia Spencer will go to trial for the murder of Corey Chan. Cheryl Grigsby was only partially aware of Terrence's illegal activities, such as ordering present employees to kidnap a former employee. We have multiple eyewitnesses that saw Terrence attempt to kill Cheryl so it can be argued that she shot him in self-defense."

"And to save Polly," Martha Swafford said.

"You're right, Martha," Vince said. "If Cheryl Grigsby hadn't shot her husband when she did, we wouldn't be sitting here with the lovely Polly Swift."

Martha had been holding Polly's hand throughout Vince's recap of the events. She squeezed Polly's hand and gave her such a tender look of concern that Polly thought her heart was going to burst.

"I just thank the Lord she's all right," Martha said. "If I think about how close she was to dying, I might just tear up and ruin my make-up."

"Is this a good time to ask for a raise?" Polly asked.

Everybody laughed and Pastor Baggs led them in a short

prayer thanking Jesus for protecting them from evil. With Vince's retelling of the case complete, people began to leave. Chairs scrapped on the floor and goodbyes were made. People lined up to shake Vince's hand.

After the last person shook his hand, Martha pulled Vince aside.

"Thank you for believing me when I called to tell you Polly was missing," Martha said.

"It's a good thing you did," Vince said. "I guess it was woman's intuition."

"You could have written it off as a silly old woman overacting and honestly, I wouldn't have blamed you if you had."

"One thing I would never call you is silly. You're probably the most serious woman I've ever known. I admire that about you, Martha."

Martha straightened Vince's collar. Feeling her hands against his face made him blush.

"Let's not get carried away," Martha said. "I still don't trust you anymore than I would a wounded snake."

Martha walked away before Vince could respond.

Polly had watched the entire exchange with Crystal and Gloria. Polly nudged Crystal.

"It looks like Martha doesn't hate Vince quite as much as she used to," Polly said.

"Don't get your hopes up," Crystal said. "She's still carrying an awful lot of hate for him."

"Don't rain on Polly's parade," Gloria said. "She just wants to see Martha happy."

"Oh spit," Crystal said. "We all want to be happy."

Gloria narrowed her eyes at Crystal.

"Really? You're never happy and I think you like it that way."

<h1 style="text-align:center">Chapter Fifty-Eight</h1>

ANITA'S FEET WERE killing her. The end of her shift couldn't come soon enough. She'd been moving through her days in a blue funk and lifting serving trays felt like she was lifting boulders. She knew that Owen had noticed that she wasn't her usual self but hadn't said a word about it.

She didn't see who had sat in the booth, just that two bodies had parked themselves there. She trudged over with menus. As she handed them to the customers, she took her first look at them. They were Dani Lewis and an older black woman. Anita stood there like an idiot, unable to speak.

"Mom," Dani said. "This is Anita, the girl I was telling you about. Anita, this is my mother, Regina."

Regina climbed out of the booth and stepped toward Anita. Anita braced for a slap in the face, but instead Regina wrapped her arms around Anita and hugged her tightly. She smelled nice, like lilacs.

"Thank you for saving my daughter," Regina said. "Dani has told me so much about you."

Regina pulled away from Anita. Anita was too shocked to speak. She looked at Dani for help.

"I told her everything," Dani said. "And how wrong I was to judge you. I'm sorry I got mad at you."

"Really?" Anita asked.

"Well. I'm still a little mad at you."

"Do you have a moment to sit with us?" Regina said.

Anita looked around the Rejoice Diner. Most of the customers had what they needed, and the rest could wait a couple of minutes. Anita slid in next to Dani.

Anita couldn't stop grinning like an idiot. Dani had forgiven her. She'd heard the saying about a weight being lifted off your shoulders and now she knew what it felt like.

"Mom drove all the way from Portland to get me," Dani said.

"I don't like to fly either," Anita said.

"I don't mind flying," Regina said. "But when I left, Dani still didn't have an ID. You can't get on an airplane without one."

Anita furrowed her brow.

"You have an ID now?" she asked.

"Mr. Grigsby had all the Kitsune employees' driver's licenses locked up in a safe," Dani said. "The police found them. That's how I got mine back."

"Do you have to testify at the trials?"

"Yeah. But that won't be for a while. The trials will be in Atlanta."

"I figured they would, otherwise I would have offered you a place to stay."

"You could also come out to Portland and visit Dani," Regina said. "You could stay in our house."

Anita grinned. "That would be nice. I'd even put up with flying for that."

"It's weird to think that Kitsune is closed for good," Dani said.

"I never did understand why it was so popular," Regina said. "A meal isn't complete unless there is some kind of protein that you can only get from meat on the plate."

"Amen to that," Anita said.

Regina held up her hand. She and Anita high fived while Dani rolled her eyes.

A young man with thick, black-rimmed glasses, a well-tended beard, an expensive haircut, and a new flannel shirt came over to their table with his menu in hand.

"Where's the other menu?" he asked, shaking the menu.

Anita cocked her head.

"That's the only one we got."

He put his hands on his hips.

"Don't lie to me. Where's the menu with the Payne family dishes? According to God Save the Foodie podcast, Kitsune's recipes were stolen from the owner of this diner. Now I want to order from that menu. I can afford it."

"Well, Kitsune didn't steal them," Anita said. "They just weren't completely honest about their main cook. Eldon and Owen were kin. Same family. Same recipes."

"So, I can get the original versions of the Kitsune dishes here?"

"I suppose you could. I'd have to ask Owen."

Anita figured that was the end of that, but then Dani jumped in.

"Sir," Dani said. "You are absolutely right. The Rejoice Diner is more authentic than Kitsune. The original dishes are made here. There is going to be a separate menu, but we were waiting for the dust to settle on the Kitsune tragedy."

"I thought so," said the young man. "Can't I order any of the dishes tonight? I came a long way for this."

"I don't know," Anita said. "I'll have to ask Owen."

"Actually," Dani said. "It's chef's choice tonight. If you'll have a seat and be patient, I'll let Mr. Tew know that someone has ordered the Payne clan dinner."

"Finally," the young man. "Make it two dinners. I brought a date."

"Two Payne clan dinners. No problem."

The young man danced back to his table. He sat next to a young woman with green hair, a knitted cap, a scarf, and a flannel dress. He whispered in her ear. She squealed, and then kissed him.

"Why the hell did you tell him that?" Anita asked. "Owen ain't going want to make something that ain't on the menu."

"He doesn't have to," Dani said. "I'll do it. I worked at Kitsune long enough. I can make most of their dishes. That will get us through tonight and then later we can talk to Owen about a complete menu."

"Have you lost your mind? You've never met Owen before. What makes you think he's going to let you cook in his kitchen?"

"When I explain to him how much money he can make being the authentic version of Kitsune." Dani turned to Regina. "I'm sorry to spring this on you Mom, but I might not be going back to Portland after all."

"Ms. Lewis," Anita said. "Please explain to your daughter that she's lost her mind. My boss is going to kick her butt right out the door."

Regina grinned.

"I didn't raise no fool. Dani sees a business opportunity. If I were in her shoes, I'd do the same thing. She should at least try to make this happen. I only ask one thing. Somebody bring me something to eat cause I'm hungry. And whatever it is better include some kind of meat."

"Thanks, Mom," Dani said. "Come on, Anita. Let's talk to Owen."

"I'll make sure to bring you dinner, Ms. Lewis," Anita said.

Anita took Dani into the steamy kitchen. The smell of vegetables cooking in bacon fat hung in the air thick enough to slice. Owen wore a food-stained apron as he moved from cook to cook to make sure things were moving along. He spotted Anita and Dani and came over to them.

"Your orders are almost up," he said. "Who is this?"

"This is Dani," Anita said. "Dani Lewis."

Owen looked Dani over.

"I read about you in the paper. Why are you in my kitchen?"

"There are some hipsters out there who want authentic Payne clan cuisine," Dani said. "Not that fake stuff that Kitsune used to peddle."

"They'll have to find it somewhere else. People around here like Rejoice Diner the way it is."

"I told you so," Anita said.

"I agree, Mr. Tew," Dani said. "You'll have to open a second place. But for tonight, I can take care of the hipsters. I just need a space to cook."

Owen stared at Dani. There was controlled chaos all around them as the other cooks prepped old fashion southern food.

"I'm just a simple country boy," Owen said. "I don't quite comprehend what it is you're trying to sell me, young lady."

Dani grinned.

"I worked for Kitsune, so I know how to make some vegetable dishes that will please that foodie couple out there that drove God knows how far to eat here. They will then go online and tell all their foodie friends that your food is the next big thing, and you aren't hip unless you eat here. Foodies will line up outside your door. You will make a lot of money and probably get your picture in some gourmet magazines."

Owen crossed his arms.

"And what do you get out of all this?"

"I want to run your new restaurant. I want to make a lot of money too."

"And you know how to cook?"

"Good enough for tonight."

"And just where am I supposed to put this new restaurant?"

"There's a lot of empty stores in town," Anita said. "The business would help all of Red Fox."

Owen turned his attention to Anita.

"And what do you get out of all this?"

Anita wanted to say that she got her best friend back but shrugged instead.

"She helps me run the place," Dani said. "I can't do it alone."

Owen looked at the two women standing side by side. He didn't want the headache of a second restaurant, but he could smell an opportunity.

"I'll think about it," Owen said. "First, show me what you can do. The aprons are in that closet over there. The freezer is back there. You can use that station over there."

"Thank you, Mr. Tew," Dani said.

She hurried away. Owen put his hand on Anita's shoulder.

"As for you, young lady. Orders are piling up. Get back to work!"

Chapter Fifty-Nine

POLLY RANG THE doorbell. Martha pulled back the frilly curtain covering the window before opening the door.

"Sorry I'm late," Polly said. "But the traffic getting here was insane."

"I know what you mean," Martha said. "That flight of stairs from your place to mine gets so backed up during rush hour."

"I brought wine." Polly held up a bottle of pink wine with an alcohol level so low it wouldn't get a hamster drunk. "I hope that's okay."

"I'm not a complete teetotaler. I like to have a glass of wine now and then."

Polly entered the house and was greeted by the heavy scent of potpourri. She had been nervous all week thinking about tonight. Martha had invited her to have dinner with her. That would have been special enough, but Martha suggested that they prepare the dinner together. For Polly, this would be a genuine mother daughter experience.

Whenever Polly came into the main house, she noticed little changes Martha had made since Brad had lived here. Tonight,

Polly noticed that Martha's collection of religious salt and pepper shakers in the dining room cabinet were missing. Among them had been Jesus and Mary shakers, angel shakers, Santa and Mrs. Claus shakers, praying children shakers, and ten commandment shakers with commandments one through five for salt and commandments six through ten for pepper.

The religious shakers had been replaced with cute animal shakers. There were bunny rabbits, baby bears, baby birds, puppies, and in a rare nod to Eastern culture, Japanese lucky cats. Polly assumed that Martha's switch from religious shakers had more to do with wanting something different than a possible crisis of faith.

Once in the kitchen, Polly opened the bottle of wine and the two women got to work. They gossiped about their customers at Martha's Hair Done Right as they prepared meatloaf, mashed potatoes, green beans, and buttermilk biscuits. The kitchen filled with the comforting smell of a home cooked meal. The only thing that Martha had made in advance was a peach cobbler.

"You know your way around a kitchen," Martha said as she checked the meatloaf. "Your mamma taught you well."

"Yes, she did," Polly said as she mashed the potatoes.

They had two glasses of wine while they cooked and a third glass with the meal. They ate at the small dining table. Martha sat with her back to the salt and pepper shakers.

"Your new pet hardly makes any noise," Martha said. "Did you have any trouble housebreaking him?"

"I was lucky," Polly said. "Butterbean was already housebroken."

With the death of Eldon Payne, his leash of tame foxes became orphans. Kitsune's ex-employees quickly adopted them for their connection to their fallen leader, but Polly insisted on taking Butterbean. The old red fox took to her apartment immediately and claimed a comfy chair in the living room as his bed.

After dinner, Polly helped Martha clean up. When they got to the dishes, Polly washed while Martha dried. Then they had coffee and peach cobbler on the front porch.

"There's a certain feeling in the air this time of year," Martha said. "It's starting to get cold, but not too cold. The haze of summer is gone, and everything looks sharper."

Polly held her coffee cup in both hands and gazed at the sky.

"You'd never see this many stars in Atlanta," she said. "Too many city lights between you and the sky."

Martha put her plate down. She had only taken a couple of bites of her cobbler.

"That day you were kidnapped. When you didn't show up for work, I knew immediately that something was wrong. You're a very responsible person. You would have told me if you weren't coming in."

"You've done so much for me," Polly said. "I don't want to let you down."

"The shop has done more business this past quarter than it has in a very long time. I have you to thank for that. Your customers love you. You've brought in people who have lived in Red Fox their whole lives but have never set foot in my place before."

"Maybe this is where I ask for a raise."

"How much do you want?"

They both laughed.

"Seriously," Polly said. "I don't need a raise. It's so cheap to live in Red Fox I really don't need more money."

"I was thinking more along the lines of a partnership. I'd like to make you co-owner."

Polly put down her cup so she wouldn't spill it on herself.

"Oh my God," she stammered. "Really?"

"I don't think we should change the name. It's been Martha's Hair Done Right for too long."

"I wouldn't think of changing the name. I can't believe this is happening."

"With you as co-owner, I could finally take a vacation. I haven't been able to take a vacation in twenty years."

"Of course. You deserve a vacation."

"With all the extra business you've brought in, I've finally been able to save up enough money to go on the vacation I've been planning on taking for years now."

"That's wonderful. Where do you want to go?"

"Take a guess."

A feeling of dread cut through the euphoria Polly had been enjoying.

"I'm going to say either a Caribbean Cruise or a tour through Israel."

Martha nodded.

"Those aren't bad guesses but come on. You know where I want to go."

"No. I really don't."

"Denmark! I want to go to Copenhagen and see Brad."

Polly felt like all the blood in her body drained to her feet. A chill in the air cut through her like a knife. It was all she could do not to run from the porch screaming.

"Of course, Denmark," Polly said. "That was going to be my next guess. Brad must be so excited that you're coming to see him."

"Brad has no idea that I'm coming," Martha said. "I want it to be a surprise."

Polly thought that somebody was certainly going to be surprised, but not the person Martha thought it would be.

"When are you going?" Polly asked.

"I have a lot of things to take care of first," Martha said. "We need to do the legal paperwork for the partnership. I need to show you how to run things while I'm gone."

"And you probably don't want to go there during winter. I heard Denmark winters are brutal."

"You're right. I didn't even think of that. I'll go in early Spring. I don't want to wait too long. I'd like to be there when there's still snow on the ground. So, I'm going to say four months from now."

"Four months?"

"Yes. Four months."

Four months. Sixteen weeks. No matter how she did the math, Polly was screwed. She had to stop Martha before she left. If Martha went all the way to Denmark to find out Brad wasn't there, it would destroy her. Regardless of when Polly told Martha, the truth would destroy her. Only now Polly had a definite deadline. Four months.

<h1 style="text-align:center">Chapter Sixty</h1>

Harper liked to dance. This was something Tracie had only recently discovered. Since Connor had started first grade, Harper had come out from under her brother's shadow. One day Tracie had the TV on while she was ironing, and a commercial for a four CD set of Motown classic songs came on. When Harper heard the music, she started dancing or rather the movements a four-year-old makes in her attempt to dance. Since then, Tracie played music and danced with Harper every morning after Connor and Skyler left the house.

They were dancing on a Wednesday morning when the phone rang. Tracie's first thought was that something had happened to Connor. She rushed to the kitchen and picked up the receiver.

"Hello?" she said.

"Tracie, darling. It's Ivy Cox. Remember me?"

Tracie put her fist against her hip.

"Yeah, I remember you. What do you want?"

"Did you take care of your problem?"

To take care of her "problem," Tracie had turned to Polly again. Polly drove Tracie to the clinic and sat in the waiting room with Connor and Harper while the doctor removed the fetus from Tracie's womb. Afterwards, Polly drove them home, made Tracie hot tea, and watched the kids while Tracie took a nap. By the time Skyler came home that night, Polly had gone home, and the kids were in bed. It was if the whole thing had never happened.

"Yes," Tracie said. "The problem is gone."

Tracie could hear Ivy sucking on her More cigarette and blowing out the smoke. She could practically taste the nicotine.

"Good to hear," Ivy said. "Deon, Tyshawn, and Reggie have been asking for you. They told their friends about what a great time they had and now their friends are asking for you. Ready to make some real money?"

Tracie's muscles tensed and she felt like she'd swallowed a burning chunk of coal. She could see Harper in the living room still dancing her little heart out.

"Hell no!" Tracie said. "I came too close to losing everything I have. I won't make that mistake again."

"Okay, okay. If you don't want to, you don't want to. You don't have to bite my head off."

Tracie leaned against the kitchen counter. She brushed a strand of hair out of her eyes.

"I'm sorry. What I went through was such a nightmare and made me appreciate what I have. I learned my lesson. I'll never do it again."

"It's a shame," Ivy said. "I watched the video feed from that night. You have real talent. You convinced me that you were enjoying it. Oh, well. You said never and that's that."

"That's right. Never again."

"Okay. But if you ever change your mind."

"I won't change my mind."

"But if you do. Change your mind. You have my number. Call me."

Ivy hung up before Tracie could tell the horrible woman that she would never call her. Not in a million years.

The call unsettled Tracie and left her in an impotent rage. She went to the bathroom she shared with Skyler, locked the door, and took out the tampon box she kept in the bottom drawer of the bathroom cabinet. Inside the box was the money left over after she paid for the abortion. She had spent some of it on a couple of nice blouses she found on sale at Wal-Mart, but there was still plenty remaining. With the roll of bills was a business card for Xtra Special TLC Massage.

Tracie got ready to tear the card in two, but she couldn't do it. Sometimes she dreamed about that night with Deon, Tyshawn, and Reggie. She always woke up wet between her legs. She would never call Ivy, but keeping the card was Tracie's way of preserving the memory.

At least, that was what she kept telling herself.

Chapter Sixty-One

BUTTERBEAN SAT IN his favorite chair and watched Polly pace back and forth. Polly stopped and scratched his head.

"What am I going to do, Butterbean?" Polly said. "I have four months before Martha leaves for Copenhagen. That's like no time at all."

Polly resume pacing.

"I'm not ready to tell her. I just want to enjoy this time with her a little longer. Is that so terrible? I can tell from your expression you think I'm being terrible. You're right. I am being terrible. I should have told her when I first came back to Red Fox."

Butterbean got out of his chair and trotted to his food dish. Polly put her hands on her hips.

"How can you think of food at a time like this? I need to come up with some way to delay the trip. Maybe Brad can tell her something that will make her change her mind about visiting him? That's a good idea, but I can't think of anything that doesn't sound suspicious."

Butterbean finished eating and lapped at his water dish. Then, he trotted back to his chair, curled up in a ball, and closed his eyes.

"You're not being helpful. I need ideas and you're taking a nap. And what the hell is that noise?"

The noise was a tapping on her window. Polly peered outside. Skyler was on her roof. He waved at her. Polly opened the window and a breeze carried Skyler's scent directly into her face.

"What are you doing here?" Polly asked.

"I came to see you," Skyler said.

"You can't be here. Martha's going to hear you."

"I've come and gone through this window hundreds of times and Martha never heard me once."

Polly ran her hands through her blonde hair. She had enough to worry about without Skyler trying to play high school boyfriend with her. Brad already played that game with him.

"Don't do this, Skyler," Polly said. "Tracie's a good person. She needs you. Your adorable kids need you. I don't need you."

"But what about what I need?" Skyler said. "I need you, Polly Swift."

"Please, Skyler. Don't do this."

"I should have seen it. I've looked into your blue eyes enough times. In this very room."

"You aren't making any sense. Please go home."

"You're my home."

"No, I am not. Now go away!"

She put her hands on the sill so that she could close the window. Skyler reached in and grabbed her forearm. Polly tensed, but he gave her his best puppy dog eyes. She never could resist his puppy dog eyes.

"Please, Brad," Skyler said. "Don't leave me again."

Polly's lower lip trembled. He knew the truth. She couldn't lie to him any longer.

"Come in. We have a lot to talk about."

Skyler climbed inside and Polly closed the window behind him.

The End

www.ingramcontent.com/pod-product-compliance
Lightning Source LLC
Chambersburg PA
CBHW040330020826

48978CB00013BC/1045